ALPHA WOLF
ALPHA COMPANY SERIES

SIERRA WOODS

ALPHA WOLF

An Alpha Company Series Book

by

Sierra Woods

UNTITLED

"I AM IN LOVE! Captivating, visceral, and startlingly sexy, the beasts of Alpha Company will steal your hearts and never let them go. BUY THIS BOOK!"

--NY Times Bestselling Author Darynda Jones

THANK YOU AND NEWSLETTER SIGN UP

Dear Reader,

Thank you so much for buying my new book. I hope you fall in love with the characters and the story as much as I have. Connecting with my readers keeps me going, and I would love to hear from you. Please let me know how you liked the book by giving a review. You can also mail me directly at:
Sierra@sierrawoodsbooks.com

https://BookHip.com/CZZXTM

is where you will find new a newsletter sign-up form. There is a *free ebook* when you sign up for the newsletter. If you discover any errors in any of my book, please email them to me, so I can fix them right away. I appreciate and value the input and feedback of my awesome readers.

Now, go read something awesome!

Love,

Sierra Woods

CHAPTER
ONE

New Mexico, USA

Four members of the Alpha Company pack crested the ridge above the targeted house in the small, isolated canyon below.

In human form.

They didn't need communication devices to hear each other. If they could hear the movements of an insect under a pile of leaves half a mile away, they could hear the whisper of a wolf on the wind.

"Take it off, baby. Take it *all* the way off," Dane said and adjusted the military binoculars, tuning in to their quarry in the house below, trying to visualize what they were walking into. By the sounds of it, it was either food or a female.

Vic Stone listened to their chatter as he readied his equipment, and one *special* item stowed securely in his vest pocket. If they succeeded, he'd give it to someone who was going to need it very soon and very badly. If Alpha Company wasn't successful, if Vic died on this mission, he just hoped no one would think he was some pansy-assed soldier for getting killed with a toy stuffed in his pocket.

"Come on, baby. What have you got for me?" Dane's voice distracted him. Subtle was not Dane's middle name.

"Settle down, pervert. Don't you think about anything but sex?" Vic asked. This was his company, and he was in command. The others were his brothers in arms. They'd been through some tough shit together, but when in the field, he was their commander, not their brother or their friend.

"Are you kidding? Dinner's on the table down there, and it's covered up. I'm *starving*." A fact made apparent to all of them when Dane's stomach growled loud enough to startle birds in the nearby trees.

"Holy hell, Dane. You're gonna give our position away with that racket." Eros, Vic's second-in-command, complained from his position on the opposite ridge, where he'd gone to get a different view of the situation.

"Sorry." Although Dane apologized, none of them believed it.

"Focus on the mission. All of you." Vic shouldn't have to remind them. They were all seasoned vets. They'd been together for years, in the Middle East, on other secret missions, and they trained until their teeth bled. Everyone knew the drills. Now was not the time to screw it up.

Dane cleared his throat and tore his gaze away from the house. "I'm ready now. Sorry, boss." He cleared his throat. "Won't happen again."

"Like I believe that." It would happen again, to all of them. They were creatures of their appetites. Vic, of course, had scented the enticing fragrances wafting up the hill and had to agree with Dane. At the moment, though, food was the last thing on his mind. He, too, had to force down the ravenous animal living inside him. The one that wanted to roar to life. That wanted to rip out of him. To run through the woods. To claw at the dirt and sink his teeth into something warm and meaty, savor the blood dripping down his chin. He understood Dane's distraction. They all did. Unfortunately, now wasn't dinner time for wolves. They were ass-deep in a mission. A young life depended on them. Their expertise. Their focus. When the life of a child was in danger. Nothing else mattered.

In the last five years, this group, this band of wolf brothers had never failed any rescue mission, and they weren't going to start now.

Failure was never an option.

Reconsidering your plan while running for your life from crazed mercenaries shooting at you certainly was. That had happened more than once, but they'd always succeeded. Today would be no different. They had to believe it or none of them could race down that hill.

"Dark in one. Shift." Waiting while the others shifted into their wolf forms didn't take long, but it took all the resistance he could muster to remain in his human form. The energy of their changes pulled at him. The beast inside him begged to shift. To revel in the power, the muscles, the vibrancy of the earth beneath his paws with his brothers. His heart thrummed wildly as he connected with the others in their primal form, feeding off of their beasts and regaining some of the energy he'd lost trying to resist.

Acknowledge, Vic said on their inner comm.

Yeah, boss.

Ready to rock and roll.

On it.

A chorus of three short yips cut the evening air as the beasts answered him. Vic focused his attention down the side of the ridge, looking for hazards to trip them up on the way, but found nothing obvious. A band of ruthless kidnappers could hide traps of any sort to stop intruders. Bombs. Motion detectors. Animal traps to snap a foot in half. Any number of destructive devices could be employed against them.

Luke had nearly had a foot blown off by an IED on a mission. Others hadn't been as fortunate. Dozens of soldiers, friends, had died or been badly maimed because of hidden weapons of varying destruction. Looking below again to reassess the hillside they'd traverse, Vic raised his head and sniffed once, but didn't sense anything he hadn't already known about.

For once, maybe, they'd get lucky and finish this mission without injury. In his mind, that was his number one fear. One of the boys, or himself, getting seriously hurt. They could handle the little stuff at the compound, but for big stuff they had to go out of their comfort zone and that meant risk of exposure to their secret life each time. Shaking off the negative vibe threatening to drag him down, he focused on the now.

In a strategically planned location, a small canyon protected the house on three sides, making it nearly invisible from the road. Their target was inside. Their quarry unsuspecting, cocky in their confidence, not even considering they'd been found out and were about to be invaded. That not only made them stupid, but predictable, making the team's job that much easier.

As leader and commander of this rag-tag group of shifter wolves, Vic wouldn't send his pack into a rescue mission without having every angle worked out. That had been his way during the war and continued to be his way now. Their intel had been checked. Twice. That relieved only some of the stress he carried. But it would do.

Go on three.

Everyone was ready. Vic gave the count, stepped over the edge of the hill and bounded over fallen logs, branches, tree limbs and other debris.

With three massive timber wolves running close behind him, Vic led the way. The wind rushed past him, stirring his senses, whipped at his face and roared in his ears. Though he wanted to shift and revel in his wolf form, someone had to be able to talk to the bad guys.

The group pulled up at the perimeter of the property. Dane remained by his side as his protector. Luke and Eros took stealthy positions at the back of the house in case someone tried to run.

And they always ran.

Then they'd run right into two big-assed timber wolves waiting for them.

Vic reached for the door. The unlocked knob twisted in his hand, and he grinned. "Sure of themselves, aren't they?" Dane stuck his nose in the door and pushed through, carefully sniffed the air for any danger before Vic entered. Though he had his own senses, they weren't what he possessed in wolf form, so he depended on Dane for the fine details. He switched to their mental link to maintain silence.

What you got?

Three males. Plus the kid. Sweating fear.

What else?

Gun oil. Stinking, man sweat. And chicken. I love chicken!

Get a grip!

Sorry, sir.

The hunger of their beasts could be overwhelming. He knew that. Understood it at an elemental level. Dane was going to get a kick in the ass if he didn't focus. There were few laws within the pack except to maintain the safety, integrity and structure of the group. Dane's job was to scent out the enemy at all costs, even sacrificing his own life if needed, to protect Vic. He hoped that never happened. The wolf and the male were an integral part of this group of ex-soldiers who'd been doomed for prison or suicide until he'd pulled them together into an elite band of brothers that were an unstoppable force. With

With his brother still missing in action there was only one alpha in this pack, and Vic was it.

Anything else?

Potatoes.

Enough with the fucking food. Eat next time.

Yes, boss. Heat in the kitchen.

Stove or people?

Unknown.

Advance. Seek.

Seek, my ass. I'm not a fucking dog.

Do your job . . . Lassie.

Bite me...sir.

Silence was Vic's only answer. Dane eased forward, dropping his tail, ears swiveling, nose high, mouth open, tasting the air, mind interpreting all of the sensations at once. Since the team was strongly connected in the psychic realm, Vic focused on Dane's energy. He sensed everything Dane did. Each scent. Each taste. Each sound filtered through Dane into Vic.

The acrid stench of urine hit Dane's nostril's hard,

almost wrenching a gag from his throat. Mingling with the unmistakable scent of fear and the salt of a tears, it seared his sinuses and watered his eyes. Vic sensed it all and choked it down with a grimace.

I'm gonna puke.

Suck it up, Buttercup. You've smelled worse.

Gack!

Two of the men argued about what to do with the kid once they got the ransom money. One wanted to kill him. One wanted to give him back. The third just wanted to kill someone. Anyone.

They're escalating. Time to move.

At Vic's signal, the other two wolves breached the house, bursting in through windows, shattering glass that clattered like diamonds on the ceramic tile floor.

"What the ... " They saw Dane first. One man raised his weapon, but the wolf was faster. The other wolves dove in. Their mission wasn't to kill these idiots, just disable them, rescue the kid, and then haul their stupid asses out to the authorities.

Screams echoed off the walls of the dining room as Dane grabbed the fleshy wrist of his quarry and shook. The man dropped the weapon from his hand and it rattled to the floor. He and Dane landed on the floor with a thud, but Dane didn't let go. He placed one massive front paw on the center of the man's using his weight hold the guy down. This wolf knew how to show who was in charge of this situation. Dane growled low in his throat, a primal sound designed to strike fear into the heart. The man stopped screaming, stopped squirming, stopped resisting. Vic wasn't sure if he stopped breathing.

"Where's the kid?" Vic demanded. "Tell me where, so I

won't have to beat it out of you." Though at this point Vic might enjoy it more than simply having the information.

"Go ahead. Try." The pudgy, stinking excuse for a human sneered at Vic.

"You obviously don't realize the position you're in." How could someone be that stupid when there was a wolf standing on his chest? "Dane? Can you give him a better demonstration of what kind of position he's in?"

Without further instruction, Dane clamped down harder on the dude's wrist and wrenched it to the side once. A satisfying snap and the man's scream let Vic know the bones were now broken.

"Stop. Stop him. He'll kill me!" Tears of pain and possibly fear rolled from his eyes. That's what Vic called an attitude adjustment.

"Then tell me what I want to know. Where is the kid?" Vic asked through clenched teeth.

"What kid?" The idiot tried one last time, trying Vic's patience.

Vic snapped his fingers, and Dane released the man's mangled wrist. With fangs bared, he closed his mouth over the man's throat. And squeezed.

The man froze, his eyes wide, looking at Vic as if he were joking.

Vic Stone didn't joke.

"All I have to do is snap my fingers again, and he'll snap your neck."

"No. Wait." The kidnapper squeaked out the words, his feet squirming against the tile floor. The rest of him remained rigidly still.

"*Where's* the kid?"

"End of hall." The voice was high-pitched, and the stink of hot piss filled the air, polluting Vic's nostrils with the

8

stench. Justice was falling into place. Pretty soon they could go home, crack open a few beers, put their feet up and laugh about the day and the humans they scared the piss out of.

Vic left Dane to control him. With a glance at the others who had their targets locked up in similar fashion, he nodded. Safety maintained.

With all three kidnappers held by his team, Vic ignored the human's pleas. Gun drawn and by his side, he moved down the hall to the bedroom. Hesitating. Taking measured steps, he approached the room in silence. Someone could still be with the kid. Their intel had informed them of only three kidnappers, but not taking any chances, Vic prepared for more. He always prepared for more, which had kept the pack alive through countless hazardous missions. No matter how good the intel was, it could still be wrong. Just the way it was wrong about his brother. He had to believe it. He had to.

The bedroom door was open a few inches, and he could see the kid inside. Tied up, thrown on a dirty mattress on the floor that smelled of shit, piss and other things he wished he hadn't interpreted. The funk of scents filled his mind, even in his human form. Vic now wanted to puke, too. The kid looked directly at Vic, the bitter stench of fear oozing from every pore.

Vic met the kid's gaze and raised one finger to his mouth, indicating silence. Hopefully, the kid would follow Vic's direction. He didn't know that someone was coming for him. He could think Vic was out to kill him, too.

Vic breached the bedroom. He slammed the door wide. It bounced off the wall flinging drywall debris in all directions. Protective instincts surging forward, he was prepared to kill anyone who interfered in his rescue of this boy. In the wolf community, the sanctity of the pack and protecting the pups was paramount. No adult wolf would allow an invader to harm the future of the group, sometimes sacrificing themselves to save the young ones. Vic wouldn't allow any harm to come to this kid. He wasn't part of Vic's pack, but was under the protection of it. That's all that mattered.

The boy squealed and fought against his restraints, trying to escape.

Vic knelt and holstered his gun. "It's okay, Turner. I've got you. I've got you." After Vic removed the gag from Turner's mouth, he screamed and kicked at Vic. Vic let him. Turner needed an outlet for the fear and frustration boiling inside of him. Vic could take it. "Turner, listen. Your dad sent me. It's okay. Your dad sent me."

That statement stilled Turner's movements, but his eyes remained wide and panicked, his breathing erratic as his chest worked to draw the next ragged breath.

"No. You're going to kill me!" Hysterical, Turner screamed again. "I heard you out there. You just want to kill me."

"I'm not going to kill you. Listen to me. Lego Batman." Vic reached for his pocket slowly, trying not to escalate Turner's imagination.

"What?" Turner fell back onto the mattress, scooted away from Vic and pressed himself into the corner against the wall as he tried to make sense of what Vic said.

"Lego Batman. Your dad said your favorite toy is your Lego Batman, right?" Vic relaxed, or at least gave the appearance of it as he knelt on the floor, taking a position that wasn't intimidating, but enabled him to flash upright if it all went wrong. He kept half an ear out for trouble in the main room, but heard nothing from that direction, nor from the internal comm.

"Yeah, so what?" The wild remained in Turner's eyes, though his breathing had slowed. The bitter scent of fear, the taste of it, lingered in the back of Vic's throat. If this didn't stop pretty soon, he was going to need a breath mint.

"So, your dad sent yours so you'd know I'm telling the truth." He paused, gauging the boy's response. All good. "I'm going to get it out of my vest." Slowly, with deliberate movements, Vic extracted the plastic toy with scratches. "I'll untie you, too. Okay?"

Tears rolled down Turner's dirty cheeks, leaving streaks of mud. He nodded, keeping his eyes on the toy he obviously recognized. "Here. You hold him. I'm going to get my knife out and cut those ties."

Turner snatched the figure from Vic's hands. His tearful gaze fastened on the beloved toy, his brain beginning to recognize it was indeed his, that Vic spoke the truth. He was about to be rescued. The kid was still going to need years of therapy after this, but at least he'd be safe. Vic pulled an eight-inch Bowie knife from the sheath at his right hip. If a gun jammed or he lost it in a fight, this weapon was his next favorite and was invaluable in hand-to-hand combat. Thank the gods for the Bowie brother who'd invented it.

For the moment, it was a simple tool used to cut a piece of rope. After Turner's hands were free, the ten year old clasped the toy to his face and sobbed. The sounds were pitiful, heartbreaking. Vic had to harden his heart against them. If he softened now, gave in to offer Turner any comfort, their safety could be compromised. "Hold on just a little longer, kid. We'll have you back with your dad in no time." The knife easily slipped through the ankle bindings. The skin was raw, red and ugly looking, but they didn't have time to deal with it now. Vic stood. "Let's get you out of here. Your dad's waiting."

"Okay." Turner sniffed, rubbed his face on the sleeve of his tattered shirt, then allowed Vic to help him up. "Okay."

"Stay behind me. The bad guys are out there. I'm going to tie them up until the FBI gets here."

"No." Turned flattened himself against the wall, his eyes wide with terror again. "They're going to kill me. I heard them! They want to kill me. Just for *fun*." Turner's voice cracked on the last word and sobs began anew with tears streaking through the dirt on his little face.

Facing the boy, Vic knelt in front of him, not to offer comfort but a lesson in logic. "Do you see how big I am?"

"Yeah." Turner looked into Vic's eyes, his attention for the moment distracted and his sobs quieted.

"I'm way bigger than those guys, right?" Vic gave a sideways smile, trying to engage the kid, keep his attention directed away from the situation behind him and moving forward with the rescue.

"Yeah." Turner nodded, beginning to see where Vic was headed.

"I've got three friends out there who aren't going to let anything happen to you. I'm bigger than those guys. There's no way they're getting through me." Vic winked at Turner.

For the first time, a small grin flashed across Turner's face, lighting up the brown eyes that had just been filled with tears. One corner of his mouth lifted, and he gave a sharp nod. "You can take 'em?"

Vic raised his brows and nodded once in return. "I can take 'em." He squeezed Turner's thin shoulder, trying to instill some sense of comfort, and stood. "Come see. My team has them wrapped up pretty good."

Vic moved down the hall with Turner hanging onto the back of his belt, still needing that connection to an adult who was going to save him. Vic stayed alert, sending his senses out to the others for any change in the situation, but there was none. The boys maintained their positions as he and Turner entered the kitchen.

Vic extracted his phone from a vest pocket, Turner sidled closer. His eyes wide and focused on the scene in front of him, he quieted, the sobs and tears gone. "I'm calling your dad to let him know you're safe." The call was answered in a nano-second.

"Yes?"

"We have him. He's safe." Vic gave the man the news with no preamble. Pride stirred in his heart at being able to tell the man his son was safe and their mission was a complete success. That this group of men, and wolves, he called brothers, had succeeded in another mission, upholding justice and holding violators of the law accountable for their stupid-assed actions. *Hoo-rah.*

These guys were going down the pike for a long, long time. In prison, Vic had no doubt they would be dealt with accordingly. Prisoners, even hardened ones, took umbrage at people who hurt children. There would be justice, one way or another.

"Let me talk to him." Emotions trembled in the father's voice.

Vic put the phone on speaker. Turner took it from Vic, but never took his eyes off the wolf in front of him. "Dad? You gotta see this."

"Turner! Are you okay? Did they hurt you?" Vic heard the desperation in the father's voice, knowing he needed reassurance from his son.

"No. I'm okay." He shrugged, his eyes wide and fixed on

Dane. "You have to see this. Vic, he's the guy who saved me, he has wolves. I mean *real wolves.*" Life and confidence had zoomed back into Turner who only saw three massive wolves in the kitchen, not the bad guys under their feet. "This is so awesome."

"Let me talk to your dad again." Vic held his hand out for the phone.

"Okay." He looked at Vic, then back at the four-legged guards. "Can I touch one?"

Before answering, Vic spoke to Turner's dad. "Tell the FBI we've secured the targets, and that your son is safe. We'll wait here until you arrive." He ended the call and pocketed the phone. "Let me get this one tied up, then you can pet Dane."

What? I don't want him to pet me. Can't you see I'm busy here? Mouth full of bad guy.

Get over yourself. He needs this.

Well, I don't. It's humiliating and not what I trained for.

Vic ignored Dane's whiny ass as he pulled out a zip tie from his pocket and prepared to secure the kidnapper's hands. In a flash, the guy pulled a knife from a hidden sheath and drove it into Dane's side. With a startled yelp, Dane released the man's neck. Without thinking, Vic had his gun in his hand and shoved it into his face.

"Tempt me." Vic growled the words.

Death gleamed darkly in the man's black eyes. "Fuck you, dog lover."

Vic pistol whipped the guy, knocking him out. He wasn't going to put up with that shit or listen to smack from this coward's ass. Vic flipped the unconscious man over, zip-tied him, then secured the other two before releasing his team members from their positions.

Dane? What's your status? He spoke to the wolf lying on

14

the floor in front of him, not wanting to admit that the pool of blood expanding beneath Dane shook Vic as nothing else could. Their safety was paramount on a mission. In one nanosecond, one brief second of turning his attention away from the mark, and Dane had suffered the consequences, might die because of a lapse in Vic's judgment.

I told you I didn't want the kid to touch me.

Fuck you, wolf. Fuck you.

CHAPTER
TWO

Dane was in trouble. Vic knew it. They all did.

Vic motioned Turner closer with him to Dane's side. "You can pet him with me."

No.

Shut up. I'm going to give you some of my energy so you don't shift back in front of the kid and scar him for life.

Oh. Gotcha. Good plan.

"Let's pet him together," Vic said.

Turner dropped to his knees, his eyes wide with excitement. "Where can I touch him?"

"Right around his ears. He likes that," Vic said and placed Turner's hand on Dane's head, but away from his teeth.

"I'll do that." With a hand that hesitated, Turner stroked Dane's ears and the back of his head. "He's so soft."

"You're doing great, kid." Vic placed one hand on Dane's wound, pressing hard. Forcing pressure against it, sending the sizzle and zing of energy from his power center into the knife wound. It hurt like a son-of-a-bitch. Dane whimpered and closed his eyes, his muscles trembling with the effort not to move, but Vic didn't let up.

Vic closed his eyes. Energy simmered hot and sharp in his gut. Twisting it into knots. Pulling it tight. Drawing power from his beast, sending it up through his heart, circulating through his arm, down into his hand, into the raw flesh of the wound, Vic forced his energy into Dane. The stench of burning fur made him open his eyes, but his focus remained inward, on keeping the channel open.

"Whoa." Turner's eyes were wide as he watched smoke waft upward, then he wrinkled his nose and pulled back a little. "Oh, man. That stinks." Singed, burnt fur smelled like shit and lingered in the memory. Yet another thing for Turner not to forget any time soon.

More of the terror left Turner as he stroked Dane. There was something to be said for animal therapy. Probably why cops carried stuffed animals with them to give to kids during times of crisis. Stuffed or live, animals always helped. Vic looked at the other two wolves and spoke on their psychic link.

You two, head out. Shift, get dressed and come back.

Roger that.

Watch your six, boss.

Eros and Luke were concerned about Dane. As their leader, they depended on Vic to keep the situation under control. Their golden eyes darted toward Vic, Dane and Turner. Heads down, they trotted on long legs and big feet out the front door. The clattering of their claws on the tile flooring was the only sound they made as they disappeared into the shadows

"Whoa. That was awesome." Turner stared wide-eyed after them, his chest working hard with his excitement.

"They're so cool. I can't believe you get to work with wolves."

"I can't believe I get to work with wolves, either," Vic said and shook his head, his meaning totally different than Turner's.

"What?"

"Nothing. They're usually good to work with, and it's rare for one of them to be injured." Really rare. Vic clenched his jaw, the muscles tightening hard as he mentally kicked his own ass for letting it happen. He was the boss. The alpha. He was the leader. It was his job to keep them safe. He'd failed Dane. Failed them all. Big time.

Boss, it's okay. Neither of us knew he had the blade.

It's not okay until you're on your feet again.

"Oh." Turner faced Dane again and continued to stroke the great wolf's ears.

How are you?

Better. Less pain.

There's less blood, too. I think you're going to live.

Thanks.

Vic halted the focused energy he gave to Dane and conserved some of it for himself and took a few breaths. Magical transference depleted energy stores, and he didn't want to be carried out because he'd drained himself.

Now, Vic turned away from Dane and listened intently. In human form his hearing was less acute, but he could still hear the sirens and the engines roaring as police and rescue vehicles headed their way. Soon they'd be overrun by humans with a lot less control than he'd like. He had to get Dane out of there ASAP and to better medical help than he could give.

Can you walk? Can you shift?

19

I can walk, but my clothes are on the ridge.

Vic sensed the others returning.

Then we wait. You'll have to stay a wolf a while longer.

Great. Just great.

The kid likes you, so deal with it.

Vic placed his hand on the floor beside Dane's head and Dane snapped at him. With a curse, Vic pulled his hand back and sucked on the puncture wound between his thumb and first finger.

You asshole. What'd you do that for?

I couldn't bite the kid, so I bit you.

Dammit, now. Just stop it, or I'll muzzle you.

Vic stood and held a hand down to Turner. "Let's go kid. I think your dad's going to be in one of those cars racing up the road right now."

"Really?" Turner stood, but didn't move away from Dane. "I want to show him your wolf. Can I?"

"Yeah." He looked at Dane who'd moved from the side position to half-sitting up. He lifted one hind leg straight up and licked his balls.

You asshole. Stop that.

What? I had an itch.

The kid is watching.

Like his balls never itched.

I'm writing you up for indecent exposure.

Hey, I'm the victim here. I'm the one who took a knife.

Forget it. Behave yourself. The cops are seconds away.

I heard.

Dane lifted his head and howled. The sirens hurt his ears, even at a distance. The vibration and tone gave him a headache. Gave them all headaches. In human form, they'd plug their ears or use ear buds and crank up the music.

Dane couldn't right then. As a wolf, Dane did what wolves did to express themselves. He howled, crying out his displeasure at the noxious sounds pounding imaginary spikes into his brain.

I'll tell them to cut the sirens.

Too late.

Dane howled as Vic called the lead investigator of the special victims' unit to go silent. The sirens stopped, but it didn't help. Dane continued to howl.

If you didn't just get knifed in the side, I'd kick your ass.

Too bad. Makes me feel better.

He raised his head and took a deep breath, preparing to vent again.

Stop it. That's an order.

Dane growled and tried to stand, but couldn't get his feet beneath him. That got Vic's attention. Maybe the injury was more serious than he'd thought at first. "Stay."

Stay, my ass. I'm not a . . . fucking . . . dog.

Dane dropped to the floor, his feet splaying out in all directions.

Eros. Luke. Dane's down!

The doors burst open and the other two males raced into the house, weapons drawn, faces fierce, eyes wide and searching for any threat.

"What happened? I thought you stopped the bleeding?" Eros asked and moved closer. His energy was sharp and piercing.

"I did. There must have more internal damage than I realized." Vic ground his teeth. "We've got to get him out of here, but the FBI is on the way with Turner's dad."

"We'll see to the boy, sir," Luke said, his eyes cold.

"No, you stay with Dane," Eros said. "I'll go get the

Hummer." The black felt hat he wore from his days as an Army Ranger perched on his head, making him seem more severe than he already was.

"Go," Vic said.

Eros dropped his weapons and sprinted out the door. Vic didn't need to tell him to hurry. He knew. They all knew. Dane was going to die unless they got him help and fast.

"What's wrong with him?" Turner dropped to his knees again. "I don't want him to die." Tears filled the boy's eyes, obviously more concerned about the wolf than with his own situation now.

"He's not going to die." Vic turned his head slightly, listening. The vehicles were almost to the house. "Your dad is going to be here in a minute, so I think we need to get you out there to meet him." He had to get the kid out of there in case Dane couldn't maintain his form. Keeping pack secrets meant keeping them from everyone, including those they rescued.

"I'll stay with Dane, sir," Luke said and gave a crisp nod letting Vic know he wasn't asking permission. Of all of them, Luke cared the most, laughed the loudest, hurt the deepest.

"We'll be out front." Vic looked down at Turner. "Let's go see your dad, kid. He's getting out of the car now."

"How do you know that?" Turner asked but headed toward the door with his Lego Batman still clutched in his hand.

"Good ears." Turner walked with Vic, but looked over his shoulder at Dane. "Let's go see your dad."

"Okay." He nodded and looked up at Vic. "He's worried about me, isn't he?"

"He sure is. He'll be really happy to see you're okay, though," Vic said.

"Yeah, sometimes Dad gets scared for me. I have to let him know I'm growing up now, so he can relax." Turner gave an exaggerated sigh.

"You do that." One corner of Vic's mouth rose at the kid's philosophy.

They exited the house as four black SUV's rounded the corner, kicking up a storm of dust.

"Turner? Turner!" A man in his forties jumped out of the SUV before it stopped. He stumbled and dropped to his knees, but recovered and raced to his son.

"Mr. Jenkins. Stop," one of the FBI agents called to the man.

"Dad!" Turner raced across the driveway and launched himself into his father's arms. They fell to the ground, but Mr. Jenkins caught himself with one hand as Turner clung to him like a lanky, blond monkey, wrapping arms and legs around his dad and held on tight.

"Are you okay, sir?" Vic asked, knowing the man wouldn't admit it if he were hurt.

"I'm fine." He rose to his knees and held onto Turner as tears streamed down the man's face. "I'm fine. Now."

"Dad. This is Vic." Turner launched into a synopsis of what had happened to him since the arrival of Vic and his wolves. "He's the one who saved me. He has this really cool wolf, Dane, but he's hurt, real bad." His voice dropped and softened as he gave the report on Dane.

"I'm sure there's a lot you want to tell me, but right now, I need to know if you're okay." Mr. Jenkins stood and wiped his eyes on his sleeve, looking casual, but somewhat uncomfortable, in jeans and a denim shirt. He looked like he'd be more at home in a board room than Vic could ever imagine being.

"I'm okay. Kinda hungry. They kept me tied up in the

23

bedroom and didn't feed me." Turner shrugged. "I don't think they know how to take care of kids."

Mr. Jenkins laughed. It was a relieved kind of bark. "Yes, well. That's probably a good thing they aren't around kids too much."

"I have to agree with that, sir." Vic had seen a lot of criminals, and those guys were lucky they got their shoes tied right. He didn't know how they managed to jack a rich kid off the street and ransom him for three million dollars.

"You're Vic Stone?" Mr. Jenkins held out his hand and shook Vic's.

"Yes. I'm the company commander." He nodded. "Pleasure to meet you, sir, but unfortunately under less than desirable circumstances."

"Agreed. Thank you, commander." Mr. Jenkins took a deep breath and let it out slowly as he regained control of his frayed emotions.

"Can I show him Dane?" Turner practically danced on his feet, eagerness pulsing in energetic waves. Apparently, he'd forgotten that he'd been kidnapped, hadn't eaten in two days and smelled like piss and vomit.

"Yes, but only for a minute. I have to get him to the . . . vet as soon as Eros brings the Hummer." Vic scanned the road looking for the vehicle.

"I hope he's okay." He tugged on his dad's arm. "C'mon. He's really cool."

Their conversation faded away as they left him. He could hear the roar of the Hummer racing down the road. The whine of the engine was distinctive, and he could pick it out a mile away.

Eros brought the olive-green Hummer, painted in camouflage colors, to the front door and hopped out as other agents went inside to take the prisoners.

"You ready?" Eros opened the back door of the Hummer, shoved equipment onto the floor, and grabbed a heavy gray tarp. It could be used to transport someone to the hospital. Or the graveyard.

"Yeah. Let's roll," Vic said.

Together they entered the house to retrieve Dane.

Eros dropped to one knee beside Dane.

"C'mon, Turner." Jenkins stood and pulled his son away. "We need to take you home to your mother and get out of their way. They have work to do."

"Aw. Can't I stay with Dane?" he asked, his gaze pleading.

"No. Afraid not, Turner," Vic said and slid the edge of the tarp beneath Dane's limp hind quarters. "We have to get him to medical help right away."

Pressing his lips together and clutching his Lego Batman, Turner rushed to Vic, hugged him hard, then returned to his father's side. Jenkins placed his hands on his son's shoulders and eased back against the wall, out of the way.

They maneuvered Dane onto the tarp and lifted. With a sharp cry of pain, Dane stirred, not happy with being moved, but there was no way around it. Once they got him onto the back seat of the vehicle, they piled in. This assignment fortunately was in their back yard, as Turner was the son of a New Mexico oil company executive, and Vic's favorite veterinarian was nearby.

"Call the doc. Let her know we're bringing Dane in and to be ready for anything." The clinic closed around six pm, so they had to haul ass to get there before it closed.

Eros made the call on the satellite phone, since there was no cell service most of the time in the deeper parts of the Sandia Mountains. Vic tried to connect to Dane on the inner comm. The inquiries hung on the air, unanswered. If the wolf couldn't connect in their psychic world, he was in serious trouble.

Vic turned the vehicle from the dirt road onto the paved, two-lane highway and floored it.

CHAPTER
THREE

Vic pushed the Hummer to its limits on the mountain highway. Dane's life was on the line. He'd put his life at risk to save the rest of them countless times. They'd do the same for him now. Vic passed car after car, people heading home after a long work day, teenagers groping each other, and tractor trailers hauling goods to market. And one lone guy sweating it up on a bicycle.

He flashed the lights, letting the slow poke in front of him know that he was coming up on the side. He wasn't backing off. Not for anyone.

"Easy, boss. Don't kill us trying to save Dane's lame ass," Luke said. The callous words were a measure of his affection and devotion to his pack mate and best friend.

"Okay. Okay. Keep your panties on." Vic completed the maneuver and brought the vehicle back onto the road safely and hit the gas again. "We'll get there in one piece. I'm not going to listen to him complain the rest of my life about how long it took to get him to the doctor."

"Yeah, you know he will, too." Luke snorted. The

tension lifted for a moment, then landed again on them. Luke placed his hand on Dane's back. "We'll be there soon, buddy." Dane's only response was a whimper and a half-hearted attempt to lick Luke's hand. Dave looked up at Luke with his golden eyes, then snapped at the hand in front of his face. "Shit. He just tried to bite me."

"Stop it, Dane. It's not his fault." Vic frequently intervened between these two who loved their volatile friendship. It was like watching two-year-old's, most of the time. Right now, he had his hands full driving like a maniac, trying not getting them all killed.

Dane growled, then woofed once in apology and nudged Luke's arm with his nose.

"Fucking jackal," Luke grumbled, and glared at Dane.

"We're all worked up. Keep it together," Eros said. "We have to get Dane looked at, then you two can argue for all eternity for all I care."

"I'm trying. I'm trying," Luke said and huffed out a sharp breath.

Finally, they reached the turn-off Vic was looking for, and he pulled onto a dirt road leading down a rutted lane with one sign that simply read *Veterinarian*.

Vic drove right past the parking area, past the front door, pulled around to the back of the two-story adobe style home. They could keep the Hummer out of sight and take Dane inside unseen by other veterinary clients. Or Alpha Company enemies.

If word got out that one of Alpha Company was down, it would signal blood in the water to rival shifter groups. The vast territory Alpha Company protected was prime real estate and open to challenge at any sign of weakness.

At all times, all places and all ways, Vic and the pack had to protect their identities. Especially when lives were on the line. Not just theirs, but the humans they rescued and FBI agents they worked with. Alpha Company hadn't come this far to give it all up in one moment of lapsed judgment, no matter the urgency.

Vic could never lose his edge or his position as alpha was over. The other pack members would replace him, or he'd kill himself first. Viable packs had no place for unproductive members. Those who were unable to hunt, defend their territory or care for pups were driven out when they became non-functional or a burden on the pack. At least that's how it's always been.

That was the old way. Vic envisioned a new way, but changes from old traditions took time. Sometimes generations. The time had not yet come for him to attempt to make major changes. Not without his brother by his side. One day the time, and opportunity, would come.

Right now, what was important was getting Dane's injury tended to. Simple healing energy hadn't fixed it, so it was obviously deep.

"I'll let the doc know we're here. Bring him in." Vic slammed the door shut. Luke and Eros carried out his orders. Vic entered the clinic and paused at the assault on his senses.

Someone had had fish for lunch. One of the employees was pregnant. Someone's dog was in heat. Great. That's what he *didn't* need right now.

"Hey, Kelly. Doc ready for us?" he asked the pregnant young woman with dark eyes and long dark hair who stared at him with her mouth hanging open.

"Oh, geez, commander. You scared the bejesus out of me." She put one hand on her chest and the other on the counter. "*Aye.* Don't sneak up on a pregnant woman like that."

29

"Sorry. We have a seriously injured wolf. We're bringing him in now." No time for niceties when a life was on the line.

"I heard you were coming, but I didn't think you'd be here so soon." She hurried toward one of the exam rooms. "Bring him in here. We'll get him fixed up, don't you worry." She pointed to the room. "I'll get Trista."

Vic opened the back door and directed them to the room Kelly had indicated. Here, they had to be careful of every word they spoke. No one in this office knew what they were, or what they did. One false move with the doc, one slip of confidential information, and she'd know they weren't what they said they were. Over the last two years he'd been able to bring the boys in for minor issues and not worry about keeping secrets, but today was a whole other level of concern.

Luke and Eros carried Dane in on the tarp and placed him gently on the large stainless-steel table. Vic tried to connect with Dane, but he'd lost consciousness during the last part of the ride. Dammit. This was not the outcome he'd wanted, not what he'd expected and certainly wouldn't accept. Dane wasn't going to die. He couldn't. Vic couldn't take the guilt on top of the loss of his friend and essential member of the pack leadership.

"Commander? What's going on? Kelly said you had an injured team member?" Trista Holiday, with blond hair, green eyes and exotic look that spoke of a northern European heritage, burst into the room. The second he heard her voice, caught her scent, locked eyes with her across the table, a zing shot through him. It happened the same way every time he'd seen her and his resistance to her allure was dropping like a rock. Something about her aroused him, stirred him, even under the most dire of circumstances.

Something about this human woman called to him, electrified his base nature and set him on fire. He liked it. *A lot.*

Green glints in her eyes sparkled with her passion to care for animals, her focus on Dane skyrocketed.

"What happened, and who is this? He's not wearing his tags. You *know* he needs to be wearing his tags," she said. When neither of the other two spoke, she looked at Vic, her emerald and gold eyes sizzling into his. "Commander?" Though the situation was serious, she lifted one corner of her mouth. "This looks more serious than any of the other injuries you've brought them in with."

"This is Dane. Took a knife. Tags were an oversight." They all wore dog tags in human form, but they often required silent, stealth mode in wolf form and tags didn't work then. Even a small clattering of tags could give them away. She was right though. Most stuff had been simple.

"Was it an accident? Give me some details." Her delicate hands parted the fur, searching for the injury. Kelly shaved the fur off of one leg and inserted an IV, then connected it to a bag of life-saving fluids.

"We were on a mission. One of the kidnappers stabbed Dane. The rest is classified." Vic watched her efficient and graceful hands move over Dane's body looking for the injury and without realizing it gave him some of her own energy. Tiny sparks flashed in his fur. Maybe it was just static. Maybe it was her own brand of healing magic.

"Kidnappers? Classified, huh? Are we going to see you on the news?" She cast an inquiring gaze on Vic, then returned her attention to Dane's abdomen.

"I hope not," he said with all sincerity.

"Did you get them, at least?" The frown that crossed her face drew her eyebrows together for a few seconds, then it vanished, but the concern remained on her face.

"Yeah. We got the bad guys. Saved the day." Could that sound more lame? It was the truth, but sounded like he was making up a story in a bar to get lucky.

"That's good." She didn't look up. "Kelly, get Garcia. Tell him to prep the OR. I have to open Dane up. I can't see a damned thing in there. Some weird scar tissue or something formed over the wound already."

"Got it." Kelly made the call to find Trista's surgical assistant.

"See this?" Without any fear, she placed her fingers into the mouth of the unconscious wolf and lifted his lips, exposing his lethal white teeth and pale pink gums. "The color should be a beefy red, not like this." A sigh folded out of her as her concern pulsed out in irregular beats. Though she hid it now, she had a fondness for Dane. For all of them, really. Her attempt to hide her feelings about them weren't very successful. Vic knew more about her than she realized. She had no idea her thoughts and feelings were wide open to him.

"They're too pale? I'm guessing that's not a hygiene issue," he said.

"Yes, they're too pale, and no it's not a hygiene issue. The color indicates he's lost a lot of blood." With one hand she patted his firm and rounded belly. "It's all right here."

"We already knew he was bleeding. We can donate blood, though," Luke said eagerly. Eros nodded.

"Are you out of your minds?" Trista asked, the look on her face incredulous as her brows shot up. "You can't donate for a different *species*. You know that, right?"

"Oh. Yeah," Luke said and looked to Vic to save him. *Help.*

"What he means is, we have wolf blood packaged and ready to go at our compound. We can retrieve it and bring it back. If you'll allow it, that is," Vic said.

Thank you!

Shut up.

"Yes. Get it back here as soon as you can," she said with a crisp nod. "I'm going to get him into the OR now. This can't wait any longer."

Go. Get as much as we've got. Vic nodded at Eros who bolted out the door with Luke fast on his heels.

"They'll be back in no time," Vic said and heard the Hummer fire to life.

"I hope so." She gave one last pat to Dane's head and opened his IV to administer fluids wide open. Concern filled every movement, and Vic sensed her trepidation over the upcoming surgery. It could go either way and she didn't like those odds. She was an excellent surgeon, which is why he'd brought Dane to her. If she couldn't fix him, then he couldn't be fixed.

Kelly turned the clippers to Dane's abdomen and shaved the fur from around the stab wound.

"I'd like to be in surgery with him," Vic said. He'd been with every one of his men when they'd been injured. He wasn't going to lose one now because he couldn't be in the operating room, connected to them in the psychic realm. Somehow, he was going to talk her into it, whether she knew it or not.

"That's not something I normally allow, not something that's even recommended." Trista looked at Vic and held his gaze, trying to figure him out, to see if he were true and could handle what he was asking for. He usually kept his mind and psychic senses closed off, protecting himself from others who would use his emotions against him. Right now, with the doc, he had to open the channel to send her the vibes that would *invite* her to agree. "He'll be sedated, he won't be able to hear or respond to you," she said. That might be true for *normal* canids, but not for *lycanthropus*.

That's where she was wrong. Dane would hear Vic. He would respond to Vic. Just not in a way Trista understood.

"In the Middle East, I led teams into battle countless times. I stayed with each one of them when they were injured and required surgery. Just because we're back in the States, and he's a wolf, doesn't mean he doesn't deserve the same respect I gave my men over there." Vic looked unblinking at her, holding the vibration between them strong. "He's still a soldier."

She stared at him for a long moment. She was making a decision based on facts in the moment, not a knee-jerk reaction based on what she'd always done. The respect he already had for her rose as he watched her.

"I'll allow you in surgery with us, but a few rules apply. Behave yourself. Don't talk to me or interrupt in any way. If you so much as twitch the wrong way, you're out of there." She gave him her best stern look that had absolutely no effect on him. He just smiled.

Leaning close until his face was just inches from hers, he locked his gaze deeply into hers. The scent of her, the heat of her, wafted over him. She stirred something deep, some primal male instinct, that took him by surprise. Not much surprised him anymore, but this he could work with. This was hot.

"I agree to your terms, but who is going to *try* to kick me out?" he asked.

Trista licked her lips, drawing his attention there. The

mouth, her lips, their fullness and curves made him want to rub his thumb over them. See if they were as soft as they looked. Made him wonder if she tasted as sweet as she smelled. Trying to look tough, she cocked her lower jaw to one side, and he tried to shove his beast back.

"*I'll* kick your ass out, commander, because you're not going to jeopardize Dane's life." She shoved him back half a step, and he let her. "Follow me, and stay out of the way. Garcia! Where are you?" She moved out into the hall and Vic followed her trying not to notice the stretch of her scrub pants across her curves.

"Here, Trista. I'm here," Garcia said. He had an array of equipment set up, ready for the patient. "I can get Dane if you're ready."

"I'll get him. He's my responsibility," Vic said. Needing a minute to reel his reactions in, Vic retreated from the surgery room and returned to the exam room where Dane lay. His eyes were open, focused on the IV dripping into his right leg. Vic tried to connect to him one more time before they put him under.

Still alive?

Yeah, bite me.

Sounds like you're on the mend.

Got enough piss left to tell you to fuck off.

Good. Then you'll make it through surgery.

Surgery? What's she going to do to me?

He whined, panicked eyes followed Vic, and Dane pulled his tail between his legs in submission.

She's gonna save your life, that's what she's going to do and you're going to submit whether you like it or not. Got it?

But boss...

Trista entered the room with a clipboard and handed Vic a pen. "Sign the consent, please. Do you want me to neuter him, while we're at it? Won't take too long, and he'll be a better animal for you."

Dane huffed his breath in and out several times, then growled at her.

She's mean. I'm going to bite her.

Don't bite her, Dane. She's just doing her job.

"He's not a pet. He's a working... animal. We'll leave him unaltered." He glanced at Dane and arched a brow in consideration. "At least for the moment."

"Okay. It's your skin if he takes a hunk out of you," she said.

Vic raised his hand, showing her what was clearly a bite wound, the skin turning red. "Already did that, so we're good."

"What?" Trista tossed the clipboard onto the counter and took his hand in hers, then cast a green-eyed glare at him. "Why didn't you tell me sooner? When was your last tetanus shot? Did you at least clean it?" Without any consideration of pain he might be having, she dragged him to the sink, turned the taps on and held his hand under scalding hot water.

"Hey. Shit! That hurts." Vic tried to pull his hand away, but she was stronger than she looked.

"Suck it up, tough guy. You'll live." Placating him only a little, she adjusted the water temperature to slightly less than Hell's steam bath and pumped the soap dispenser three times. She scrubbed his hand, focusing on the puncture marks on the pad between his thumb and first finger, the flesh already tender. Nothing she did made it feel better. Only worse.

"Holy Hell, woman. Leave me some skin," Vic said, trying to maintain his dignity and extract himself from her grasp.

"Not if you intend to keep your hand. You didn't even wash your hands after he bit you, did you? Do you know what kind of bacteria wolves have in their mouths?" Shaking her head, she clearly communicated her disgust at his lack of action. With this woman, he wasn't going to have to work very hard to figure out what she was thinking.

"No. I was kind of busy driving like a maniac to get here," he muttered.

"So, where are your buddies? We need that blood going before I can start surgery. Dane's going to need at least two units. IV fluids only help so much," she said.

"They'll be here any time. The compound is just a few miles from here." They were out of his inner radar range right now, so they were likely inside the fenced and gated property.

"The compound? You've mentioned that before," she said, and he cringed. Another almost-slip they couldn't afford. The pressure of her ministrations eased, and the pain in his hand decreased somewhat, but it still hummed with pain. "Where is it?"

"Over the ridge." She was making conversation, and he was hiding secrets.

The vague answer was deliberate. There was a lot of land and forest that direction. The secret compound only opened for a select few. Anyone else was politely asked to leave. Or chased off by a pack of wolves. That usually kept the casually curious at bay.

"*Over the ridge*? There's a lot of *over* over the ridge." She rinsed the suds off of his hand, then pressed another dispenser and applied clear, stinging acid onto his hand and he hissed through his teeth.

"That shit stings, too." The pain was instant, blazing and almost made him shift right in front of her. *Gods.*

"I know. It's supposed to. The second phase of hand washing. Alcohol gel." After a twitch of her delicate brows, she gave him a look. Where females learned that shit was beyond him, but every female he'd ever known had given him that look at one time or another.

"I prefer my alcohol in a glass, if you don't mind," he said. Seriously.

"Yes, well, now you'll live long enough to raise one with this hand. At least now it won't rot off from infection. Call your doctor. Get an antibiotic and a tetanus booster. Tomorrow." Her touch softened as she applied an antibiotic goop and a Band-aid.

"Those hurt, too," he said, trying to maintain his dignity as an alpha and trying to ignore his internal beast that was laughing at his behavior.

"Didn't you do two tours in Iraq, tough guy?" Her brows twitched again, as if she were having a hard time controlling her amusement.

Some part of him wanted to say it wasn't fair, she was being a bully. The deeper male part of him insisted that he liked it. Wanted her to keep it up. As long as it meant her hand remained on his, her body stayed next to him, and her heat melted him. That scent of hers stirred wild longings of what he'd do to her if he ever got the chance.

After today, he wouldn't in good conscience be able to hassle Dane about being a pervert. He was just as bad.

He didn't care. The beast in him didn't care. The animal in him just wanted to scent her and bend her over the nearest piece of furniture and claim her as his.

CHAPTER
FOUR

Unfortunately, he had to rein his desires in. She wasn't of his world. Didn't belong in it. Didn't have any business knowing about him, or their group that was so close, yet so far away. Tijeras, New Mexico, was her world, a tiny mountain town east of Albuquerque. At least that's what humans thought it was.

In the wild hills of the southern Rocky Mountains and the high desert, he and the boys could run wild. Any time they wanted, they could shift to their wolf forms and take off in the *piñon* forests around the compound. The sights, the sounds, the impressions of the world were so much sharper, clearer and earthier in wolf form. Nothing compared to that. Except maybe a really hot night of wild sex as a human, but that only lasted so long.

The area had been chosen carefully by previous alphas. National forests surrounded the acreage on three sides, so there would be no humans building right up against them, interfering in their freedom, getting nosy into their business, or trying to inflict stupid zoning laws. The only way in or out was the access road protected by video cameras and motion detectors.

And a pack of massive timber wolves who were so much more than that.

The entrance was barely visible from the road and only if someone knew it was there. Nothing more than a giant boulder, that looked like it had been left there at the last ice age, marked the turn-off. Their mail went to a PO Box. Not even the mailman knew they were there. Couldn't have the boys chasing him down the lane every day. Amusing, but not smart.

Vic had had enough of city life when he'd been forced to live in them. Now that he worked for the darkest part of the government and was paid generously for his secret services, he could afford the luxury of maintaining a sprawling home that was safe for him and those under his command or protection. His pack. His family. Here, he found some peace.

No one, not even the super sexy, long-legged, green-eyed siren in front of him was going to screw it up.

Once a commander, always a commander. The Middle East and now, in the States. The soldiers with him currently had all served with him there, and their loyalty toward him hadn't changed. The best place for all of them was together, in their pack, safe from humans who didn't understand or were afraid of what they were. That's why witch hunts and religious crusades began. Out of fear. Fear that would end if there were true understanding between the groups. It hadn't happened in the past and Vic didn't expect that would change any time soon, so he fiercely protected what was his.

Secrets kept them alive. Rather than risk the safety of the pack, they would all take the secrets of their origins, of their knowledge of otherworldly things, to the grave.

"So, where are you, commander?" Trista asked, bringing his attention back to the present. The pain in his hand had dulled from the fiery burn to a dull throb. He resisted the urge to bring his hand to his mouth and lick the wound. She'd have him committed for sure.

"Oh, just trying to figure out why you put battery acid on my hand," he said.

"It wasn't battery acid, you big wuss," she said with a luscious laugh. She tossed the cloth towel in the bin for washing and moved away from him, her eyes downcast, her pulse suddenly fluttering and irregular. A throb of pheromones erupted from her and blazed over him, like a fire of hot, stormy sex.

Now *that* was intriguing.

She was attracted to him. Though she found him interesting

and was irritated every time he'd brought one of the boys to her to be patched up, she found him *interesting*. That was information he hadn't expected to get right now. The beast in him tried to move him closer, tried to catch her scent, but he resisted the pull.

"Sure felt like it," he said.

"I didn't realize you were so delicate. Next time I'll sedate you before I treat a bite wound." There was some secret chick school where women were taught that sass from birth. Some women had it in spades. Sass and sarcasm. He ate it up. If he could walk all over a female, human or shifter, there was no fun in it. No sport. He loved a challenge, and she had it written all over her.

"Delicate my ass." He placed his nose within a millimeter of hers. "If you want to see how tough I am, lady, just ask. I'll show you," he said, his beast hoping she took him up on the challenge.

He tilted his head to the side, let his gaze meet her surprised one, and breathed in her scent. By the gods, he wanted to kiss her. Though she was about to operate on Dane, he wanted her naked and in his arms. He wanted to see how sweet her lips were. If her scent matched her taste. If she could take him all the way in. Give him what he wanted. What he needed. Placing both hands against the wall on either side of her head, he trapped her within his arms, but didn't touch her. She could escape if she desired. Raising her eyes, she looked directly into his, challenge blatant in those green eyes.

Apparently, she didn't want to.

Lashes of heat, whips of desire, shards of need blasted through him and his body responded to her nearness. He was half wolf. How else was he supposed to react when a female cast that kind of enticing scent at him?

Trista, you're out of your mind! Fluttering her lashes, trying to compose herself, she met his gaze and the intense heat in them startled her. He was quite the masculine man, and she'd just egged him. Some part of her couldn't stop herself. She wanted to end this little flirt thing between them that had begun the day they'd met. Every time he came into her office her pulse went through the roof and today, her body had decided to take it one step further. To see how he'd react.

Boy, did he react. She'd gotten more than she'd bargained for in that moment. But was it really? More than she wanted? From the first time she'd seen him, she'd been intrigued, curious, and desirous of him. She didn't know him. Not really. But man, he set off all her triggers, stirred

42

all her senses. When he was around, her nerve endings sizzled.

She loved and hated equally those masculine military men who risked their lives for cause and country. Something in her DNA, she supposed. Her family was full of military men, and she knew how they worked.

Trista stared at Vic, trying to decide if he was for real or not. Her late father was a classic example of men who felt intensely, but expressed little. He'd have cut his tongue out rather than admit to having tender feelings for anyone.

When he'd told the family he was deploying again, he'd promised to come back to them all. He'd promised things would be different when he returned. He'd promised it would be his last deployment. It was. Within weeks of returning to the Middle East he'd been retired by an IED. Permanently. And he hadn't lied to them. When he'd returned, things had certainly been different for all of them.

Every military relative of hers had been seriously injured or killed. In her family, there were no retired veterans. Only reunions filled with widows and orphans.

Vic Stone, should be avoided if she didn't want to end up like her mother and aunts, though something about him made her want to throw her finely honed sense of caution out and let her guard drop completely with Vic. Could he be any different than her father? Other military men?

Some bitter part of her rejected the idea. The commander was military through and through. There was no turning him into a teddy bear with a semi-auto strapped to his hip. For crying out loud, his canine companions were wolves, not Labradors.

She'd known him a few years as he'd always brought his wolves to her for care. They'd always been minor injuries, quickly treated, and he hadn't lingered for long, but the glances he'd leveled on her had certainly let her know he'd noticed her.

Of course, he always made an impression on the ladies in the office, as well as half the men. But somehow, today, there was something else about him. Something vulnerable about the way he stared at her. As if he were asking for her understanding, her compassion and amazingly, for her permission.

That shocked her. This guy didn't ask for anything from anyone. He just took it. Whatever it was. A hot flush undulated through her body, originating somewhere deep in her abdomen, deep in her core. Sweat popped out on her neck, between her breasts. She took a quick breath and blew it out, trying to dispel the surge of sexual energy trembling between her legs.

An obscenely erotic vision of him making love to her flashed through her mind, electrifying the desire to reach out to him. His hands on her. His mouth on her. Everywhere. Taking what he wanted. Giving her what she needed. He didn't ask for anything. He took what he wanted. By the look in his eyes, he wanted her.

Embarrassed she'd been caught lusting for him, she cleared her throat and dragged her gaze away. The tingle lingering in her system and the sudden pooling of moisture between her legs was enough to jerk her back to the present. Wow. Just *wow*.

Then she did something she hadn't planned, hadn't expected herself to do. She wasn't an impulsive woman, but a very methodical one who planned her life in detail. In this moment, with Vic so close to her, with his masculine sweat and fragrance so close to her body, her own body reacting to him, she dropped her gaze to his lips.

She'd seen them thin with anger and full with a smile.

44

Could those generous lips of his be warm and loving, too? The way she'd fantasized.

There was only one way to find out.

Closing the small gap between them she pressed her lips against his.

The jolt of awareness that shot through her was outstanding. She'd surprised him. That was apparent by the instant stillness that claimed his body for half a second. He thought he had the upper hand with his size and superior strength, but her action caught him off guard. Then he parted his lips to her questing tongue, letting her make the moves, control the kiss, allowing her to take the lead.

That was a sign of a confident man. One who didn't need to take control, take charge of every moment of their destiny. It was very arousing. She leaned into him, parting her lips, sliding her tongue forward, gliding it against his and fitting her mouth perfectly to his. Oh, God, she was in trouble. Serious. *Serious*. Trouble.

Unable to control her hands, she let herself cup his face and opened her mouth fully to him, stroking her tongue against his silky-soft one, wanting to crawl inside his skin with him. Or at least his clothes. She'd bet good money if she placed one hand on his crotch he'd have a hard-on the size of a tree trunk. Sweat broke out between her breasts and a fine film of it covered his face, though he stood solid, unmoving, not unaffected by the heat between them. She pulled back and looked into those blazing blue eyes of his.

"Yes. I do," he whispered.

"You...what--"

She jumped as the door crashed open and the two other company men rushed into the room.

"Commander? You're in here shagging the doc while Dane's bleeding to death?" In a move too fast to be seen,

Eros grabbed Vic by the shirt and hauled him against the wall while Luke grabbed her arm and dragged her away from Vic.

"Sorry, doc, but you've got a job to do before you can take the commander for a ride," Luke said to her.

"Let go of me." Twisting sharply, she yanked her arm out of Luke's grasp in a move that surprised him. The follow through was an open-handed slap to the face. Long ago her father had taught her a few moves when she'd started dating, and she hadn't forgotten that one.

With eyes that smiled all the way up, he clapped his left hand to his cheek and let out a howling laugh. "Yowza, Doc. You're a fire ball, aren't you?" Luke asked and nodded approvingly at her.

"No, I'm a vet. What are you?" she snapped.

He opened his mouth to respond, then apparently thought better of it. "You don't want to know, Doc. Right now I'd appreciate it if you'd save Dane's life." Holding his hands up away from her, Luke backed a few paces as staff rushed to her aid. "It's okay. The blood is here and ready." Luke pointed to a small, hard-sided cooler by the door.

"Everything okay here?" Garcia stood with hands palms out, as if he'd stop whatever was going on with that gesture. Looking with wide eyes at the very large men in the room, he apparently changed his mind and dropped his hands. "Uh, okay then."

"Yes. Everything is fine. Can you get the blood going?" Trista took a breath, willing her heart to slow down, her breath to return to normal and the flush of desire to fade from her face.

"Sure. I'll put it through the warmer. By the time we're scrubbed it'll be good to go," Garcia said. He looked between her, Luke and the other two across the room. "Uh, *are* we good to go?"

Vic's hard face was now unreadable. The only giveaway was the muscle ticking in his jaw. A new bruise was developing under his left eye.

Resuming her professional demeanor, she turned to her other assistant. "The commander's going to need an ice pack. Kelly, will you get one for him while I scrub, please?"

"Sure. Sure thing." Kelly leaned as far as she could over a short refrigerator.

"Better make it two," Eros said and wiggled his jaw. He was not amused, either. The black stare shot daggers of disapproval at Trista. She raised one brow at him and stared back for a few seconds, then turned away. She wasn't about to be intimidated or bullied on her own turf.

"Gotcha." Kelly stood upright and handed each of them a pack of frozen corn.

"Corn?" Eros asked, but took the froze package from her and applied it to his left cheek.

"They work." The commander accepted his and applied it to his eye without comment.

"I'm heading into the surgery. Commander, if you'd still like to be present, put a mask on and follow me." Without waiting to see whether he was going to follow her, she headed into the surgery to scrub and prepare to save Dane's life.

After opening up Dane's abdominal cavity, Trista found the bleeder, repaired it, fixed a small nick in the large intestine and put him back together again. An unusual bit of scar tissue had formed over the wound itself, as if someone tried to cauterize it. That was the only strange thing she noticed. The commander hadn't mentioned any treatment applied in the field, but she wasn't current on military medical techniques that could have accomplished this.

She pulled off her mask and took the first deep breath of fresh air she'd had in three hours. "Looks like he's going to make it." She addressed the commander for the first time since the beginning of the operation. In order to do the things she needed to do, she had to distance herself, not be the fuzzy-on-the-inside little girl who wanted to save animals. In the surgical suite, she had to be ruthless, cold and unfeeling. That took a toll on her, sapping her energy, her nerves and emotions, pulling out of the overload of sensations when the hard part was over.

"You did good work there, Doc. Good as any surgeon I've seen." He nodded and took a step toward Dane, his sharp gaze looking for his wolf to rouse. "Is it okay if I touch him now?"

"Yes. I'll give you a few minutes, then we'll take him into recovery 'til he wakes up." As a thought occurred to her, she frowned. "Oh. Uh, not sure what we're going to do with him after that, though. I'm not sure our kennel will hold him, even if he's sedated."

"We're taking him home with us." That was an order if ever she'd heard one. And not one she agreed with.

"Commander--" she started, not liking this direction at all.

"Vic. Please."

Lines of stress and fatigue showed clearly on his face now. She didn't know what kind of work he really did, but it looked rough. Though he tried to hide it, he was a man of emotion living in a world devoid of it, and her heart cramped a little at that realization.

"Okay, Vic. Moving him much after surgery isn't a good

48

idea at all." She looked outside and raised her brows in shock. "Oh! I hadn't realized it was so late."

"It's definitely late. We hauled ass to get here before you closed, and it's a couple hours past that." He nodded toward the front office. "I think Kelly rescheduled everyone else that was here. Sorry for the inconvenience, but I get kind of single-minded when someone under my protection is hurting."

That made her smile. "Kind of?"

"Yeah." Half a smile lifted one corner of his mouth. That mouth again. Would she ever stop watching it?

"If that's your *kind of* I'd like to see when you get *really* single-minded," she said, only half joking.

"I'd be happy to oblige, Doc, but that kind of demonstration will have to wait," he said.

"Oh...but...I didn't mean..." Dear *God*, would she ever stop embarrassing herself today? What had happened to her self-respect? Her professionalism? Her ability to have an intellectual conversation?

"I gotcha, Doc." A slow smile crossed his face, giving her an inkling of what he would do to her should he direct that single-minded focus her way. "I gotcha."

"Yes. Well." She turned away from him. She had to, or she would go from mere embarrassment to ultimate humiliation by committing a lewd and carnal act in the middle of her office. With witnesses. "Let's go to my office and have a drink. I don't know about you, commander, but I can use a stiff one right now."

A muffled laugh erupted behind her, and she glared at him, wanted to crawl under the desk and hide her head. "Stop it!"

"Lead the way, Doc," Vic said, very good at hiding his amusement at her lapse.

Trying not to hurry, trying not to think that he was watching her ass the entire time, Trista tried to focus and think about the periodic table, or advanced calculus, or why cats always land on their feet. Anything except the stirring feelings trying to take control of her body and her mind. Mostly her body.

She headed straight to the cabinet where she kept medication samples, her purse, and, of course, *the tequila*. Thank God for good tequila. With hands that trembled, she quickly unlocked and opened the door.

There, shining in all its glory, was her sacred bottle of life-saving elixir. *Herradura*.

With the bottle in her hand, she stood and looked around. "I'll find some glasses," she said.

"We don't need any." Though he kept his intense eyes on her, he took the bottle from her hands, removed the top with those long fingers of his and took a long drink. No glass required.

Trista couldn't stop herself. She *had* to watch his lips close over the mouth of the bottle. He didn't just drink from the bottle, he *devoured* it. The strong muscles in his neck worked as he swallowed several times. The defined chest rose and fell with his breathing. His hand clasped the bottle as if it were a fragile thing. She swallowed down the emotions churning up from her abdomen, through her chest, and rising into her throat. Intrigue, curiosity, arousal and something she couldn't name all roiled within her, struggling for top billing.

Holy hot flashes. The man had such an effect on her. When he released the bottle, there was a little slurp and a splash of liquid landed on his lip. It was his eyes, his gaze ravenous, that remained on her. She wasn't sure how much of a struggle she'd offer should he attempt to devour her.

He held the bottle out to her, but she couldn't take her eyes off of him. She hadn't been this star-struck since high school. Her fumbling hands reached for it. It almost slipped from her grip, but Vic hung onto it.

"Thanks. I wouldn't want it go to waste." God. She was so *on* it. Such the witty conversationalist.

"Let me help you," he said.

"Oh, no, that's okay." Though she willed her feet to move her away from him, they didn't listen and actually moved her closer.

"Drink." He held the bottle to her lips, and she clasped her hands around his as he tilted it back. The first splash of the liquid in her mouth was so welcome that she moaned. She closed her eyes and savored the heat, the burn, the warmth pooling in her stomach. After the last few hours, she certainly needed it, and gulped down two more swallows before opening her eyes.

When she did, she looked right into the heat of him. For a second, his eyes shone with a fiery golden glow. She tried to swallow, but choked and nearly snorted tequila through her nose. She coughed, and gasped for breath, inhaling through the firestorm in her throat. His intense blue gaze met hers and she realized she must have been hallucinating, influenced by the lust-filled-hormone-craze currently holding her hostage.

"Oh, God," she choked out and coughed.

"You okay, Doc?" Vic took a wide stance, his feet spread apart, his weight balanced evenly. The man was solid as a rock, and she wanted to climb all over him.

"Yeah." *Cough, cough.* "I'll live." *Gasp.* She shoved the bottle into his hands. Maybe tequila hadn't been such a great idea after all. Resistance *was* freaking futile. She wanted to assimilate her body with his. Change of subject needed, stat.

"Back to the subject at hand. You can't seriously be thinking of taking Dane out of here. I won't allow it," she said. No way.

"Won't allow it?" Vic gave her a cold and calculating smile. "You don't have a choice, doc."

"Are you threatening me?" She narrowed her eyes. He couldn't be serious.

"Oh, no. Not at all," Vic said. He took a step back, giving her some space and a crooked smile lifted one side of his mouth. "I'm just telling you we're taking Dane home. Tonight. We have an excellent medical facility at the compound. We can monitor him overnight better than you can."

That made her brows shoot upward. That was a challenge if ever she'd heard one. "Seriously? You're *seriously* telling me you can do a better job than I can?" The sizzle in her started to fizzle.

"Are you going to stay up all night with him and monitor every breath he takes, every twitch he makes, and every beat of his heart?" he asked, challenging her to what her protocol for the night would be.

"Uh, no. No, I'm not," she said. That was a concession she had to make.

"We will. So get him ready for transport," Vic said.

"Really, commander. I must object." She followed him out the door of her office and into the hallway where the other two soldiers stood sentry beside the sedated wolf.

"Object all you want, but he's coming with us," Vic said as she marched along behind him.

With all the strength she could muster, she grabbed hold of his arm and dragged him to a halt.

"Then so am I."

"**N**o, you're not." There was no way this human woman was coming with them. As intriguing and entertaining as she was, he didn't need the distraction.

"Try to stop me. I have a duty to animals, the same way any doctor has to their patients." She released his arm and placed her body between him and the door to the surgery. "If you're taking him, you're taking me." Determination covered her face, she crossed her arms over her chest, and stared at him.

"You're not invited." With one arm, he brushed her aside, dismissing her words and the silly notion she had. Dane was starting to wake up. He could hear his beast crying out in the psychic plane. This conversation was over. He had to get to Dane. Had to reassure him. Had to make sure he didn't give them all away.

"Then I'll follow you." On quick feet and silent sneakers, she hurried after him.

"Don't. You'll regret it." Though he meant it, he didn't want to fuck up the relationship they had going with this vet. They'd been working together for a few years, and he didn't want to start all over with another vet he didn't know or trust. The only other vet in the area was old and not nearly as hot as Trista. That appealing quality couldn't be overlooked.

"Oh, goodie. Another threat. Do you want me to call the police? I will." She shoved her hand into her pocket and extracted her phone, holding it out to show she was serious.

"Doc. You're pushing it." Vic lowered his brows and took a step closer to her, using his physical presence to try to intimidate her into backing off. It worked with most humans, but not her. She took a step closer, a glow in her eyes, looking like she was actually enjoying herself. Dammit.

"Whoa, whoa, whoa," Eros said and approached them. "Everybody back it up and just chill." He pushed Vic away from Trista and waited until Vic looked at him.

"What?" Vic snapped.

"We don't need the police involved." Eros glanced over his shoulder to Trista. There she stood, arms crossed, feet wide apart, glowering at them, looking like she was going to make them do what *she* wanted and not the other way around. "If the doc wants to come with us, then she should. Might be good to have her around if Dane heads south," Eros said, offering the sensible suggestion.

With his jaw clenched, Vic nodded once, then stepped back. Though he spoke to Eros, he kept his eyes on the woman in front of him. Every breath she took lured in his arousal, stirred his anger and teased his lust. "She can come, but I don't like it."

"Roger that." Eros blew out a breath, then spoke to Luke. "Gear up."

They spoke out loud for Trista's benefit. Normally, communications like this would be psychic. They had no need to waste words when all they had to do was think about it.

"Good. I'll get my emergency pack and follow you in my vehicle," Trista said, as if she were preparing for a pleasure outing.

Vic didn't respond as she left the room.

"What the hell's the matter with you?" Eros asked and gave him a shove in the chest, knocking him back a step. Though Vic was the leader, the alpha, he wasn't above getting challenged by the others, especially when their secrets were involved.

"Watch it," Vic said and growled at Eros.

"No, you watch it. Once second you're sticking your tongue down her throat, then next you're pushing her so hard she's going to call the cops. We don't need cops, sir," Eros said, his intensity adding weight to his statement.

"Why can't he stay here overnight? Why do we have to move him now?" Luke asked. He stood strong beside his friend, one hand resting lightly on Dane's head.

"She's going to put him in a little wire cage. Can you image what happens if he shifts in his sleep? What happens when they find a naked man in a cage where they'd left a wolf the night before?" Vic huffed out a harsh breath. "Use your brain, Luke."

"Oh, yeah. That would be bad." Luke nodded, then leaned over to Dane. "Sorry, man. He's right. We gotta go."

"Has he responded to you? I can't connect to him." Vic tried to get hold of his emotions. Eros was right. He had to get himself under control. Mistakes were not acceptable. If something he did jeopardized the pack, he'd never forgive himself. Neither would they.

"No. He just twitches when I say his name. That's it." Energy snapped and boiled around Eros. Dane wasn't the only one he couldn't connect with at the moment.

"Okay." He looked at Eros. "Pull the Hummer as close to the door as you can. We'll bring him out."

"I'm ready, too." Trista returned with a huge pack on her back and carrying one in each hand. Looked like she was ready for an apocalypse.

"That's a lot of stuff, Doc," Luke said with a laugh.

"Need a lot of stuff if we're going to be away from here. I feel better having more and not needing it, then needing something and not having it," she said.

"Typical female." Vic snorted.

"Excuse me? You're dissing me for being prepared? You of all people should understand the need for having everything you need," she snapped back.

"If we don't have it, we improvise, Doc," Vic said. Like he was improvising now.

"I can see that in a military situation, but for now, I'm taking everything." She tossed her head. "Don't worry. You won't have to carry anything for me. I carry my own gear." With that, she headed out to the parking lot to her vehicle.

"Woo-hoo-hoo!" Luke gave him a look, practically dancing in place. "She is a *fireball*. I like that in a female. Makes the challenge a lot more fun."

"Stay away from her, Luke. She's off limits." Eros began to tie up the IV and get Dane ready for the move. "To everyone."

"What do you mean? She's got challenge written all over her," Luke said.

"That challenge is not for you, you idiot," Eros said and shook his head. "Sometimes you don't have any more brains than a rock. I don't know how you survived Iraq."

58

"Hey, now," Luke said and placed a hand over his heart. "That hurt."

Eros just shook his head.

Vic watched the two of them bantering like a couple of teenagers. Basically, that's what they were. In wolf years.

With wolves, they never seemed to grow up. At least some of them. He'd never experienced frivolity as a teenager, at least not much. With his history, his family upbringing, he'd been an adult since he could remember. Strife and chaos had filled his home pack. With no one to take over and pull the pack together, he and his brother had stepped up until an adult leader had emerged. When the pack became stable, they'd joined the military, leaving the pack in their uncle's hands.

Trista popped her head back in. "Are you guys ready to go, or what? We're burning daylight." She looked at the men frozen in front of her. "I thought the military moved with efficiency. I don't see any of that going on here. Get him loaded, and I'll lock up."

"Okay, Doc," Luke said and clasped one end of the tarp while Vic held onto the other end. Eros stood guard at the Hummer, a weapon in his hand, eyes and ears searching out any intrusion, anything that didn't belong. This was one of their most vulnerable times, when they were focused on an injured team member. This defenseless time made it easy for their enemies to ambush and do their worst. With all of the years and the miles they'd put on, they'd accumulated enemies near and far. One very close to home. The Ridge Runners in particular wanted to exterminate them, take their territory and use it to run guns, drugs and women for profit. As long as Vic lived, that wasn't going to happen. This was his home, too, and he wouldn't stand by while someone destroyed it.

"One. Two. Three." They strained to carry the heavy beast through the doorway with as little jostling as possible.

"When did he get so fucking heavy?" Luke asked, the muscles in his arms straining and his face contorted with effort. "Put him on a diet. Please put him on a diet."

"Didn't you guys just carry him in here a few hours ago?" Trista asked, a quizzical look on her face.

"Yeah, but we were pumped with adrenaline. Now, he feels like a fucking rock." Luke slashed a hand across his forehead and flung away the sweat.

"He's put on a few pounds," Vic said, strain in his voice. "Remind me to put him on an exercise program when he's better."

"Okay." Luke groaned.

Somehow, they managed to get Dane through the doorway and onto the back seat of the Hummer without hurting him or blowing out a testicle. Hernias weren't for sissies.

With darkness upon them, they settled into their designated positions in the vehicle. Glancing in the rearview mirror, he watched as Trista got into an SUV rigged for the outback, and pulled in behind them. With any luck, he'd lose her on the winding mountain road. He was still not happy about having her come to the compound with them, despite the logic Eros had offered. They'd guarded too many secrets for too many years to let anyone fuck it up now. Even one so charming, helpful and sexy as Dr. Trista Holiday.

They headed west on Route 314, south of Tijeras, into the wilderness of the national forests where homes were few and far between. Only fiercely independent and hearty souls lived out there. They depended only on themselves and their skills for survival. Though 911 services extended to this area, most people would be dead before help arrived. These tough people had learned to cope and help themselves.

At the compound, they'd installed every convenience known to modern civilization and some that weren't. Some of their toys were prototypes they tested for another division of the government. A research and development division of Sandia National Labs designed and built top secret items on the Air Force base south of Albuquerque. A staunch supporter of the pack, one of their scientists brought tools and weapons for them to try out, work the kinks out of, and returned to the lab to perfect them. They certainly made life more interesting.

"Relax, man," Luke said and grabbed an apple from the pack on the floor at his feet. "She's okay. For a human chick. Stop worrying about it. If she's a problem, we'll just eat her," he said.

"We can't just eat her, you idiot," Eros said and reached back to whack Luke upside the head.

"No?" Luke laughed, a deep hearty chuckle. "I think Vic wants to."

"Can it. Nothing is going to happen to the doc while she's on our property. I'll see to that," Vic said and hoped he wasn't going to eat his words as they approached the first of three gates all designed to keep out the causal passerby or stray livestock that happened down the wrong road. This situation was not going the way he wanted it to. Not at all.

"Sure. We'll can it when you get her naked." Luke laughed. "That's something I want to see."

"You're not going to be seeing anything 'cause it's not happening." Vic huffed out a breath hoping those words were true. "I made a mistake back there. I overstepped the boundaries and now look what's happened. She's driving onto the fucking compound, invading our space."

"Seriously. How long has it been since you've been laid?" Eros asked, turning to look at Vic with a quizzical expression.

Vic didn't answer. Not because he didn't want to engage in their little teasing banter, but because he wasn't certain. Not like he kept track of it on his phone or anything. There wasn't an app for that, was there?

"You don't know, do you?" Luke asked in astonishment from the back and pushed forward, hanging between the two front seats. "Geez, man. As commander of this group, you have a duty to take care of yourself so you can take care of the rest of us. That includes getting some on a regular basis." He pushed back against the seat. "No wonder you're a grumpy bitch lately."

"I am not," Vic said, trying not to sound like one. He slowed down, clicked the remote and waited impatiently until the black iron gate opened, pulled forward and waited until Trista pulled through. He pressed down on the gas pedal, taking it slow, resisting the urge to go too fast and jostle Dane unnecessarily. He repeated the process through the final gate, which opened up into the main area of the compound. Motion activated flood lights kicked on to illuminate the yard, and he pulled into the front of the building that doubled as a medical clinic.

"Yes, you are. Do your duty. Fuck the doctor and get her out of your system. You'll feel better. And so will we." Eros had his say, shoved his way out of the front seat, and opened the door to the building as Trista parked nearby.

Lights clicked on in the building, and Luke busied himself in the back of the Hummer.

"This is quite a place you have here," Trista said,

looking around at the little village comprised of adobe-style buildings, all built to blend in with the landscape and not draw attention from the outside world. Upon close inspection from overhead, a chopper or other aircraft would have a hard time finding the place.

"Yes, it is." He watched as Luke and Eros lifted Dane from the back seat and carried him into the building.

"This is your medical facility?" Trista asked, her eyes glowing green in the artificial light, her golden hair shining. Looking at her like this, Vic decided she could be part cat with those green eyes of her. That could be bad living among wolves.

"Come in. I'll show you we've got things under control, and then you can go." It would be a relief to have the temptation of her gone.

"Lead the way, but I'm not going home. I'm going to check out this medical facility you claim is better than my own practice." Trista moved toward the doorway, her hiking boots crunching in the gravel driveway. "That's insulting."

He grabbed her by the arm and spun her around. "That wasn't our agreement, Doc." No way was he letting her hang around all night. Other males, lots of them, were due back from other missions. People came and went all the time around there, and he didn't want her seeing males morphing from human form to wolf, or vice versa.

"It is now." The curiosity in her eyes as she looked up at him was almost enough to make him change his mind. For her protection and everyone's safety, he couldn't afford to give in to her green eyes or her alluring scent, no matter how much he wanted to feel her beneath him.

"Where did you get the idea you're running the show around here? You're on *my* turf now, Doc, so like it or not,

I'm in charge. I'm going to continue to be in charge. You'll do as I say, when I say it, and how," he said and eagerly awaited her response.

"Oooh. You like bossing women around, don't you? Misogynist." In a move that surprised him, she yanked her arm out of his grip. Her speed and strength were worthy of him as a mate. Too bad she wasn't a wolf female. He'd mate with her in a heartbeat if she were. His groin pulsed in response to that thought. He liked certain qualities in a female. All that sass and spit and fire Trista possessed turned him on like nothing else. That's why he'd kept his dick in his pants for so long. No female he'd met recently had interested him enough to bring it out to play, not even for a one-night-stand.

Until this moment. Until Trista stood there with her face tilted up to him, defiance in every cell of her body. Gods, he wanted her. Wanted her in a primal way that could get both of them hurt.

"Only in certain situations," Vic said, answering her question. Like when he got her in his bed. Then he'd enjoy it.

"Ever known a Taurus, commander?" She asked and pushed her way past him into the medical building, and stopped short, her eyes wide and her mouth soft, her breathing puffing through her parted lips. "Wow. I mean, just *wow*."

She glanced at him with renewed respect in her eyes and some force surged within him, liking the feel of her gaze on him, her chest rising and falling with her rapid breathing. So much about a person was revealed in their breathing, and they never knew it.

"You were saying?" He parted his feet and crossed his arms over his chest, settling in for a debate with the most interesting woman he'd met in a long time. "You still think our facility is *inadequate*?"

"Uh, no. No, I don't." She licked her lips as her eyes took in the entire length and breadth of the building. "Not anymore." Spread out before them were five patient bays with shiny metal gurneys, tricked out like any hospital ER. If not better. Way better.

"You have everything here, and I mean *everything*, don't you?" Turning her eyes to him, she blinked several time. It was a lot to take in.

"Well, we're still hoping for an MRI machine, but that's down the road," he said, admitting the one fault in the system. Though they were deep in the government and had access to more money than they knew what to do with, they still had budgetary restrictions.

She gaped at him. "*Seriously*? And MRI machine? Of your very own?"

"Yeah, why not? We have men who need medical attention and diagnostics as well as the wolves. We have to be prepared for both," he said in a reasonable tone he didn't feel as his body tightened in reaction to her reaction.

"I see." Almost reverently she ran her hands over the stainless steel table in one of the bays.

"You look like you just walked into a church, doc." There was a reverence about her that just glowed.

"I feel like it." But she gave him a glance and then relaxed some. "I have equipment envy. You've got everything here I could ever dream about," she said, her voice soft.

"Well, maybe we can work something out there." He couldn't fathom what at the moment, but he'd have to figure out something fast.

"What did you have in mind?" The questions in her

green eyes made him wonder what the hell he had in mind, too.

"Another time. Come on over and satisfy yourself Dane's in good hands for now, then we'll talk, have a drink, get something to eat. I'm fucking starved." He led her to where Dane was rousing. Eros had strapped him to the table in case he decided to lick his nuts again and fell off. That would be bad if he ripped himself open for something so stupid.

"How do you have this? I mean, *why* do you have it?" she asked, sputtering in disbelief. "How in the world can you have this place out in the middle of nowhere and be better equipped than any healthcare facility I've ever seen?" Now, instead of staring at the equipment in adoration, she stared at him with unrelenting curiosity. "I'm not leaving here until you tell me what's going on." Now she crossed her arms and waited for him to reply.

"Don't believe that was part of our agreement, either, Doc," he said, but enjoyed himself too much to stop this conversation.

"I've just amended it," she said and narrowed her eyes at him.

"Taurus, are you?" He was beginning to understand her a little better. Stubborn. Bull-headed. Independent. Also, sensual and fucking hot.

"Horn to horn," she said slowly. This blond-haired gypsy thought she could out-stubborn him.

"I see." Stepping closer to Dane, Vic tried to connect with him again, but couldn't. Maybe it was on purpose. Maybe it was the aftereffects of the drugs she'd used on him, and he couldn't help it. Maybe it was because he wouldn't let Dane bite Trista. In any case, with his metabolism on fire, Dane would be waking soon. Vic didn't want Trista to see anything she wasn't supposed to see.

"Do you guys work for the..." She closed her eyes briefly and gave a long sigh. "I can't believe I'm even going to ask this, but do you work for the shadow government?" A light flush surged beneath her skin and cast a pink glow to her face as she struggled with controlling her feelings, her emotions. Though she hid it well on the outside, she was an emotional and sensual creature. He stared down at her, trying to figure out how to answer her question when Dane stirred beside them. Stretching first, then realization hit him and his eyes opened wide in panic. He struggled, trying to get his feet beneath him when he howled, then began to shift right in front of them.

"Oh, shit." Vic rocked his head back and crunched his eyes shut. "Un-fucking-believable." The series of events that had happened today was going to destroy their entire organization. He couldn't let that happen, no matter what. Unfortunately, he was going to have to do something he didn't really want to do to protect everything he'd worked so hard for.

"What the..." Panic filled Trista eyes and fear tainted the sweat now pouring off of her. "What the *hell's* going on here?" She stepped back from the table, her face pale, eyes wide and staring. She tried to put distance between herself and the now-naked man strapped to the table. She pointed to him. "Did I just see that? I didn't just see that, did it?" Panic was flooding through her. Her pulse kicked up a few hundred notches. The breath that had been calm in her throat now rushed in and out of her lungs. He didn't have a clue what she was going to do. Fight or flight? It was fifty-fifty at this point. Even as tough as she was, he was betting she'd run after seeing what she's just seen.

"Doc, take a breath." Though she wasn't on the psychic link, he could reach her, could influence her, could give her a little mental push, fiddle with the image in her mind and not hurt her.

"I can't." Yet, there she was, breathing.

"You're hyperventilating. Slow it down," he said and dropped the tone of his voice.

"I can't." She huffed in a few more breaths. At least she hadn't keeled over.

Eros tuned in to him as he took a stance in front of the table between Dane and the doctor.

Get her out of here.

"Doc, we gotta go. There's some explaining I have to do," Vic said.

Instead of listening, she sprinted for the door.

"Well. Hell." Vic dashed after her. Even if she were a world-class sprinter, she wouldn't get far. He was a wolf and made it to the door in two seconds, faster than she could get halfway across the large room.

The chase was on.

CHAPTER
SIX

Trista was out of her mind. Out of her freakin' mind. She suddenly became aware that she was alone in a remote compound full of military men. Mercenaries no doubt. In the mountains. No one knew where she was.

No one. No one at work knew she'd gone with the men. They'd all left before the commander had said he was taking Dane back to the compound. She became aware of Eros watching her, of Luke, having materialized from somewhere and several other men of equal impressiveness, eyes glowing, emerging from darkened corners of the cavernous building. Eyes wide, her heart about to beat its way out of her chest, and if something didn't change soon, she was going to wet her pants.

"Relax, doc." Vic held up his hands, palms out, trying to put her at ease. Nothing could explain what she'd seen. "Just relax." He took a step toward her. It wasn't outwardly threatening in appearance, yet everything was a threat right now. Everything. Including the commander. If she died here today, it was her own stupid fucking fault.

"Stay away from me." She pointed a finger at him, like that was going to help. "Just stay away from me." Little stars appeared in the periphery of her vision. Great. She was going to faint like a little girl who'd just caught sight of her first naked man.

"Doc, I know you're freaked out now, but there's an explanation for everything you think you saw." Vic's eyes mesmerized her, she couldn't look away.

"*Think* I saw?" Now that maddened her. "There's nothing wrong with my eyes or my mind, commander. I know *exactly* what I saw." She cocked her bottom jaw to the side, trying to decide best how to get out of this situation alive. She wasn't going to play nice. Wasn't going to pretend she didn't see what she just saw. Even though denying it would be the most likely way to stay alive.

"Then tell me, what did you see?" Vic asked.

"That...that...that fucking wolf t-t-t-turned into a man." She glanced back at the table and gaped. There was no man there. It was Dane. A *wolf*. She flashed around to Vic with her jaw open, her eyes wide. Now she knew she was losing her mind. "But...but..."

"Come with me, doc. I think you need something to eat and maybe another shot of tequila." He held out his hand, his eyes holding hers and some amazing light, some sort of energy emanated from him. She began to relax, if just a little. "Listen to my voice. You know me, Doc. Come with me. You have nothing to fear from me. Nothing at all."

A sarcastic snort emerged from deep within her, and she raised her brows at him. "Really? Nothing to fear from you when there are six guys surrounding me?"

"I see what you mean." Vic did nothing more than nod and the others dispersed into the shadows where they had morphed from. "See? Just you and me, now. Nothing to be afraid of."

"You haven't inspired me to let my guard down. There's still Eros and Luke."

"That's not going to change. They're both field experienced and trained military medics. We need them here." He dropped his hand, having realized she wasn't just going to walk to him. "Dane needs them."

"Let me go home." She held her position. "Now."

"Let's go have that tequila, and we'll talk," he said, trying to direct her.

"You won't release me? You're holding me prisoner? Eventually, my staff will realize something's wrong when I don't show up for work on Monday. They'll call the police to come looking for me," she said in a rush.

She'd never felt more like a rabbit about to be eaten by a predator than right now. The commander took a few steps closer to her, slowly, as if he were stalking her.

"And you think we won't be able to hide your body and make any evidence that you were ever here disappear?" There was a calculating coldness in his eyes she'd never seen before. She'd seen it plenty of times in her father, brother, and other military men she knew. Never in the commander. She swallowed.

"No. That's not what I'm saying at all," she said. Well maybe she was. Perhaps she'd deluded herself that he was different, that he could be trusted, that he wasn't as fragile as the others she'd known who'd returned from the Middle East broken and dangerous.

"Listen. I'm not going to hurt you. I don't want to hurt you. You've got to realize how dangerous it is for you to be here. For you to know this place even exists," Vic said, revealing what's she'd begun to suspect.

"Dangerous? For me or for you?" she asked.

"For all of us. No one can ever know you were here. No one can know anything you've seen tonight. Ever. Or we'll all be dead," he said, his face serious.

That surprised her, but explained things. Slightly. The pace of her heart slowed a bit and the tightness in her throat eased. "So you really *are* shadow government?"

"Doc, we're so dark, the shadow government doesn't even know we exist," he said.

"Whoa." That information made her relax. These guys didn't want anyone to come looking for her and expose their situation here. Whatever that situation really was. So really, *she* was the one in control. Some of her energy, her power, came back to her. She didn't need to give it away as she had in those last few moments when she'd panicked. Panic did not save the day. Being calm and level-headed did. "I see." When she thought back over the last few moments, the images were fuzzy, distorted. She couldn't recall what she'd seen clearly. Maybe she *was* losing it.

"Ready to have that drink now?" he asked, his eyes less guarded than they had been moments ago, and he seemed to relax, too. The mutual dance of learning to trust each other had begun.

"Make it a double," she said.

The tension leaving his face was visible. "Good. I'd hate to have to kill you, now."

"What?" She stopped short, not certain she'd heard correctly.

"Kidding, Doc. Kidding." He blew out a long breath and gave a short, caustic laugh, needing the release, knowing his little memory interruption had worked. He only performed that sort of interference with another when the situation was desperate and right now it was. "It's been a hell of a day, doc. A hell of a day."

"I have to agree with you on that." One of the weirdest days she'd ever been through, and she'd experienced some strange ones in her life. Caution in her step, she followed him through the door and out into the cool night air. There was no way she was going to walk through the doorway with him behind her. That was something her father had taught her. Never give the enemy a chance to put their hands around your neck. So she put some distance between them. Even though the night was full upon them, small motion-activated lights and solar garden lights illuminated paths all around, taking some of the fear out of the dark. If she weren't in the middle of a secret military compound, the effect would have been quite charming. But they weren't, and it wasn't.

"We'll go to the house, to my office," he said.

She was so confused. Her instincts were that of the rabbit, and telling her to run for her life, but some other deep instinct made her pause, use her intelligence, her ability to reason and logic to make the decision to follow him into the large adobe-style home. "Promise me you'll let me go."

"I don't have to promise. You're not a prisoner here," he said.

"Really?"

"Really. You're an invited guest, a medical consultant, if you will, to keep Dane stable," Vic said.

"I see." That sounded so reasonable, but her gut didn't feel that way.

"Since you're not a prisoner, I don't have to promise to let you go," he said.

"I'm going to hold you to that. I don't want to worry

73

about whether you're going to slit my throat while I sleep tonight," she said and suddenly wishes she hadn't.

Instead of answering, he moved closer to her, eased into her space, invaded her boundaries and she let him, wanting to see how far he'd go.

"If I wanted you dead, you'd already be dead," he said. "I don't. And you aren't."

"Okay, then. Lead the way." He was totally right in that. If he didn't want her around, she wouldn't be.

Vic opened the door. They walked into a foyer that was as big as her first apartment. The vaulted ceilings gave the impression of huge space. Since all of the men she'd met were huge, she imagined they needed the room to breathe and accommodate their bulk. A wide, curving staircase moved off to the right. The bedrooms were probably up there. Ahead a great room with a floor-to-ceiling stone fireplace held court, not a typical small kiva-style fireplace common to the area. She could envision lying in front of it with a glass of wine, naked and entangled with Vic. Exchanging long, deep kisses with him as he slid deep into her body, riding her until they were both sated with pleasure.

Realizing the direction of her thoughts and the carnal nature, Trista turned quickly away from the fireplace and bumped right into Vic's chest. "Oh."

"Got a problem with fireplaces?" he asked. The a light in his eyes said he knew exactly the route her thoughts had taken and his weren't far off.

"No. Not really," she said. She swallowed and tried to take a step back, but he caught her by the arms and drew her close to him.

He didn't respond with words. His demeanor changed as he held her close to him. He looked into her eyes, then at her mouth, focused intensely. The stance he took was strong, with his feet braced apart. He held her close to him, almost nestled against his chest, against his thighs. The heat of him pulsed into her, and her mouth went dry.

God, she was so freaking attracted to him. She wanted to throw any caution she ever had to the wind, give in to the lust currently circulating within her body, experience the pleasure of a man hot and hard between her thighs again. Then something, some memory, surfaced. Back in her office she'd wondered if his cock would be hard if she placed her hand on his crotch, and he'd said yes, it was. Was this guy psychic, too? Did he want her the same way she wanted him? Was that it? Or could she just think something, and he'd know?

Giving it a try, she let her gaze meet his intense ones. *Wanna get naked with me, Vic?*

"Yes," he whispered.

It was a simple answer. One she hadn't expected, but it gave her the information she needed. She'd better watch her thoughts around these men.

Leaning toward her, he parted his lips and placed his face next to hers, almost touching, almost giving in to what they both wanted. She swallowed as he grazed his lips against her jawline, teasing and torturing her, tickling his light beard against her skin. The sensation created a curious feeling deep inside her, and she wondered what it would like to feel that same sensation of his beard mixed with his hot breath against her thighs.

"You may find out soon enough." His words were a whisper in the air and pulled her deeper into the fantasy of having his skin against hers. Again, she realized he'd listened to her thoughts.

"How about that tequila, Vic? I really need it now." Like really, really needed it.

"Coming right up. Neat?" he asked and moved away from her.

"Yes." Ice only diluted the punch. He strode to the wet bar in the great room. As he did so, she took a minute to examine him, trying to figure out what it was about him that turned her on so much. What attracted her enough to want him naked and sweating on top of her? He was pretty tall, which she liked. About six feet. Maybe more. His hair was a little longer than a Marine cut, but not enough to grab a handful of in the throes of passion. His face wasn't classically handsome, but looked like he'd been carved from one of the sandstone rocks common to the area. Each feature was finely etched. A few scars marred the terrain of his tawny skin, but then again she wasn't a fan of perfection.

He had shoulders a woman could hang onto, or weep on, if she needed to. Just above the collar of his black tee shirt, the edges of a blue tribal tattoo peaked out, but she couldn't make out what it was. A tan, long-sleeved shirt topped it off. It was buttoned up most of the way, sleeves rolled up, revealing muscled forearms. Scars and scratches blemished his arms, but they looked like they could hold onto a woman all night long without any trouble.

Black, tan and green camo pants covered his legs. She imagined a multitude of weapons filled the pockets. The fabric pattern hid any definition of muscles in his legs, but she could imagine he was as well-developed there as everywhere else. Black military combat boots completed his attire.

"Like what you see?" He turned back to her with two short, wide, glasses in his hands, each filled with double shots of golden liquid that she hoped was really good tequila.

"Yes. I was going to ask you where you got the boots," she said, trying to cover her unguarded inspection of him.

"Nice one, doc." He handed her a glass, and she took it. The touch of his hand lingered on hers, as if he wanted to know what her skin felt like, in the same way she wanted to know his.

"How come you don't call me by my given name? Always doc?" she asked and kept her gaze on him.

He gave half a shrug as he contemplated his answer. "Can't. Too personal." He shot half the drink back into his mouth and swallowed. She did the same. The heat and sting of the liquid hit her on the back of the throat. She swallowed, keeping her eyes on him, trying to figure out his next move before he knew it.

"You want to get into my pants, and you can't say my name? Say it." She wanted to hear her name on his lips, to hear his voice hold her name on his breath.

"No." Glittering ice frosted his gaze.

"Why? Afraid?" Normally, she didn't challenge anyone, but now, filled with liquid courage after a mind-bending incident and a desire that wasn't settling down, she couldn't help herself.

"I'll let you in on a little secret, doc. Relationships are temporary. It's why we use last names or nicknames mostly in the military. You know this already, right? You get used to calling someone by their first name, it's a subconscious thing. You're going to want them around more. Expect them to be around more, when in reality, they could get killed or leave you any time they want to," he said, giving her some insight into his world that saddened her.

"Leave you? Really?" That was a slip, she was sure of it.

When he looked down at his drink, he was buying a little time. He hadn't meant to reveal that tidbit of himself to her. Yeah, there was more depth to this man than he let on. She liked it. It intrigued her more than she cared to admit. Being attracted to strong, dangerous men wasn't her deal, but resisting the pull of the commander was not happening despite her best efforts. If anything, she was being more drawn to him the longer she stood there savoring the tequila sloshing its way around her brain.

"People can transfer any time, get injured or ship out. It's self-preservation to not get too close. To anyone." The shrug he gave was as telltale as any words he'd used. Body language among animals was something she'd become an expert in analyzing, and that skill came in handy here. He'd been hurt. Badly.

"That's not what I'm seeing, Vic," she said, deliberately using his name. She tossed back the rest of her drink, ready to end this stalemate they'd been circling around.

"Really? What do you think you see?" he asked.

"I see a bunch of guys so tuned in to each other, you read each other's thoughts. You're like brothers, but even closer, right?" she asked.

He finished his drink and set the glass on a table. "You're pushing it now," he said. The muscle in his jaw twitched.

She was getting to him. Good. She didn't think he'd had anyone shake him up for a long time, and she was going to do it right now. Apparently, today was the day she was going to live dangerously, despite her life being designed to the contrary.

"Say my name." Turning to face him, the full effects of the alcohol hit her system. With no food for hours, it was a main-line to her bloodstream and into her brain. *Yee-haw*, there was a buzz coming on. She was going to ride it as long as it lasted. She'd ride the commander as long as he lasted, too.

"No." Though he said the word, his feet brought him closer to her. Those tingles and pulses in her body got hotter and faster, making her want things she shouldn't want. After today, she was willing to let her libido come out and play, if only for one night. After today, she might never see him again.

"Say it." She clasped the lapels of his shirt and clenched her fists, prepared for him to pull away, to withdraw or push her aside. A muscle clenched in his jaw, and she knew he was having trouble controlling himself, the same way she was having trouble. Being a tall woman, she was able to lean closer and whisper into his ear. "Say it for me. Just once. Say my name," she said, drawing the words out to linger in the air between them.

"You don't know what you're getting into," he said. He turned his face toward her and inhaled, as if scenting her, sizing up her readiness, bringing her essence into him. That was fucking hot.

"I know exactly what I want to get into." She allowed one hand to stray to the front of his pants and lightly traced her fingers across the telltale bulge there. "The question is, do you want me to get into it?" She closed her hand and squeezed. It was as hard as she'd hoped it was going to be. She could ride that all night long, too.

In a flash, Vic grabbed both of her hands and shoved them behind her back. Bringing her hips against his, pressing his cock against her groin, his breath fast, his gaze locked on her mouth. He leaned against her ear and traced the outer shell with the tip of his tongue. Her heart raced.

Her mouth went dry. Her breathing came in short gasps. Eager anticipation consumed her.

"Trista." The whisper of her name made her close her eyes, savoring the sound of his voice in her mind. "Trista. I want you. Right now. Is that what you wanted to her?" He sighed a hot breath into her ear and tremors broke out within her, need curled her toes. "I hope you came prepared."

Drugged with pure, unadulterated lust, she opened her eyes as he pulled back an inch, looking deeply into him. She licked her lips, somewhat confused. "Prepared for what?"

"The ride of your life," he said and grinned.

Still holding her hands behind her, he opened his mouth over hers. He didn't just kiss her, he possessed her. Devoured her. Let her know how much he wanted her.

Resisting never crossed her mind. She parted her lips and accepted his tongue into her mouth, sliding hers against his, reveling in the sensation of silk gliding against her silk, loving the sensations he created in her. Her body responded as he held her against him. Her heart raced. Her breasts swelled. Her nipples ached for his touch. Another ache grew between her legs. Pulses of desire bloomed as her body responded to his. Moisture surged in her core, getting her ready for what she wanted.

Tugging her arms against him, she wanted him to let her loose, she wanted to touch him. "Let me go." Pulling back slightly, she spoke the words into his mouth.

"No." But he released her hands and moved his to her hips, pulling them tighter against him. His fingers dug into her ass, pulling her pelvis upward.

The heat of him. The hardness of him against her created more want. More need. More desire. To rip her clothes off. To feel his skin against hers. To ready herself to accept his body into hers.

Vic pushed her lab jacket off of her shoulders, but kept his mouth plastered to hers.

With hands that didn't seem to want to function, she tugged at his shirt, pulling it from his waistband. Sinking her hands inside to press against his skin, she moaned into his mouth. Though he was a tough man, the feel of his skin was pure satin. She shoved the shirt up, desperate to feel his skin against her. He released her to rip it off over his head. He clasped the hem of her scrub shirt, pulled it off and cast it aside.

The look in his eyes scalded her skin, seared his desire across her body. Leaning back against the wall, she let her gaze move over his naked chest. A sprinkling of hair between his nipples led to a fine line of darker hair that crossed over the defined muscles to below his navel, disappearing below.

He was a magnificent piece of man flesh, and she wanted to take a bite out of him. Unfortunately, they were in the middle of his living room and someone could walk in at any time. "Is there somewhere else we can go?" She licked her lips and squirmed as desire filled her and boiled over. "I mean, someone could walk in on us."

"Don't worry. No one's coming in here 'til I tell them." He dropped his gaze to her breasts hidden behind the cups of her lacy white bra. So un-sexy, so plain-Jane, but she'd had no idea when dressing this morning she'd be in a man's arms tonight. "You're beautiful, Trista. Just beautiful." Slowly, reverently, he tucked his thumbs in the cups of her bra and dragged them down, revealing her hard, tight nipples to his eager gaze. Leaning into her, he kissed the side of her neck, spreading kisses upward until he reached her ear. Somehow he knew her weak spot, a place of centered desire. A place that stirred her passions. He pulled her earlobe into his mouth, then released it. "I want to kiss you. Touch you. Bury myself inside you until you scream my name," he whispered.

God. He didn't say much, but when he did, it was something.

The energy surging between them overwhelmed her. She didn't want to speak and break the spell, so she spoke with her body. Raising her arms to his muscular shoulders she tugged him closer.

His hands cupped her face, and he kissed her deeply. One hand strayed down to stroke her breast, to tease her nipple with his thumb, to stir her desire more thoroughly. As if his desire for her had somehow managed to find its way *inside* of her, and she now felt his need from his eyes, his point of view. A tremor shot through her as his need surged.

Leaving her mouth, his lips nibbled down her neck, across her chest and over her breast. Her breath caught in anticipation of the first wet sensation of his mouth when it closed on her taut flesh. A gasped filled her throat and tightened her chest. Her head dropped back when he took her nipple into his mouth and sucked hard. The flash and heat of lust pulsed straight to her core, her arousal strong and powerful. Unstoppable.

"Oh, God, that's good," she said.

He teased her nipples, stirring her to a height of frenzied desire. She clutched his shoulders. Every movement, every muscle twitch, every nuance from his skin moved into her as he lifted her breasts to his mouth and teased her nipples, somehow knowing how to stir her body to the height of desire. So close to him, so into him, she almost felt a part of him.

Yes, very good. His tongue eased out, teasing her sensitive nipples further.

Somehow, she thought she heard the words in her mind, but in the hazy fog of desire, she couldn't be sure if she were hallucinating or merging with him.

"I want you inside me. I want to feel you slide inside me." Until now, she could only imagine how it would feel to have make love to her, but now, on the verge of it, she couldn't wait any longer.

You will. Very soon. Again the words emerged in her mind as his touch held transfixed. Every cell in her body was tuned into his and stood at attention.

She reached for the button on his pants, urgent to take him in her hands. He caught her, preventing her from achieving her goal. She squirmed, her desire overwhelming.

"Please. I want to touch you." Needed to touch him.

You will. The waistband of her scrub pants fell away beneath his hands as he stripped them and her panties down to her feet, flipped her shoes off and dropped to his knees in front of her. "I get to touch you first." Breathing in her scent, he wrapped his hands around her hips and pressed his face into the V of her legs.

"Oh, I must smell bad." She hadn't taken a shower since this morning, and it had been a long, sweaty day. She hadn't even considered this.

"Don't you know, wolves smell each other before they mate?" He inhaled again, taking in her feminine fragrance, saturating himself in it. The moan of pleasure in his throat pleased her.

"Yes, I know that, but... *oh*." Any words she could have

thought of making ended when his tongue snaked out and parted her slit. The sensation nearly dropped her to her knees beside him, the muscles in her legs suddenly gone rubbery.

The heat of his tongue on her swollen and tender flesh drove her over the edge. Closing her eyes, she gave herself to him, beyond able to stop the reaction of her body, lacking any desire to do so. Clutching his shoulders, she dug her nails into his skin as he used his mouth to take her down a path she hadn't been down in way too long.

The magic of his mouth was indescribable. The heat, the soft rasp, the quick flicks. The surge of orgasm rushed in on her from all sides. Pulses of pleasure filled her center. Awash in a storm of sexual heat, she gave in to the sensations pounding through her. Her breath came harsh in her chest, and her legs trembled.

He maneuvered himself upward, then fumbled to release the fastening on his pants.

～

VIC STOOD, savoring the scent of her all over his face. Standing tall, he looked at her, desire filling him as he took in her all-rumpled-and-sexy-from-the-first-orgasm-of-the-day look. Messy blond hair, eyes dewy with desire and the sight of her breasts spilling out of her bra fueled the fire sizzling inside him. This vet, this champion of animals, was the sexiest woman he'd seen in a long, *long* time. And she was here, in his arms.

The taste and smell of her arousal filled his senses. Spoke to the beast in him. Urging him to conquer. To mate. To take her as his own. The beast had to be pushed aside when making love to a human female. They weren't as sturdy as wolf females, and he didn't want to hurt her while he took his pleasure with her.

When her hand reached for him and closed over him, he stilled and closed his eyes, taking her touch inside him, reveling in the sensations she stirred in his body. Months and months had passed since he'd been with a female and taking care of business in the shower didn't cut it. His body craved her touch, craved her scent and longed to join with her.

"If you keep that up, it's going to be over before either of us wants," he said and clutched her wrist in one hand.

Her gaze dropped to his mouth, and she squirmed against him. "Now."

He kissed. By the gods, he needed this. Needed her. He lifted her by the hips and pressed his chest against hers to hold her. She wrapped those long legs of hers around his hips. The moans in her throat stirred him, tortured him and his beast urged him on.

Unable to wait any longer, he pressed against the sweet entrance to her core. The heat of her seared him. Little moans of pleasure escaped her as she gasped, and threw her head back as he plunged all the way inside her. Pressing his forehead to hers, he took in a few gasping breaths, trying to hush the urge to let it all go now. He paused as the sensations overwhelmed him.

She was everything he wanted. Everything he needed. Everything he couldn't have. Throbs of pleasure, waves of pure sensation churned through him in an explosion of energy. His universe was centered at the place where they joined. His animal insisted on pushing through. Taking its pleasure. Taking what it needed. Growling from deep within him.

With her legs tightening around him, the muscles in her

thighs holding onto him let him know she felt the same needs as he. A good alpha ensured his mate was satisfied. A great alpha ensured his mate took her pleasure *before* he achieved his. Each pulse of his hips ensured her enjoyment was as great as his.

Nothing had ever felt as sinfully delicious as joining with this woman. In the psychic realm he connected with her, eased into her unguarded mind, teasing awake pathways she didn't even know existed. Her pleasure became his own. Doubling the feelings hammering through him, doubling the ones thrumming through her. The moment she dug her fingernails into his shoulders drove him over the edge. Her hoarse cries in his ear ended him.

The demanding pulses of his body took over, and he drove into her. The orgasm of a wolf lasted until there was nothing left. When he had nothing left to give, he kissed her again, relishing the taste of her lips and dropped to his knees with her still hanging on tight.

CHAPTER
SEVEN

"Trista, you okay?" Vic asked, finally having enough muscle strength to lift his head off her shoulder, to wipe the sweat off his forehead. He hoped eventually he'd have enough muscle function to stand again. Perhaps the feeling would return to his legs. Some day. Maybe next week.

"Yeah," she panted and took a ragged breath. "I'm good." Then she snorted. "Not sure I'll be able to walk for a while, though."

"Sorry about that. Well, not really, but you know what I mean," he said and hoped she did. His brain wasn't firing on all cylinders yet.

"I got it," she said and cupped his face with one hand, then looked deeply into his eyes. "You were right."

"About what? I'd like to know so I can lord it over you later," he said. When a female told a male he was right, the male paid attention.

"The ride of my life," she said. Closing her eyes, she nodded. "Awesome. Ten out of ten." She gave him a sarcastic two thumbs up vote.

"Happy to oblige." He pressed a kiss to the tip of her nose. "I gotta move, or I'm going to be permanently stuck this way," he groaned and cringed. The fire of a leg cramp was creeping up the back of his thigh.

"Yeah. Got it," she groaned.

Somehow, they extricated themselves from the floor and put body parts back into clothing where they belonged. Trista smoothed her hair back from her face. "How do I look? Okay?" she asked, an artificially bright smile on her face.

Vic took a good look at the swollen lips, the red beard burns on her neck, the contented look in her eyes and the flush of her skin. "Like you've just been royally fucked."

A laugh barked out of her, and she clapped a hand over her mouth. Something in him shifted at the sound, and he smiled. "Good. I'd hate to think all that effort with nothing to show for it," she said.

"Doc, you're something else." After steadying himself, he held out hand and directed her toward the kitchen. "Let's eat. I'm starved."

"Hmm. Didn't you just . . . uh . . . eat . . . never mind," she said, teasing light sparkling in her eyes.

He gave her a lingering glance, seeing her anew in this moment. This woman was surprising him at every turn. Nothing surprised him. *Ever*. Except now. Except her.

"Yeah. Now I need to eat something with nutritional value." The memory of it, of her, her fragrance filled his mind. He'd be able to find her anywhere now. She was imprinted on his mind, seared into his memory banks. Should he take her as his mate, it would tie them together forever. Nothing could stop him from finding her scent on the wind.

"Lead the way," she said and fluffed her hair again.

Together they entered the kitchen, which was really a misnomer. It was a chef's wet dream, a galley of stainless steel and granite worthy of any high-class restaurant around the world.

"Got anything in mind you'd like?" he asked.

"Holy shit. You can feed an army in here. It's bigger than my *house*!" she exclaimed, her jaw hanging open, eyes wide as she took everything in. Her reaction amused him though he kept it hidden.

"We do on occasion feed masses of men when we're on larger missions or have training sessions here." He rummaged in the refrigerator drawer of the island, looking for something fast and easy.

"Vic?" The look of wonder on her face puzzled him as she approached, her footsteps hesitant, uncertain. Eyes wide, those lips parted, her breathing in short little gasps. The heart beating wildly in her chest made no sense. What the hell was going on with her?

"You look like you're about to have another orgasm, doc," he said and stood. Puzzled, he braced a hip against the counter watching her.

"If that's a refrigerator *drawer*, I am." She clasped her hands to her face. "I covet. Oh, I covet."

"If you'd like to touch it, you can. I don't mind," he said, teasing her.

"Really?" Reverence filled the eyes, and she took a step toward the drawer.

"Seriously?" He crossed his arms over his chest, watching her. Unbelievable. "You take on an elite unit of special forces, with *wolves*, and *now* you're melting like a little girl over a refrigerator drawer?"

"Yes. Well." Flustered looked good on her as she tucked her hair behind one ear, then licked her lips, buying time as she tried to come up with a good answer. Finally, she dragged her gaze away from the hidden appliance. "Okay, fine. It's a girl thing. You wouldn't understand."

"That's the best you can do?" Amused, he shoved the drawer closed with his knee, just to see how she'd react.

"Oh." Those green eyes shot to him, pleaded with him to stop. "Leave it open, please."

"Doc." He shook his head, uncertain of the feelings churning within him. The woman intrigued him like no one else.

Is it safe to come in? Luke's voice penetrated his focus.

Yeah. In the kitchen.

Naked?

No, you idiot.

We felt a disturbance in the force.

You did. It's over now.

Let me just say, it was fucking awesome.

During a wild lovemaking session like he'd just had, his ability to focus, shield his thoughts and feelings from the others was impossible. They knew exactly what had happened, how it happened. They felt nearly everything he did. Secrets didn't exist in this group.

After the alpha makes love, when the others are in close proximity, they approach. With shifters things could get wild, and safety was paramount to the mates. They also paid their respects to the female the alpha had chosen to mate with. An alpha could go to bed with whomever he wanted, but after he chose his permanent mate, he'd never *make love* with another for the rest of his life. Therefore, it was in everyone's best interest to keep both of the alphas healthy and safe. For now, the others were just curious. Once the alpha chose a permanent mate, the hierarchy and structure of a pack changed, affecting everyone.

Heavy footsteps approached the kitchen and destroyed the moment. Trista pulled away, and he masked his senses from the others.

"We're about to be invaded," Vic said.

"Seriously?" Panic flashed in her eyes, but she hid it quickly. "I'm not ready for that."

"Just act natural," Vic said.

"What's that, after you've been royally fucked by the military commander of a rogue group of special forces soldiers?" she asked and scratched her nose with one finger. "Not sure what the protocol is for that."

"Me, either." He'd never brought a lady to the compound before. Not that this was *that* situation, exactly, but the end result was the same. There was a lady at the compound and they'd acquired carnal knowledge of each other.

"Oh, good. You're getting food. We're starving," Eros said, taking the lead and burst through the kitchen door. He was one of the quieter males, but no less deadly. He held back, watched, read others like a book and when the time was right, struck at their most vulnerable point. An essential asset to their pack.

"Like you haven't eaten all day," Luke said and yanked open the drawer Vic had just closed. "Where's the chili? I've had that on my mind all day."

"Dane finished it in the middle of the night. I heard him in here last night." Eros picked up an apple from the fruit bowl and tossed it up in the air, caught it and took a bite.

Luke spun around, the horror of that travesty written on his chiseled face. "Don't tell me that! I was gonna make love to that chili with my mouth."

"Don't listen to him. It's in the other drawer," Vic said and directed him to the correct place. Although he enjoyed the boys bantering around, they had to watch it in front of Trista. Who knew what would happen if they got into a scrap over food? They could shift on each other in a flash and destroy this whole fragile trust thing he had going with her. There were serious limits to what she could see or have knowledge of at this point. For their protection, of course, but for her own as well.

They had enemies, dangerous and deadly ones, who'd think nothing of using her to get to them by any means possible. In the dark days of shifter groups, many an alpha male had found their mates disemboweled, or torn to shreds by their enemies. Though Vic would fight to the death for her already, she wasn't his mate, and that offered her some protection. For the sake of all of them, the less she knew about them the better.

"There's steak marinating in the cooler," Vic said and pointed to the massive Sub-Zero appliance.

"Awesome. Commander, fire up the grill. We're having steak," Luke said and rubbed his hands together in anticipation. He pulled the large container of chili from the other drawer, set it on the granite island, then strode with great intent to the cooler for the rest. "Let's get it going."

"I CAN HELP, too. I make a pretty good salad." Trista made the offer, but paused as every man in the room froze like she said she wanted to have a discussion about feminine hygiene products. "What?"

"Meat, woman. We need *meat*. We don't *do* salads," Eros said and cast a cold glance over her. Change was something he obvious didn't like and for some reason was seeing her an interloper in their tightly-knit group. Maybe she was.

Maybe she really wasn't wanted there. They'd been telling her that for hours, but now, she really felt like the interloper in their space.

"Perhaps I should go then and leave you to it," she said. "It's late." Suddenly she felt like an intruder in their midst. Maybe it was just her, maybe it was the newness of the discoveries of the day, or possibly the last hormones of her post-orgasmic-high fading away.

"No. Don't leave because of one sex-starved, grumpy-ass guy," Luke said, holding the steaks in his giant hands and faced her. "There's plenty. We'd like you to stay for dinner, wouldn't we, Eros?" Luke kicked Eros in the shin. For his efforts, he got a sizzling glare that should have cooked the steaks in his hands.

"Yeah. Sure. Not my decision." Eros couldn't have sounded less enthused.

"Right. It's mine," Vic said. Though he didn't move a muscle or raise his voice, only spoke the three words, it was enough and the atmosphere in the room changed. Though she couldn't really get a handle on it, she knew they bowed to his authority. Impressive. "Go ahead and make a salad, Doc. We can all use a little more fiber," Vic said.

"Now you sound like my mother," Luke said and grinned. He was obviously the more lighthearted of the two and she liked his demeanor immensely.

"Could you direct me to where your salad stuff is?" she asked. Happy for something productive to do and get her hands on that fridge, she looked to Vic for the answer.

"Uh, not sure. Have a look and see what you can find," Vic said.

"Last time we had salad was a couple of weeks ago, during that mini-training session we had," Luke said, cast a glance at Vic, then back at her. "We had a cook then, so who knows what's left."

"Why don't I just have a look?" Rubbing her hands together, she moved closer.

"You just wants to get her hands on the appliances," Vic said with a softening in his eyes as he looked at her.

"Hey, now." Facing him, she put her hands on her hips and gave him a pointed look. "You're the one who pulled it out and showed it to me, and then wouldn't let me touch it."

All the men erupted in riotous laughter.

"*That's* what he did while you were in here?" Tears filled Luke's eyes as he cracked up. "He *showed* it to you? That's it? *That's it?*" Luke set the steaks down and braced his hands on the counter.

"What?" Trista looked to Vic, then thought about what she'd just said and how it could be interpreted. A flash of heat burst from her chest upward and colored her neck and face. She slapped a hand over her eyes. "Oh, dear God. It's not what you think."

"Really?" Luke wiped his eyes with the heels of his hands. "Really?"

"Oh, man. That's totally embarrassing," Trista said and shook her head. "I'll be leaving now," she said and closed her eyes, hoping she'd disappear into the tiles below her feet.

"It's okay, doc. We needed a good laugh today," Vic said, mirth in his voice. "Thanks."

"I'll just have a look in the cooler and see what you have in there," she said and opened the door. The blast of arctic air calmed her flaming cheeks as she rummaged for salad items. There was little left and the lettuce had turned an ugly shade of slimy brown. With a grimace, she held her breath and removed it, tossing it into the trash. Fortunately, she found enough to make a side dish of diced red beets, feta cheese and walnuts.

In short order, they had a meal.

"So tell me, guys. How long have you been together?" Trista took a bite of the perfect steak and savored it. Red meat had been out of her diet for a long time, and this rare treat was fantastic.

"Uh..." Luke looked at Vic for input, permission or something else she wasn't getting. Curious. Though they weren't in a combat situation, they still deferred to Vic in so many ways. The military men she'd been around didn't maintain that hierarchical structure in their personal lives or on down-time.

"I'll take that question. We've been here about two years. We relocated from another place as our missions and commitments to the community have changed and grown." Vic frowned at the beet dish, then took a bite and his brows shot up. That simple reaction of pleasure created a hum of satisfaction in her chest.

"So, you started coming to see me right after the compound was built?" she asked. The timeline made sense to her.

"The house was already here. We bought the property and put up some new buildings, this house, the infirmary, tore down a few others and remodeled what we could," Vic said.

"Wow. That's awesome. How many buildings are here?" she asked, only having seen two or three as they came in.

"Seven, though you've only seen two. The others are away from the house," Vic said and took another bite of the salad.

"It's quite a place," she said. Seriously. She'd lived in

this area for years and never knew about or even heard about this place. That said something for the amount of secrecy they'd gone through to obtain it. In communities like this, someone always knew something about everyone.

"We're prepared for a zombie apocalypse," Luke said and cut into his steak. He ate like he hadn't seen food in a week. "By the gods, this is good. You outdid yourself this time, bro'." He pointed to Eros with his fork.

"Tried out a new marinade I found online," Eros said. Though he shrugged and appeared to blow off the compliment, she could see he was pleased.

"I approve." Luke shook his head and dove in for another bite. "Totally. Get a case of it."

The remainder of the meal was filled with tame stories of neutral subjects. By the end of it, Trista hadn't gotten any better feel for who these men were, what they were all about, and why the vibe she was suddenly getting from Vic was so intense. He'd gone motionless. Eyes closed, brows furrowed and lips pressed firmly together, he looked like he was about to have a seizure.

Something was wrong. Seriously wrong. The two others cocked their heads as if listening to something far away, tuned into a vibe only the three of them could hear. Their postures took on equal intensity. Vic dropped his fork and opened his eyes, his gaze communicating something to the other two. They knew exactly what was going on. She was the only one out of the loop. It must be some kinda loop.

"Commander?" she asked and placed a hand on the table near him. "What's going on?"

"Let's go check on Dane," Vic said and stood abruptly, leaving the rest of his meal. "Doc. With me."

"What's wrong?" she asked. Not knowing what the situation was, but trusting his lead, she followed him outside and they hurried in the direction of the infirmary. "Did you get an alert or something?"

"Just a feeling, Doc. Just a feeling." His steps were long, purposeful, chewing up the ground beneath him, and she struggled to keep pace with him.

Vic burst through the door to the infirmary, heading straight to the wolf lying on the table. "What's wrong, Blaze?" Though he spoke to the medic tending the beast, he looked at the wolf. "Dane. Can you hear me?"

"He was doing fine, then his pressure dropped. I opened up his fluids, all his labs looked good, but I don't know what else to do," Blaze said to Vic, then at her, his eyes guarded. "You need to talk to him, sir. You're the only one he'll listen to. Stubborn bastard."

"Talk to him?" Trista asked, and moved away. Vic changed right in front of her. The eyes she knew as bright blue changed to a golden glow.

"Move her back," Vic said. Even his voice sounded different. His breathing changed. His eyes closed.

"Take a step back, Doc," Luke said and pulled her away. "He has to concentrate a minute." Unable to do otherwise, she moved back a few paces with Luke. Something was going on here, but she had no idea what.

～

WITH TRISTA CONTAINED, Vic could do what he needed to do to get Dane's attention. He pressed his forehead to the top of the wolf's head. Both hands pressed into the side of Dane's face.

Dane, you stupid dick. Get your ass back here.

Don't want to. It's nice here. Pretty. Blue.

97

You have a job and a mission. And they're not done. You're AWOL if you think you can leave without my permission.

I'm leaving. My ancestors are calling me.

Don't listen. We need you here. You must stay with us.

It's too hard. Too hard to--

Fuck hard. You've had hard times. You never backed down from them. Don't back down from this.

But--

Your alpha commands you to return to this plane.

No.

Do not deny your alpha.

Sorry, Vic.

~

"Do not defy your alpha." Vic pulled out of whatever mental thing he was doing and spoke out loud to the wolf. Yelled, really. Trista was puzzled he referred to himself as *the alpha*, not the commander as she knew him. He was speaking to the wolf like he understood English. "You must not defy your alpha. Return. Now," Vic said, his voice hardened, lowered to an animal-like growl, as if he were having trouble speaking. Muscle spasms shuddered through his body, and he sank his hands into the ruff of fur at Dane's neck.

The medic took a step back. "This isn't the usual way we do things around here," he said, but his words didn't offer her any comfort.

"What's happening?" Fear. Panic. Uncertainty. They all ran through her as Vic broke out in a heavy sweat.

The medic paused a second, then looked at her, his eyes now guarded and wary when minutes ago they had been open and cooperative. "I don't know how much the commander told you, so I can't answer that. The treatments I've done for Dane aren't working. The only reason he isn't responding is because he doesn't want to." He nodded at Dane. "The only way he'll come back is if the commander directs him to."

"How does he do that?" she asked, trying to process those words, to understand how they affected an animal who wasn't capable of understanding that much English.

He withdrew, looking like he was tuning into some inner conversation, just like the others, though she hadn't met this one. "You'll have to wait for him to answer that question."

"Hey, Doc? How about you wait outside with me?" Luke asked and took hold of her arm, leading her away. "It might get kinda weird in here, and you don't need to be a part of it."

"*Kinda* weird? Like it isn't weird enough already?" Although she allowed him to draw her away, she looked over her shoulder. Feet stopped moving. Body stopped moving. Brain stopped processing. "What the--" Her brain didn't want to comprehend what she thought she saw. What she knew couldn't be the truth. Things like that didn't happen. Ever.

Luke looked behind her and uttered a foul curse, then whipped her around to face him. "I'm really sorry, Doc. You shouldn't have seen that." Luke pulled back a fist, and her world exploded in a shower of sparkling stars.

CHAPTER
EIGHT

Zane Cavalier watched from the road. Waiting. The stinking odor of humans lingered in the air long after they'd left the area. The downside of having an advanced sense of smell? You could literally smell the past.

He'd been watching the lady vet for months, waiting for the moment that would change his life. He'd lead the Ridge Runner pack to a position of supreme power and control of the entire southwest. Only those who excelled in their positions got his attention. Those who didn't became kibble for the others, were torn to pieces and consumed by the pack. Werewolves didn't waste meat. Of any kind. Zane wasn't going to be kibble for anyone else. He was patient. Waiting for the right moment to strike.

Anticipation. Planning. Layers of protection in his organization were all going to pay off very soon, and he could put his ambitious plan into motion.

Years had gone into selecting the right players around him. Years of trips to South and Central America. Making contacts. Cultivating business associations. Eliminating others who wouldn't join his game. He'd created a pipeline from Central and South America, up through Mexico, straight to the intersection of major highways in Albuquerque. From there, the entire United States, even Canada, would be under his control. If you couldn't have it all, why bother?

Guns. Ganja. Girls. They were all his to command, distribute and profit from. Everything was finally falling into place. All his work. All the bloodshed. There was no better feeling than taking what he knew to be his.

All the loss. All the trauma. All the destruction had been worth it. Even the friends he'd killed to take the pack from the former worthless alpha had been worth it. Zane was now the leader of the Ridge Runner pack. He didn't need any friends.

Only one thing stood in the way of his magnificent plan. Only one group had caused him any grief.

Alpha Company.

That pack of fucking jackals that wouldn't go away.

The cops, the FBI, Homeland Security and the Border Patrol hadn't posed any problems. They'd been eluded, bought off or killed outright and buried in the desert where they wouldn't be found.

Ice caves and fields of old lava beds were perfect places to dispose of bodies. No one went to those place on purpose. Discovery by a casual passerby was unlikely. Zane only killed the humans. Nature took care of the disposal process.

The only beasts standing in his way were those military wolves, growing stronger, growing larger all the time. Something had to be done about them. And he was going to do it very soon.

Their lair had yet to be found. None of them left the

compound alone. They never were seen in public alone, so Zane couldn't catch one to torture for information. When he found their stronghold, he was going to--

"Boss, what are we doing here? You've been staring at this fucking empty house all fucking night. Nothing's happening," Buster, his second in command, complained.

"Patience, pup," Zane said, not bothered by Buster's irritability.

"You know I hate when you call me that," Buster said and growled from the passenger seat of the large black SUV they occupied.

"That's why I use it." Zane cast a sideways glance at the younger wolf in human form.

"Can't we go? Nothing's going on. That vet has either flown the coop or is outa town." Zane flopped back into the seat, a perpetual, petulant child.

"The longer you pout, the longer we're staying," Zane said and looked through his night-vision goggles again, watching for any sign of the human female.

"I'm not pouting, I'm fucking bored. You know I hate being bored. Sitting on our asses all night is not my idea of a good time. At least we could go to Maggie's and score some tail, you know?" Buster took out his knife and cleaned beneath his fingernails.

"A little longer, then we'll go." The stench of Alpha Company hung in the air. They'd been here recently. He knew it. Could taste it in the air.

The shadow of something triggered motion detector lights, illuminating the entire front of the veterinarian's home and office, yet all remained dark inside. Then a small creature from the *Felis Catus* clan emerged from its hiding place in the shrubbery.

"Just a damned cat. Can we *go* now?" Buster groaned

and flexed his hands, forcing his claws out the ends of his fingers in frustration.

"It's not just a damned cat. It's *her* damned cat." Zane kept his gaze on the black and white feline. It parked itself by the front door, licking its paws as if it didn't have a care in the world. Fucking cats. Always thought they were the center of the universe. He'd show the damned thing. As quietly as possible, he opened the door to the SUV, eased out. "Stay here."

Zane practically oozed from the vehicle and closed the door softly. Small pieces of gravel shifted beneath his boots, destroying his attempt at a stealthy approach. The cat would hear him no matter what he did, anyway. Those from the *Felis* clan had outstanding hearing. Even better than his. Flashing into his beast would be more satisfying, but it took time, and the cat could dash off any second into some hole Zane couldn't get into.

He remained hidden in the shadows for several yards, then broke the plane of light. He was going to catch this cat and put it to good use. There was more than one way to score some pussy tonight.

The second his feet touched the pavement the cat froze, eyes wide, glowing green, reflecting the light from the porch.

"Come here, little pussy," Zane said in a sing-song voice, trying to draw it closer. He cast out a soothing energy toward the feline. Well, as soothing as he could manage.

The damned cat was smarter than he'd anticipated and scampered off like its life depended on it, which it did. Zane had no qualms about gutting this little distraction.

Giving up wasn't in his makeup when he wanted something. He'd worked hard over the years, and he wasn't letting a fucking cat get in his way. Making his way through the parking lot in the direction it had gone, Zane trod lightly, stepping over branches and around rocks, engaging his night vision to differentiate between light and dark, shadow and night.

The cat was there. Frozen in fear. Trying to hide its sorry ass behind a tree. A light breeze had blown its tail into view, and Zane grinned as he moved silently through the night. Crouching, he took one last step and grabbed the unsuspecting cat.

Several things occurred to Zane in the nano-second it took to leap around the tree.

The wind was blowing the wrong way.

This wasn't the cat he'd followed.

And he was one big fucking idiot.

The skunk in his hands reacted violently, spraying noxious fumes into the night, lighting Zane's senses on fire, as if he'd inhaled jet fuel and lit a match. *Ka-boom.*

"Fuck!" He launched it as far away from him as he could, which wasn't far enough. Tears filled his eyes, and he cried like a fucking baby. He pressed his hands to eyes that burned like the hottest pepper juice had been squirted into them. Choking, he dropped to his knees, the breath of fire trapped in his lungs. "Goddamn, fucking son-of-a-bitch." *Choke. Cough. Wheeze. Snort. Sneeze.*

He struggled to his feet and staggered back to the SUV. Falling forward, he caught himself on the hood of the vehicle, startling Buster from his focus on Snack-Chat, a foodie app.

Get out here and help me.

What's wrong? Cat got your tongue? Buster laughed.

Get the fuck out here!

All right. All right.

Buster opened the door and instantly recoiled, jumping

back inside and locking the doors. "No way. No way you're getting in here with me."

"Open the goddamn door before I break it and then your face." Zane was beyond seeing red. He was going to choke the ever-loving shit out of Buster if he didn't open the door.

"Where's the cat?" Buster's face screwed up, his eyes disappearing into his skull. With obvious reluctance, Buster unlocked the doors, then pulled the front of his shirt up over his nose and mouth.

"It got away," Zane wheezed, then crawled in and started the SUV. He coughed and choked again as he put it into gear.

"See? We should have left when I wanted to, and this wouldn't have happened." Buster opened his window and hung his head outside, sucking in fresh air. "You never listen to me!"

Pissed, Zane grabbed him by the jacket yanked him back inside. "Get back in here. You look like a fucking dog hanging out the window."

"You stink! It's going to set off my asthma," Buster said, his voice cracking.

"Asthma, my ass. You don't have asthma," Zane said in disgust, reconsidering his leadership positions.

Buster looked away from him and raised his nose in the air. "I have allergies."

"Forget about it. This is serious," Zane said.

"No shit. Theo's gonna have a fit. He just detailed this SUV last week after we took that load of sluts up to Colorado," Buster said.

"Shut up. I need to think." Zane wiped tears from his eyes that had begun to swell.

"Just sayin'." Buster glanced at him, brows raised, upper

lip curled in disdain. "You know, opening the windows might help the stink go away sooner."

"I said shut up!" Zane coughed again and wiped the snot from his nose.

Looking out the window at the night rushing by, Buster turned his back on Zane. A wolf signal of displeasure.

Zane pulled out his phone, but cell service was spotty in the mountains. He opened all the windows in the vehicle, hoping it would help and tried not to drive off the road.

"What are you doing? You know you shouldn't drive and text!" Buster said.

"Then you Google how to get rid of skunk piss," Zane said and squinted through the windshield as the lights of Albuquerque came into view. They needed supplies and Albuquerque had them.

"Technically, it's not piss--"

"Google it!" Zane gripped the steering wheel, fighting the urge to bash Buster in the face.

"Fine." After choking a few times and wiping away the moisture dripping down his face, Buster squinted at the screen on his phone. "You know reception's not very good out here."

"Buster...I swear, I'll skin you alive..."

"Hang on." Brushing away more tears, Buster used his fat fingers on the tiny keyboard. "Got a few tips, but we'll need to stop by a store."

"I can't go into a store like this, moron," Zane said. "Plus, it's three A.M. Everything's closed, dammit." How was he going to live through this night?

"Then you'll be sleeping in the garage until you get rid of it. No one's going to let you in the house like that, alpha or not," Buster said.

Several miles and a hundred curses later, Zane punched

the steering wheel with one hand. "Okay. There's a 24-hour store on Eubank and I-40. We'll go there and you can get whatever shit is on that list you looked up." He hoped to the gods that it was normal stuff and nothing that had to be ordered.

"Thanks to you, I now smell like skunk piss, too," Buster said, with some attitude.

"Well, what the hell are we going to do? I can't stay like this for days. I have meetings, I have--" Zane stuttered, thinking of all the things, all the details that would have to change because of one stupid lapse in judgement.

"*We?*" Buster gave him an incredulous look. A laugh cackled out of his thick throat. "I don't know about *you*, but *I'm* going to take a fucking shower and go to bed. I'll be fine after that. You, however, are going to have to figure it out on your own." He tucked his phone back into the outer pocket of his leather jacket. "Not. My. Problem."

"Buster..." Zane shifted to his wolf eyes, let some of his beast emerge, reveled in the power roiling through his veins, the tingle and thrill zinging across his muscles. The growl vibrated his throat, rumbled in his chest. Power emerged, filled the vehicle and then was swept away on the rushing wind. "Don't make me--"

"Okay, okay. Dude. Dial it down a notch." Buster shrugged and tilted his head to the side in a reluctant gesture. "I got a guy I can call."

"*You got a guy you can call?* Seriously?" Zane glared at his second-in-command in disbelief.

"Well, a minion, really," Buster said dismissively. He pulled the phone from his pocket again and hit some buttons. "He does shit for me."

"Since when do you have a minion?" Zane snorted. Then chuckled. Then threw his head back and barked out a laugh. "That's funny. You...with a minion?" He pounded one fist on the steering wheel. "Good one."

"Everyone else has one. Why shouldn't I?" Buster asked and shrugged keeping his eyes low, intimidated by Zane's wolf eyes. "I wanted one, too," he said, his voice meek and submissive.

"Well, call your fucking *minion* and have him get the shit I need," Zane said and coughed again.

"How do you know it's a guy?" Buster asked and looked at Zane with narrowed eyes.

"Don't make me laugh. *Again*. No female is going to let someone like *you* boss her around like *that*." He laughed again and shook his head.

"But--"

"Do it! We'll meet him outside the store on Tramway and Central," Zane said and started to relax. This hiccup in his night was going to be over soon and he could get back to his mission of dealing with Alpha Company.

Ignoring Zane, Buster made a call, spoke a few seconds, then hung up. "He'll be there in thirty," Buster said.

"Good." Zane breathed out a sigh, letting the air rush out of him. At least he'd stopped choking, and his eyes had quit watering. "I'm gonna catch that fucking cat and skin it alive."

"Wasn't that the plan tonight?" Buster asked.

"Shut the fuck up before I decide to skin you alive instead," Zane said. He didn't need the reminder.

Buster shut the fuck up and sent a follow up text to his minion.

Take a piss in the bottle of neutralizer, too.

~

TRISTA STARTLED AWAKE TO AN OVERWHELMING, threatening dark night filled with storm. Flashes of brilliant white light snaked in through the closed window blinds followed by the rumble and roll of thunder. Her throat pulsed with the echo of her heartbeat thrumming in her chest.

The tic-tac of rain pelting against the window drew her attention away from the dryness of her throat and mouth. They felt like she'd been left on the mesa for a week without water. Swallowing past the desert inside her, she tuned into an ache in her jaw and frowned, having no memory of injuring herself. Now that she'd noticed it, she realized the pain had been throbbing for some time, stirring her from sleep.

The wind exerted the force of its energy, raising ethereal arms to shake the cottonwood branches of the ancient tree outside the window, showing her the power it wielded.

The heat of another body lay beside her, and she lifted her arm from beneath the covers. A large, heavily-furred canine lay on the bed beside her. At her touch it lifted its great head. With eyes downcast, it licked her arm twice. After releasing a heavy sigh of contentment, it resumed its position and slept.

With the next sizzle and flash of lightning she realized a large, German Shepard lay in bed with her, and there were two problems.

There were no cottonwood trees outside her bedroom window, and she didn't own a dog.

Angry male voices drew her attention away from her current predicament and onto a new one. Where the hell was she and why were there two men arguing outside the door? More curious than afraid, she tuned in to their voices.

"She should have awakened by now."

"I know. I'm sorry, sir. I must have, uh, tapped her too hard."

"*Tapped* her? That's what you call what you did to her?"

"You weren't exactly available for a consultation. Sir."

"Excuse me?"

At that, Trista rolled out of the bed, startling the dog beside her, which probably wasn't a great idea, but she had to find out what was going on. Those men on the other side of the door were the only ones who could tell her.

She yanked the door open, her breath rushing in and out, stars appearing at the periphery of her vision. The scream of pain in her legs reminded her of the unusual sexual activity she'd engaged in as well. "Wow. I got up too fast." Clutching the door frame, she didn't want to embarrass herself in front of the two men standing there. Luke and the commander. Especially the commander.

Vic reached for her waist and drew her against him for support. "How are you feeling?" he asked, his voice soft and silky, but with a tinge of irritation in it.

"Like I anesthetized myself," she said. Her legs wobbled a little, and he used those magnificently muscled arms of his to hold her tighter against him. Could anything on earth feel so damned good?

"Anything else?" he asked, his gaze assessing her for injury.

"Dizzy. Hungry. Thirsty. Grumpy." She paused and did a quick body scan. "That about covers it."

"So, back to normal then?" he asked, and one side of his mouth tilted up.

If she'd had any strength in her, she'd have belted him one, but as it was, she didn't and only nodded. Vic tightened his arm around her waist, the heat of his large hand seeping into her bones, giving her some of his strength.

The dog had taken up a position at their feet and appeared to be awaiting orders. He sat with his full attention on Vic.

"Rico. Downstairs. Wait." The dog scrambled to obey the command.

"I could use something to drink, though," she said.

"Let's get something in your hour of need," Vic said, and nodded at Luke, who eased away, looking grim. Apparently, their topic of discussion was going to be tabled for now. It was reassuring to know that she took precedence over their discussion for the moment. It would remain to be seen if he continued to turn his attention to her for more than sex.

"The reason I even have an hour of need is because one of your boys clobbered me one," she said. "Luke, I think." The memory was coming back now and she wiggled her jaw. She tried to get a sense of what had happened, what she'd done to invite such treatment. Had Vic changed his mind and decided to treat her like a prisoner after all?

"That was an unfortunate event," Vic said.

"Unfortunate? That's what you have to say about it?" she asked. A slow burn started in her gut.

"C'mon, doc. We'll get you something to drink, then I'll brief you," he said.

Vic sat her down on a stool at the granite island with a cup of something hot and steamy.

"Green tea?" Her brows rose at that discovery and she tried not to curl her lip that it wasn't something stronger. "I thought you guys only ate red meat and turned your noses up at the finer things in life?"

"Generally, that's how it goes for the others, but I enjoy a cup of tea now and then." He shrugged and reached for a stainless steel skillet hanging from an overhead rack. The black shirt stretched tight over his pecs and the hem lifted out of his waistband, revealing hard abdominals and a light dusting of dark hair drawing her eyes downward. She remembered quite vividly just what that dark hair pointed to.

Vic lowered the skillet in front of him, but didn't move toward the stove. Trista raised her gaze upward over his abdominals, over his pecs, past that strong jaw covered with a light beard, until she met those blue eyes looking at her. "Like what you see?"

Raising her nose primly in the air, she raised her mug to cover most of her face and sipped the brew, eyeing him over the rim of the mug. "I don't know what you're talking about. I was merely seeing what you were doing," she said.

A grin flashed over his face. "Liar," he said and moved to the refrigerator and removed a few things. Vic cracked a few eggs into the skillet and whipped up a savory omelet for her, stirring an appetite she hadn't realized until then was enormous.

"Thank you," she said quietly.

"You're welcome."

"How's Dane? I should probably have a look at him soon," she said. "If you don't mind."

"No problem, but let me fix you something to eat first, then we'll go to the infirmary, and you can see for yourself that Blaze has been monitoring him all night," Vic said and then made her a savory omelet that she wolfed down quickly.

"That was..." Trista started, then paused.

Vic wasn't even paying attention to her. He was staring into space, like he wasn't even seeing her in the kitchen. His eyes were open, but he appeared to be looking far away, focused on something elsewhere, not there in front of him.

Something was wrong. Seriously wrong.

Heavy boot steps rushed toward the kitchen. Rico clattered in behind the others, tail up, ears forward. Even he knew something was wrong. He stood at the commander's feet, awaiting orders.

"What's--" Eros began, then halted when Vic's hand went up. He hadn't moved, but his eyes glowed a crazy yellow color, not his usual blue. Trista moved away from the kitchen table and watched the trio who seemed to have forgotten her presence. She just wasn't getting it, whatever *it* was.

"Draco. And Silver. On the western perimeter," Vic said.

"That's National Forest. Everyone knows it's off limits," Eros snapped. The intensity in the room shot up a thousand percent. The air around them vibrated and the hair on her arms rose in reaction. There was danger in this room. She was just glad it wasn't directed at her.

"We need to go," Vic said.

"On foot or with the Hummer?" Eros asked.

"Foot. Go. I'll catch up," Vic said.

Eros and Luke stripped their clothing off right in front of her and dashed from the kitchen. Although she appreciated the fantastic show of man flesh, she had no idea what was going on. Vic whipped off his shirt, then looked at Rico. "Stay. Guard her."

Vic planted a hard kiss on her mouth, then dashed after the other two. Rushing after them to the side door, she stopped as Rico tugged at her pant leg, slowing her down, trying to keep her in place. Her jaw dropped as an entire pack of wolves streamed past the house racing in the direction the others had gone. Wolf after wolf. Black. Gray. Brown. They seemed to come out of nowhere, racing after

114

the others. It was both the most beautiful and the craziest thing she'd ever seen.

She looked at Rico who was doing his best to herd her back into the house.

"Something is definitely wrong, boy, isn't it?" she asked him and dropped her hand to the top of his head. "Definitely wrong."

CHAPTER
NINE

The wait was awful. The not knowing. Why were they rushing away like that? Why did they take their clothes off? The energy in the house and the compound was unnatural, even though she'd never been there before, the vibe of the house changed when the men left. It was bizarre. As if the world waited on hold for something to happen, like in the seconds before a wave crashed, or a bomb exploded. Silence filled the compound where previously sounds of life, of activity, had come from everywhere.

Not even the night crickets called out to each other. It was just silent. Nervous, she realized Dane would be alone in the infirmary if all of the wolves and men had taken off. Unwilling to leave him alone, she outmaneuvered Rico and slammed the door to the kitchen on him. With his frantic barking right behind her, he'd found a way out of the house through a window or a doggie door. Smart dog. With him fast on her heels, knowing she'd incite his primitive instinct to chase, she ran toward the infirmary. Nothing was going to stop her from getting to Dane. In the absence of the men, she was now his only protector.

Rushing through the door with Rico storming in behind her, she took a deep breath. Rico yipped and growled a few times, verbalizing his displeasure at having been outmaneuvered.

"Sorry, Rico. I had to get over here," she said.

He grumbled low in his throat, but settled down by the door to observe her movements. Apparently, he took Vic's order seriously.

Dane lay where he'd been, on his side, but a warming blanket had been placed over top of him. He must not be doing well if he couldn't hold his body temperature. That was a bad sign.

"Hello?" A male voice addressed her.

"Oh." Jumping, she clutched a hand to her throat. "I thought Dane was left alone, so I came to check on him."

"Nope. Never alone. Ever." The medic she'd seen earlier gave a crisp nod. He was cut from the same cloth as the others. Intense. Wound tight as a drum. Everything about him said military though and through. The muscles in his chest and shoulders were accentuated by the tight black shirt he wore. Must be the dress code around there. He wore his dark brown hair in the same high and tight haircut as most of the others, except a strip of platinum blond hair marked one side.

"Blaze, right?" she asked.

"Yes," he said. "We didn't really get introduced earlier."

"No, we didn't," she said. "But things don't follow the usual rules around here, do they?" she asked, knowing the answer to that question already.

Blaze barked out a laugh and relaxed a little. "That's an understatement."

"So, how is Dane? Any changes? I see you put a warming blanket on him." She stepped closer, wanting to assess Dane's condition, see for herself that he was okay.

"He's not changed much from when you were in here before," Blaze said. "I just added the blanket a few minutes ago."

"The last I saw him, he was trying to die, but the commander did something... said something to him." A vague memory surfaced as she recalled what had happened before Luke knocked her out, and she placed a hand to her jaw. "I remember Vic... did something." She raised her eyes to Blaze, trying to see the answers in his eyes, but he wasn't giving anything away. "I just can't think of what it was."

"He has a special connection with his soldiers, and the wolves, so what you saw may have been...unconventional... but it works for him. For all of us," Blaze said without really saying anything.

"Not SOP, then?" Trista smiled, trying to engage the man and set him at ease.

"No, ma'am," Blaze said and grinned. His teeth reminded her of the wolves these soldiers associated with. White teeth in perfect condition, with slightly elongated canines. "Not standard operating procedure by a long shot." He broke his gaze away from hers. "That's what makes Vic so successful. This unit would be nothing without the commander," Blaze said and she heard the respect in his voice.

"I see." More information she'd have to think on. "Has Dane awakened?" Changing the subject away from Vic's hidden capabilities, Trista focused on their shared patient.

"No. He's still unresponsive." Blaze shook his head and a frown crossed his brows. "There's no good reason for it, though. His vitals are stable, we've got fluids going, and his labs have come back normal. The only reason he's not rousing is because he doesn't want to wake up yet." He clucked his tongue in disgust. "Damned stubborn wolf."

"I wonder if he has PTSD? That can happen to animals the way it happens to humans," she said. It definitely made sense, especially for such higher functioning animals.

"For sure," Blaze said, picked up a clipboard and wrote down some numbers from the monitor on it, just like a nurse would do while monitoring a human patient. Fascinating. "He'd just taken a knife to the gut. That's enough to trigger this reaction."

"I see." She'd have to do some research on PTSD in wolves. Tension in the air seemed to sizzle across her skin, and she rubbed her arms to rid herself of the odd sensation, like the rush of a breeze before a wave struck. It was just like the air in the kitchen when the men had gone on alert. "Do you have any idea when the others will be back?" she asked.

"Soon. I hope." The full lips pressed together and thinned for a moment. Though he hid it, he was worried. He knew what was going on, but didn't want her to know. Or couldn't tell her.

"The worst part is being left behind, isn't it?" she asked. Some bit of insight flashed in her as she watched this soldier monitoring his patient. His gray eyes flashed to her, studied her, wondered if she could be trusted.

"Yes, ma'am," he said. For a second, his shoulders relaxed. "Someone has to keep watch over those who can't watch out for themselves." His stance returned to that of being on alert, his senses tuned for any sign of danger. Though he didn't have a weapon in his hands, he was on guard as if he were on sentry duty. Nothing was going to get past him, and he'd die to protect those under his care.

"A good soldier always protects the weak, the women, and the children. Don't they?" she asked.

"You surprise me, Trista," Blaze said and faced her, the intensity in his eyes searching hers. "You *do* understand."

"I'm a military brat. I understand what it is to be a soldier, though I've never been one," she said. Her father, brother, uncles. They'd all sacrificed some part of themselves and so had their families.

"Thank you," Blaze said.

"Be at ease, soldier. You're doing a fine job," she said. Her words seemed to mean something to him as he stood more upright, but without the tension of a few moments ago.

"I thought since you're a doctor, a vet, you'd be uber critical of what we do here," he said A small smile lifted the outer curve of his mouth to one side. Apparently, he was rethinking his position on her.

"No, way. I couldn't do at my place what you do here. The commander was right, but don't tell him I said that," she said. "You have way more cool toys than I do." At that she laughed, recalling Vic's description of the infirmary, though it had annoyed her at the time.

"That's true. The commander's got every piece of equipment known to man--"

Rico stood now and faced the door, on alert. Ears forward, tail high.

"They're coming," Blaze said and set the clipboard down, moved around the table and stood in front of her.

The door to the infirmary burst open. Rico went crazy barking and then whining when he recognized his companions and the other wolves flowing in through the door behind them.

Vic and Eros held an injured man upright, his arms over

their shoulders, his head rolling to the side. The lot of them were covered in scratches, bruises, dirt and blood. And they were all naked.

"Commander!" Trista rushed forward to help, but was cut off by Rico trying to keep her contained, trying to herd her away from perceived danger. His orders had not changed. "Will you stop?" She hated getting cross with animals, but this one was about to drive her crazy with his protective ways.

"Let's get him on a table," Vic said. He and Eros eased the unconscious man onto a stainless-steel table and positioned him on his back. Immediately, the pack of wolves surrounded them, each of them trying to get closer to the table to see what was going on. Trista's brows shot up. She'd never seen so many wolves at one time, nor been in such close proximity. Were they all his? Were they all friendly? Were they all trained well? She turned her back to Vic, not sure she was as safe as he seemed to think she was.

"Doc, why don't you back up a bit? Give us some room to work?" Vic said.

"I was going to help." Though she spoke to Vic, her eyes remained on the wolves, who now found her of great interest. Dozens of golden, gleaming eyes focused on her and a primal instinct to run bubbled inside her.

"You don't work on humans. But--" Vic started.

"Uh...help? Vic?" She tried to remain calm and professional, but this situation totally freaked her out. Her breathing rushed in and out of her lungs, she knew she exuded fear, which is what wild animals needed to attack. "Commander? Help!" she cried.

"What?" He glanced over with a frown at the distraction. "Rico. Herd. Protect." Stone gave more commands in German to the dog, who immediately went into action and herded her from the pack of wolves and away from the table.

The wolves kept their intense gazes on her as she moved, slowly, trying to follow Rico through the mob of furry bodies. Many of them leaned forward, sniffing at her legs as she passed by. A few bold ones stuck their noses right into her crotch and her butt for a quick sniff.

"Hey. Cut that out," she said. Without thinking, she swatted at the nose in her butt. She received a quick growl and a snap of teeth that barely missed her hand.

"Back off!" Vic commanded and the wolves parted to give her some room. Though they looked like they wanted a piece of her, none of them moved after Vic's words. Some sat down, others lay down and a few groomed each other. The tension eased and only remained high at the table with the injured man.

"Wow." Trista had never seen such a thing, such power over wild animals. She was seriously impressed. More than she already was with Vic.

A flurry of activity at the door drew her attention as Luke entered with a gray wolf draped over his shoulders. "I've got Silver," Luke groaned, straining under the weight of the injured wolf. Luke lumbered forward and Blaze helped him to ease Silver onto another table. After catching a few deep breaths, Luke helped Blaze work on Silver. The gray wolf whimpered as they inserted an IV into one leg, but remained still. Luke placed an oxygen mask that was shaped to accommodate a pointed snout over his face and leaned close to him. "Deep breaths, my friend. We'll take care of the bastards who did this to you. Don't worry about anything. We'll take our revenge on their asses, and you can sleep on their hides in front of the fire," Luke whispered urgently to Silver. After one last stroke down Silver's back, Luke straightened. "You got it from here?" he asked Blaze.

"Yes." Blaze gave a stiff nod. "I'll take care of him."

Still naked and unconcerned about it, Luke turned away from them and moved to the other table. "I'm ready to go, sir."

Vic lifted his gaze and looked between Luke and Eros. "Gear up. Pick four others. The rest stay," Vic said.

"What's going on?" Less afraid of the pack now, she hurried over to Vic. Placing her hands on his chest, she had to touch him, feel for herself that he was okay, that he wasn't hurt.

"It's okay. I'm fine," Vic said, his voice softening as he spoke to her.

"You're covered in blood," she said. "Scratches, abrasions and bruises, too."

"None of the blood is mine," he said. He placed his hands on her shoulders and squeezed, the heat of him surging into her. Leaning closer, he placed his forehead against hers and took in a breath, taking her scent in, or that's what it seemed he was doing.

"Okay. Okay," she said. Relief washed over her. Emotions swirled in her chest. So much had changed in a few short hours, her head was just spinning with it. "Can you tell me what's going on?" The heat and intensity of him was overwhelming, out of control, and she didn't like it. A bead of sweat trickled down her back.

"We're in the middle of a turf war, and you're caught in the crossfire. That's as much as I can tell you right now," he said. One hand stroked down her back and brought her hips against his. His other hand curved her hair behind one ear in a tender gesture. How could he be so gentle, so affectionate, after being in a brutal fight just moments ago? "You have to stay now."

"I thought you said I wasn't a prisoner," she asked. She tried to pull back, knowing there was no way she'd escape, even if she wanted to try. Now, she didn't want to leave, didn't want to go back to her normal life. At this point, she wasn't even sure she could. Something had changed inside her. Something she didn't want to change back. Whatever it was had taken a strong hold inside her.

"You weren't before. Now you are," Vic said and placed a kiss on her nose.

"I'll could call the police, or the National Guard," she said, threatening him with something she knew she'd never do now.

"They won't come." Vic quirked a smile.

"Why not?" she asked. This she had to hear, even though she had no intention of calling for assistance.

"They're afraid of us," Vic said.

That made her gape and then laugh. "Seriously? The National Guard is afraid of you guys?"

"Yes. For now, just stay put. Please." His gaze searched hers for answers or a hint as to what she was going to do. "Don't try to leave. Let me do my job, and then we'll have it out when I get back," Vic said, offering her a promise that he'd come back to her.

"But--" What happened if he didn't come back? Then what would she do?

"You'll be safe here. I can't guarantee your safety anywhere else. You have to be safe for me to do what I need to do next," he said, his gaze locked on hers.

"What are you going to do?" Her hands drifted to his hips and held on, her hands moist, the blood in her heart racing fast, surging through her veins as if every cell in her body waited for his answer.

"I can't tell you. But there will be blood. Lots of blood," he said. Cupping his hands around her head, he pressed his lips hard against hers. He filled her with the scent and taste of him, insanely strong. Reclaiming her in front of the others.

He pulled back and left her standing there as Eros, Luke and four wolves fell into line behind him.

She took another breath and pressed the back of her hand against her mouth as tears pricked her eyes.

What in God's name did that mean?

VIC PUNCHED in an access code to the door of the armory building. He, Eros and Luke entered the building made of steel and reinforced concrete. If anything ever blew up in here, it would be contained, wouldn't torch the entire compound and wouldn't start a forest fire that would draw attention their way. They geared up, grabbing packs and bags that had already been prepared, slipped into camouflage suits and heavy boots. Everything was ready for special ops at a moment's notice. Like firefighters preparing for a blaze, they could be ready in no time. In less than five minutes they were headed out the lane in the Hummer, three men in seats, four wolves in the back.

The only sound was the whine of the engine working, straining hard as Stone pushed it to its limit, taking them to their goal.

"Where are we going?" Eros asked.

"To kick Zane's ass." Vic grinned and loosened the hold on his beast a little. He glanced at Eros. Everything about him spoke death and pain. From his cold, calculating eyes, to the stiff way he sat in the seat fondling the knife in his hands, to the way he used his senses, feeling for the enemy. Vic could feel it. There was no wolf he wanted at his side more than Eros. And Luke. Dane would be with them if he hadn't been injured. These were his pack mates. His brothers.

"Where else did you think we were going?" Luke asked with a laugh from the back seat and poked Eros in the shoulder. "Costco?"

"Back off, ass-hat. We don't know where their stronghold is. No one's been able to find it. The same way they can't find ours." Eros shook off Luke with a snarl. "Do you know where they are? Did you get a sense from the others? I've been looking, but can't tune into them," Eros said. He took the blade and pushed the tip into his thumb until blood welled up from the wound. It pushed his energy higher. His vengeance deeper.

"On a Friday night in Tijeras? There's only one place they'll be. Maggie's Bar, baby," Luke said with glee. The one and only joint where shifters of any sort could hang and not be out of place. Since everyone who went there was odd, everyone fit in. Vic glanced at Eros as he smeared blood on his arms. "Save the cutting for them," Vic said.

"Gonna kick some ass tonight, boys." Luke bounced up and down in the back seat, his excitement palpable, then he leaned forward, hanging over Vic's shoulder. "You know that's asking for it, right? Charging onto their turf?"

"They're the ones who asked for it by crossing the boundary lines, ignoring the treaty," Vic said.

"Draco and Silver were alone by the time we got there. There were no witnesses. It ain't gonna hold up at council," Luke said, his face tightened, his eyes narrowed.

"Couldn't you smell the stench of the Ridge Runner pack on them?" Eros asked and grimaced. "And fox piss. Whatever that was all about."

"I could smell it. But if we're going to be working within the boundaries of the treaty, it won't help. Can't prove smell in council either," Eros said to Vic, but kept his gaze on the road, looking out the window, checking the mirror in case they'd been followed.

"We aren't going to council," Vic said.

"Awesome." Luke rubbed his hands together and flopped back against the seat. He grabbed the face of the wolf nearest to him and stuck his face close. "We're definitely gonna kick some ass tonight." The only response was growling and excited breathing. Everyone was on the same wave length.

In minutes they arrived at the neighborhood bar that doubled as a meeting place for the Ridge Runner pack. They ran with a rough crowd of outlaw bikers and drug runners. All things Vic despised and wanted to rid from the state of New Mexico. At least the area surrounding Albuquerque. If he could stop the influx it all running through there, it would put a huge dent into the financial empire of the group. Zane didn't play by the rules they were all supposed to abide by. Why should Vic? If he crippled Zane financially, he'd leave. Or at least Vic hoped it could be that easy.

Sure, once in a while someone would forget to pay their parking tickets or abide by the human rules and get themselves arrested. They all did stupid things, but the shifter community rules had been set down and agreed upon by their kind for the last five hundred years. Of course, with updates for the modern era. Since werewolves had been coming to the new world from Europe and more shifter

128

groups appeared every year, there had to be some law and consequences.

Rules had to be followed by everyone or there would be all-out war.

All shifter groups in the area had agreed, the national forests were claimed by no one. Free range for everyone, the ranchers, the humans, and the wolf packs. If humans were scented, they all backed off until the risk of exposure was gone. Livestock that grazed in the forests and mountain pastures were fair game. To a point. A group could pinch a few head of cattle now and then when there were no other options.

Twenty years ago there had been rogue bands of wolves traveling through New Mexico, Colorado, Wyoming and Montana killing livestock for sport, not survival. They'd tortured and mutilated cattle, then left their carcasses to rot in the sun, which brought serious investigations down on everyone. Those packs had been driven by force out of the region up and into Canada or had been killed outright. A few of the betas had been assimilated into local packs, but would never be alphas or allowed to breed in case something in their DNA emerged in their young.

As it was, the ranchers and the general public believed the mayhem could be attributed to anything from aliens to secret military operations. As long as the local werewolf packs weren't blamed, that was fine with everyone. Eventually, the furor had died down, and the secrets of the shifters remained hidden.

It was the one time in recent years that area packs had banded together *with* the Ridge Runners to rid the area of the rogue wolves. After the job was done, they returned to hating each other.

"Looks like it's a full house tonight." Eros noted the row

of heavy-duty motorcycles, trucks and work vehicles stationed around the low building that looked as if it should have a condemned sign on the front. A shoddy wooden post held up the roof over the porch, someone had spray painted graffiti on the side and one of the front windows had been shattered. The coyote fencing around the parking area didn't look like it could keep out coyotes, let alone werewolves on a rampage. It was all for show. Keeping a low profile and looking run-down kept the majority of tourists away. Only the locals knew what was going on there. Wisely, they mostly kept their distance.

Luke stuck his head out the window. "Fucking trash, Ridge Runner pack! I can smell your stinking asses from here!" he yelled at the vehicles.

"So much for stealth," Eros said and shook his head, then sheathed the knife.

"We're not here for stealth. We're here to put them on notice and shove it up their asses." Vic parked the Hummer in front of the row of motorcycles, not caring that it blocked half the vehicles in the lot.

The males and wolves emerged from the Hummer. Vic in front, Eros and Luke flanking, wolves bringing up the rear. He didn't need to give any commands. They all knew what to do.

As Vic approached the door to the historic establishment, he had to take a breath, to force back the beast in him that wanted to emerge and tear the Ridge Runners to shreds and damn the consequences.

The desire to bring his teeth in, to allow his muscles to mutate, to transform himself into a killing machine nearly overpowered him. Blood lust didn't easily take a back seat. Trembling with the need, fighting the urge to strike out, he stood with his hand on the heavy wooden door, sweat pouring from his face and neck.

"Commander?" Eros jabbed him one in the ribs. Vic snarled, but the distraction did the trick, and his beast receded inside to brood and growl its displeasure. "You got it?"

"I got it." With that, he shoved the door wide and it banged off the wall. The place was packed with bikers, women, and a few locals who knew to beat a hasty retreat out the back door. As they left, the wolves entered the building silently, searching out the main players in the rival group. They scented and surrounded one table where three wolves in human form sat. The threat was clear.

You move, you die.

Three males, dressed in black leather jackets, openly wearing sheaths with deadly knives leaned back in their chairs, taking in the scene. Amusement shone in the leader's black eyes.

Vic approached. Eros and Luke behind him. Those in wolf form behind them. Should there be any trouble, they knew what to do, who to kill first. Whose hide to put on his wall.

"Zane."

"Vic."

"There seems to be an issue with your ability to comply with the Rio Grandé Treaty of Weres. Or did your boys simply forget the rules not to engage others in neutral territory?" Vic asked. He didn't expect to get much out of Zane.

"*The Rio Grandé Treaty of Weres?*" Zane barked out a. "Are you shitting me? *Seriously*? Who talks like that anymore?" He picked up his beer and downed the remainder, then wiped his mouth on the back of his hand. "I don't follow that worthless treaty. No real alpha does. It's old and outdated." Zane looked Vic up and down pointedly. "Just like you."

Can we jump 'em, boss? Luke asked. *I really wanna beat Buster's face in.*

No. Not yet, Vic replied.

"Is that so?" Vic asked with a grin, barely containing his beast who wanted to shred Zane to pieces.

How about now? Luke asked. *I feel the need. The need to feed!*

Not yet, Vic said.

Slowly, Zane stood, the threat imminent. He almost matched Vic in height, sinew and strength, but not in brains. "You and your pups should be on a leash and fed like dogs, 'cause you lost your taste for blood. You don't have what it takes to be the supreme leader of this territory." He flashed his wolf eyes glowing golden as he let some of his beast show.

"And you do?" Vic had to ask. He already knew what Zane was going to answer.

"Yes," Zane growled, letting more of his beast show. "Consider yourself notified. We're coming for you. All of you. Including that pretty little vet of yours. Nice piece of ass you got your hands on-"

Now boss?

Now!

The room erupted in chaos. Vic seized Zane by the throat forcing him backwards across the room and bent him backwards over the bar, trying to break his back, striking the head of the snake first. Zane's resistance fueled Vic's appetite for blood. Wolf claws out, he forced them into Zane's fleshy neck, ready to slice through his vessels and end the bastard right there. Trista's safety was paramount.

Vic wouldn't allow Zane to even speak her name. His beast demanded that blood be spilled.

"Stay away from her. Stay away from my pack or I'll come for you with everything we've got," Vic said. A low growl emerged from his gut and moved up his throat. The glasses over the bar rattled at the power building and sizzling inside of him.

"Or what? What are you going to do? Human lover." Zane flexed his hands, forcing his claws out and sliced them into Vic's arms.

The pain only fueled Vic's determination. Sweating, straining against the pain and the energy it took to hold his beast back, Vic ground his teeth together and bared them at Zane. "Back. Off."

"Or what?" Zane strained against the power Vic exerted against him matching Vic's power with his own. With his beast chomping at the bit to be released, he could take Zane, could kill him right now, but not without consequences. Vic had already engaged in combat once today. His muscles were fatigued. His power not replenished. not ready for another round. Zane was fresh, ready for a fight. Vic's chances to take Zane would be better when they were on even terms. With no witnesses.

Vic pressed his nose against Zane's. "Or I'll kill you." He whispered the words from his soul. "I'll tie your carcass to the Hummer and drag you down the highway until there's nothing left but a few teeth and some fur."

"Like that threat's going to bother me," Zane said and barked out a laugh, not bothered by the threat.

"You going to let one of these jackals take over your pack? Take over your business you've worked so hard for and run it into the ground? You know that's exactly what'll happen," Vic said and nodded toward Zane's men who were dangling by their throats in front of Eros and Luke.

Eros pressed the tip of his knife into the throat of one. Luke held his frightened quarry in a choke hold, grinning the whole time, blew a kiss at Zane. "Think about it," Vic whispered. "Think about Buster sitting in your chair. Sleeping in your bed. Fucking your females." Vic leaned closer still. "You haven't bred the next generation. One of these idiots is going to be your legacy. Going to take over your pack. Is that what you really want?" Vic said, dropping the psychological bombs in Zane's ear.

Zane stopped struggling as Vic's words penetrated his brain. He retracted his claws and pulled them out of Vic's arms. He looked at his men and then back at Vic. "I see what you mean," Zane said, considering Vic's statement. "There is wisdom in your words I hadn't considered." Zane gave a nod of acknowledgment to that. "Coming from you only means I'm coming from you harder. Got it?" Zane asked. A hint of respect flashed in Zane's eyes, but was quickly replaced by hatred that Vic had outsmarted him on his own turf.

Vic released Zane with a shove as the pain in his arms flared to life. "Keep your boys off my land. Stay away from the borders. If I see anyone near the human female, I'll bleed you." He shoved his face into Zane's again. "All of you."

"What are you so huffy about that vet for?" Zane shook his jacket into place. "It's not like she's your mate or anything. Just a female. And human at that." Confusion clearly showed in Zane's expression as his brows met.

"She's under my protection. Back off." Vic leaned a fraction closer and sniffed, then pulled back quickly in distaste

134

and released Zane with a shove. "Take a fucking shower, man. You stink," Vic said.

"What?" Zane flashed around to glare at Buster. "You said that spray would take the skunk smell out."

"It did. I swear, boss, it did," Buster raised his hands in the air as fear showed in his eyes. "You don't smell like a skunk anymore."

"You smell like fox piss," Vic said and backed away. Luke and Eros released the other two. "Be warned. We'll be watching. We'll know when you fuck up." Vic smirked. "I'm sure it won't take long."

Vic gave a piercing whistle through his teeth and those in wolf form retreated. All but one. After a quick growl, Torch spun around and bit Buster in the ass, then raced out after the others.

CHAPTER
TEN

Trista waited and waited. And *waited*. Although the time that passed wasn't that long, maybe an hour or two, it felt interminable. When waiting with no word from someone who'd just gone into battle, the wait became unbearable. The mind took images and intrusive thoughts, added a little catastrophe, and melted them all together to cause the maximum amount of worry possible. The clock seemed to run backwards. Time became an illusion.

Though she didn't know the exact circumstances of what was going on, she knew the commander and his men had jumped into the Hummer and gone off to war. What kind of war, she didn't know. But she knew the signs. Felt the lethal energy of them all.

That much she knew. The danger in their eyes. The threat in their stances. The tension in their jaws. All of it spoke death.

She didn't know if she'd ever see Vic again. Ever know what happened to him. Ever know his touch, his heat, his fire and passion again.

Not that that was all there was to him, but she'd just gotten to feel him against her skin, feel his touch stirring her body taking her to the height of passion. Was it just because he was in such superb condition? Or that he was the leader of this bunch of men she didn't know anything about? Or was it the passion, the tension, the intellect she sensed just beneath the surface he kept hidden most of the time?

"God. This waiting is awful." She paced the floor of the infirmary, moving back and forth between the two men and the wolf that Blaze was charged with keeping safe.

"I know. I'm sorry, ma'am," Blaze said hardly looking up from his duties as he tried to offer her some compassion.

"I'm the one who's sorry, Blaze. You've got three patients and all these wolves to keep track of." She glanced around the room. It seemed that the number of wolves had decreased, gone somewhere, as only a handful remained. "Well, where did they all go?" she asked.

"Uh..." He glanced at her, but didn't hold her gaze. "Maybe they went to find something to eat. After the energy expenditure on a day like today they have to eat, have to replenish their energy reserves."

"That's true." Her brows shot together briefly. "Is there enough small game in the woods for all these wolves?"

"Yes. I'm sure there is," Blaze said. He cleared his throat and busied himself with something on the monitor. "A few will probably band together and find a deer or two to share."

"That's good. I wouldn't want any of them to go hungry. Now that the wolf has been reintroduced to New Mexico, I'm more concerned than ever about their safety and ability to be successful predators here without driving the ranchers crazy," she said.

"The commander keeps an eye on the numbers and helps to relocate some when there is danger of overpopulation" Blaze said absently.

"Really? I thought that was Department of Fish and Game did that stuff," she said, pleased that he was so thoughtful and caring about the wolves in New Mexico. The thought of his humanitarian nature, of his concern for animals created a little warmth in her chest. The more she learned about him, the more intriguing she found the man.

"Yeah. He helps them too by managing the numbers," Blaze said and gave a cringed smile, for some reason. "He's into all kinds of--" Blaze paused and cocked his head to the side. "I think they're coming now."

Rico shifted into high alert. Though he still lay on the floor beside her, his attention had moved from her to the door and his ears perked forward. Waiting. Watching.

Trista turned, her heart thrumming in her chest. Would she see Vic again? Would they all return or only some of them? Unable to stand the suspense any longer, she hurried toward the door as the glimmer of lights shone through a window and moved across the room as the Hummer approached the infirmary.

The hair on the back of her neck stood up, on alert for danger. She paused and waited as Rico stood his ground in front of her, not allowing her to get to the door. This time she didn't try to push him out of the way. She dropped her hand to his head, deriving some comfort from the warmth of him standing strong beside her.

The door burst open. Three men and four wolves rushed through. The relief, the happiness, the pure joy that flooded through her made her limbs weak.

"Commander." Unable to stop herself, she hurried toward him, and he grabbed her against him, pulling her body tightly to his. In that moment she knew he was okay, he wasn't seriously injured, and she could take her first full breath in hours.

"I'm fine, Doc. We're all fine." He pressed a chaste kiss to her forehead and moved her against his side, keeping a hand on her hip. "Good to see you."

"I was so worried when you raced out of here," she said, admitting the truth. The tremor in her hands, in her throat returned. The fear in her heart fluttered away, now that she had her hands on him again. Her imagination could take a hike, and she was no longer envisioning him lying dead on the side of the road.

"We're all back. Unscathed," he said as he gaze sought out hers.

Her eyes widened. "How can you say that when there are bloody scratches all over you? And Eros and Luke?" *That's* unscathed to him? What would scathed look like?

With a grin that went from his lips all the way to his eyes, he laughed. "We made our point. Loudly," he said.

"I see," she said.

"Don't worry," Vic whispered.

She realized her hand on his arm was wet and she pulled it back to look at it. "You're bleeding! Look at your arms. Let me see them," she said in a rush.

With a glance at one of his arms, he gave a shrug. "It's just blood. It'll be fine." He released her as his attention moved to the men on the tables and the wolves beside them. "I want to check on my men first," he said, squeezed her waist and moved away.

"Okay." Thus dismissed, she crossed her arms over her middle. If he wasn't going to worry about it, why should she? The disappointment of being brushed off so easily hurt. Maybe she was just imagining things. Seeing things between them that just weren't there.

"You coming?" He paused and held out his hand to her, waited while she closed the distance between them and slid her hand into his larger one. The heat of his skin on hers incinerated the feelings of dismissal.

"I wasn't sure if you meant you wanted to do that alone," she said. Reading people was a fine art. Reading Vic was going to require the Rosetta Stone."

"No. You can help with the wolves if you'd like," he said.

"Oh, for sure. I'd love it," she said. That would give her something to do and to hide the tremors in her hands. So quickly, so easily, she was becoming enamored with Vic and his group of soldiers.

While she examined Silver, she noticed his eyes were open and looking at her, unafraid, curious and calm. That surprised her. He was obviously an intelligent animal.

"Uh, Vic?" she asked as she watched Silver.

"Yeah?"

"Silver's looking at me," she said.

"He has good taste in females, what can I say?" Vic said. She moved closer to the table, looked at the gray wolf whose coat was interspersed with silver streaks of fur. If he were human, he'd probably be prematurely gray. She snorted to herself. Now, she was humanizing wolves. Probably since Vic had such control over them.

"So, Blaze, can you let him up? Lighten up his sedation now," Trista asked the medic.

"Oh, he's not sedated," Blaze said. "He's just waiting to be given the okay to get up."

"Given the okay to get up?" Trista repeated. Stunned. "That is one well-trained wolf."

"Not always," Vic said with a snort. "At the moment,

he's doing what he's supposed to do." He turned to Blaze. "Did you find any more injuries?"

"Just stitched up one ear and a place on his lower lip where someone took a piece out of him, but nothing else. I think he won the fight," Blaze said, but he'll have a scar the ladies will love.

"Good. Release him when he's ready," Vic said and placed a hand on Silver's shoulder. He leaned toward Silver, as if he were going to speak, but just looked deeply into the wolf's eyes. Silver closed his eyes once and opened them again, in silent acknowledgment of the message he'd received from his commander.

"You are something else, Vic. I've never met anyone with such control over animals that normally can't be controlled. Are you like, the Wolf Whisperer or something?" she asked, words a whisper of awe.

That made him laugh, and he placed his arm around her shoulders, drawing her closer to him. "No. I just have a way of talking to them at their own level, in a way they understand," he said.

After seeing to Draco and assuring himself that the man was on the mend as well, Vic sighed. Fatigue lined his face, lowered his shoulders and his energy seemed to have left him.

"How about we go get you something to eat now? Some hydration, too, or you're going to be hooked up next to your boys here. You could use a rest, too," she said, trying to walk the crooked line between a female in a new relationship to a doctor making a recommendation.

"I'm fine." He gave a crisp nod. "I appreciate the concern, but--"

"Sir, no disrespect intended, but Trista is right," Blaze said. "Let her see to your wounds at least. Part of your job is to take care of yourself because you're needed here." Blaze held Vic's gaze a beat longer.

Ready to protest, Vic frowned at Blaze, then looked at Trista. Something softened in his gaze then, and he closed his mouth, swallowing down any objection he was going to make. "Okay. But I'm fine. Really. I've been through tougher battles than this one," he said.

"Humor me," Trista said and took him by the arm.

The clattering of toenails on the cement floor caught her attention as Silver jumped down from the table. He limped, favoring his right shoulder, as he headed to the door beside them. Vic let him out, and they followed him part way to the hacienda. Silver paused and then looked back, his eyes flashing a glowing green. He turned and disappeared into the night as shadows of the deep forest swallowed him.

~

"I'LL SHOWER and get most of the mess off of me." Vic stripped off his bloody fatigues and stepped out of them as they entered the kitchen. Nudity and being naked were things he and the boys were very comfortable with. They wore clothing mostly to keep the humans from freaking out. Wolves didn't cover their exposed sexual parts, or compare sizes of those parts, so why should they do it in human form? Nudity was a natural state.

Trista spun and turned her back to him when he picked up the clothing and tossed into the nearby laundry room. Apparently, she wasn't as comfortable with nudity as he was. "Okay. Uh, you do that."

"I'll be back in a few, and you can doctor me up then," he said, speaking to her back, wondering if...

"Okay. I'll just wait here," she said. "Do the dishes or something useful."

He started to leave her there in the kitchen, but paused, focusing his attention, his empathic senses on her. She'd been through quite an ordeal in the last day. Her shoulders were up around her ears again, her back rigid, and those long arms of hers hugged her middle. The heat of her pulsed out in undulating waves as he let his wolf senses explore her. Heart beat erratic, breathing too fast. Definite signs of stress. He pulled his senses back in and took a steadying breath.

"Unless you'd like to join me. There's plenty of room for two," he said, liking the idea. Imagining her hot, wet and naked against him in the shower made his groin pulse. There would be no hiding his. Exposed. Vulnerable. Thoroughly turned on.

"Uh, yes. I'd like that," she said and turned toward him, her eyes drifting over him from the scratches on his face, neck and chest, downward over his abs, and lingering on his arousal pointing at her. "I haven't had a shower. Either. And I could... um, use one." That pink tongue of hers peeked out as she licked her lips. Nervous now, he felt the rattle of her pulse coursing through her veins. The rush of adrenaline and the pulse of sex hormones.

Allowing his beast a little latitude, he let his wolf senses reach out to her, let his eyes droop downward to cover the most visible sign of his inner animal. Taking a deep breath, he scented her from across the room. Her fragrance filled his mind. Sweet. Earthy. Musky. His mouth watered at the memory of how she'd tasted, her essence now deeply etched in his mind. Her scent filled his mind and made his heart pulsed faster. Her heart thrummed wildly as she watched him watching her. A fine sheen of sweat exploding with pheromones covered her body and a trickle of it snaked down her back, tickling the fine hairs along her spine.

Sauntering toward her, he kept his eyes on hers. Looking another wolf in the eyes would only cause trouble, but with her, he could see into her soul, see what she was thinking, feeling, and the moment when her flimsy resistance deserted her. He cupped her face in his hands and kissed her, parted her lips and slid his tongue against hers. Her taste, her fear, her relief, all translated into her want and need for him in those few seconds. The temptation of her was almost too much for him and for his beast. Trembling against the need to mate, to prove his dominance, he drove back the overwhelming desire to take her hard and fast, pushed it back to snap and growl in a corner.

Vic didn't want to hurt Trista, wouldn't allow his beast to harm her, either. If he didn't control it, he could harm her and for that he'd never forgive himself.

"Come with me," he said.

She preceded him up the stairs to the second story. The sweet curves of her ass drew his attention. Unable to resist the temptation of her, he hooked his fingers in the waistband of her pants and pulled. The startled cry that emerged from her throat was enough to stir his wolf, bring him to high alert.

"Commander!" Giggling, she squealed and tried to elude him, but he had her by the waist and brought her up against him.

"You sounded like a frightened rabbit. That's dangerous around wolves. They'll only want to snap you up and eat you," he said.

"But I'm not frightened. Or a rabbit," she said and placed one hand on his chest. She stopped squirming and the playfulness in her eyes faded as he brought her hips against his. The feel of her heat, even through her clothing, set his senses on fire.

"I'm aware of that." With his hands on her hips, his eyes on hers, he backed her up against the door to his suite and leaned into her. "You're definitely a woman." His gaze roamed from her full lips to the curve of her jaw, past the elegance of her neck and to sweet breasts that rose and fell with her breathing, rapid now with want and desire. He itched to touch her silky skin again, to caress her tempting body, to stroke the enticing flare of her hips and bring her fully against him. To dig his fingers into her ass as he pulled her over him, sink into her, feel her muscles tighten around him. "You're all female to me."

With a small cry, she parted her lips and reached for him. This time she was the aggressor, the seeker, as she slipped one hand over his shoulder and one hand between them. "Vic..."

He led her through the bedroom, pulling off her clothing as they moved toward the bathroom. "You're beautiful, Trista, just beautiful." Now it was *his* breath that raged in his throat. *His* chest that pumped as she revealed more and more of her skin to his view. The tight peaks of her pink-tipped breasts and the flaring arch of her hips drew his gaze to the feminine V pointing to the place his mouth watered to taste again. Tearing his gaze away from her, he turned on the dual shower heads and adjusted the water temperature.

Blond hair tumbled over her shoulders to tease her nipples, her desire-saturated gaze held his. She walked toward him tall, beautiful, naked and wanting. By the gods, she was *all* female.

He swallowed hard as the full impact of her hit him

hard in the chest, in the gut, in the deepest part of his human form and to the beast within. He wanted this female as he'd wanted no other. Together now, they were as vulnerable as either of them could get, reaching out to the other to fulfill their needs. Each flawed in their own way, but perfect with those imperfections. The scars on his back. The scars on her heart. The weight of his responsibilities to the others. Right now, nothing else mattered.

She was the female he wanted. He was just the man she desired.

Unable to speak past the lump in his throat, he held his hand out to her, and she took it. Unable to control himself any longer, he pulled her closer until she looked at him.

The full lips that parted, those green eyes that lifted to his was all the encouragement he needed. He leaned toward her, a tremor filling his gut. Heart racing the way it did when he stretched out his muscles, racing through the forest and over the high desert lands, he pulled her against him. Lowering his head, he took her mouth with his and devoured her. She was the epitome of everything he wanted in a female. Soft and tough. Fragile and strong. Innocent and wise.

For the moment, she was his.

Keeping his mouth against hers, he led her into the shower as steam billowed out through the open door. The snap of the latch closed them into a cocoon of heat, water, and pure, unadulterated lust.

As the water hit him, hit his injuries, the dirt and debris clinging to his back, the scent of pine sap wafted up and swirled around them in the small tile room.

"What did you do, roll around in juniper?" Pulling back a little, she wrinkled her nose at him.

"Actually..." That wasn't far from the truth. "The fight

was around some juniper bushes and cedar trees, so yeah, I guess you could say that." He backed into the steaming spray overhead and saturated his head, letting the hot water wash over him. He reached for a bottle of body wash, poured a generous amount into his hands.

"I'd like to do that," Trista said. "Turn around, and I can do your back."

"Something stings a bit back there, so can you see what it is?" he asked.

"Sure, just—geez!" She gasped. "*Vic!*"

The shock in her voice made him look over his shoulder. "What is it?"

"You've got a splinter the size of a telephone pole in your back," she said. "Oh!" She placed her hands on him and turned him back around. "Geez! How did you not feel this before?"

"Adrenaline." He bounced his head to the side and had to admit it. "And lust. Those two things tend to dull everything else," he said.

"You have to go to the ER and get that out. Hurry up, and I can take you in." She used the body wash all over her with hurried motions and rinsed.

Buzz kill.

"No ER. You can do it, or Blaze can take it out. That's what we have the infirmary for, you know?" Rinsing his face in the water, he realized they were done. For the moment. With the amount of fear racing around in Trista's system right now, there was no way he was going to push her to satisfy his carnal cravings. There would be another time. Or not. Not would be better for both of them.

Sudden irritation broke out over him, filled his mind, his senses, and he let the anger rage. This life of his was no place to bring a female. Let alone a *human* woman who couldn't defend herself against the kind of war he'd just escalated. It was going to be bloody. His conscience wouldn't let him drag an innocent into it, no matter how much he wanted her. He couldn't expose Trista more than she already was. *Doc*. He had to call her Doc.

"You can't let Blaze take that out. You need a physician," she said, her voice raised in irritation.

"Blaze is a battle trained medic. He's handled worse than a giant splinter. If that's not good enough for you, then you can do it. Finish up and get dressed. I've got some spare fatigues you can wear," he said.

"Fine." She nodded, and the set of her jaw looked as if she'd come to a decision. The wariness in her eyes certainly let him know she had. He'd hurt her with his words. But better that than her getting killed on account of him. "I'll take out your damned splinter, Commander, then I'm done playing whatever game you've got going here," she said.

Keeping her back to him, she rinsed the soap from her hair, let it sluice down her body. Without a word, she turned off the taps and took the towel he handed to her. He wrapped a towel around his hips in deference to her. In silence, he entered the large bedroom closet and extracted some older clothing he no longer wore, and handed them to her.

"You can wear these home. I don't need them," he said, trying to keep his voice even.

"Thanks. I'll get them back to you," she said, her voice clipped.

"Don't bother. I said I don't need them."

"Fine. I'll see to your back, then I'm leaving." Pulsing waves of hurt, disappointment and anger throbbed off of her. He didn't need his wolf senses to pick that up. It was for the best if they didn't take this little tryst any further.

Each of them had separate lives. Separate responsibilities. And they didn't mesh. Couldn't ever mesh.

"As I said before, you're not a prisoner here. You're free to leave whenever you want to." Although the words came out of his mouth something in him had changed. Something about the way he looked at her, something in the way his beast wanted her had changed in the last two days. Remaining silent was the only way he was going to get through this situation.

She gathered her clothing from the floor and walked out. Only when they reached the infirmary did her steps slow, did the focus of anger and hurt shift. She was angry, but there was no help for it.

He couldn't take a human woman as a mate. In that Zane was right. Fuck him to hell and back. The goddamn wolf was right.

Steam practically rolled off of her as she crossed the infirmary to the first bay. "Blaze, do you have any numbing medication for injection? Lidocaine or--"

"I don't need it, Doc. Just do it," Vic said.

"Seriously?" For a second she hesitated, then her expression shut down, and she raised her brows, pressed her lips together. "Fine. Sit down." She shoved her clothing onto a side table. "I need a surgical kit."

"Yes, doctor." Blaze looked between the two, questions in his eyes, but he remained silent.

"You ready?" she asked Vic as she snapped on a pair of sterile gloves. Everything a human physician could want was laid out at her fingertips.

"Yes." He took a breath to say something else, then a searing pain sliced into his back below his left shoulder blade. "Fuck!" He stiffened, unprepared for the sudden pain. His beast almost erupted from his skin. Gritting his teeth, he punched down the fierce reaction that caused some fur to push through the skin on his hands and arms. Fortunately, Trista was focused on his back and didn't see it or the canine teeth that shot through before he could control it. Vic panted, in pain, and with the strain of pushing back his beast.

Blaze, keep her field of vision to my back.

Yes, sir.

Blaze moved to his side under the pretense of assisting Trista, but he blocked her view with his body, giving Vic a chance to take a breath and force his body to remain in its human form.

"Don't move," Trista said, barking the order at him.

"You didn't say it was going to hurt that much." Did he sound like he was a baby? Sounded like it to him.

"Whiner. You're such a bullshitter, commander," she said and clucked her tongue.

Blaze stiffened and his eyes widened, looking back and forth between them. "Relax, Blaze. It's okay," Vic said.

"Yeah. I can insult him any time I want, but you can't," she said. She continued to slice through the flesh on his back with the fine scalpel in her hand. "He's the dumb-ass that wouldn't take any numbing medicine, so he gets to suffer. I hope it hurts. A lot." The tough words hid her pain. That was apparent. He took no offense, because he was the one who'd hurt her.

Vic jumped again, but ground his teeth together to keep from making any noise. The beast in him growled and snapped at the pain, but Vic pushed it down, pushed it back. He used the pain to fight his beast, to keep himself focused for the next battle and the next one after.

You okay, Commander? Blake asked.

Fine. Is she almost done? Vic asked.

Yes. The last stitches are going in now, Blaze said.

Good. At ease, soldier.

Yes, sir.

"You've got quite a long suture line there. Keep it clean. No rolling around in the dirt, fighting or otherwise ruining my work," Trista said, her voice flat. The energy keeping her anger fueled, slipped away. He sensed her fatigue, the need to hide and lick her wounds. That's what any wolf did after a fight, or after a loss, and he couldn't fault her for her need to do the same. In his wolf form, he'd heal in a matter of hours, but still would have had to have the splinter removed. Now, he was in human form and it would take longer, but it couldn't be helped. Vic stood, jerked on a shirt over his head.

"Eros will go home with you," Vic said.

"No, he won't. I'll see to myself, like I always do, Commander. I don't need any help from you or your men," she said. The look in her eyes was flat, void of the recent vibrancy he'd seen in them. It had to be done this way. If she hurt, if she hated him, then it'd be easier for her to leave and never come back.

It would kill him. Slowly.

"Thanks, Doc. I appreciate your efforts here," he said.

"I'll expect a full report from Blaze on how Dane and Silver are doing. Email me. And I suggest you find another vet to treat the wolves after this. You won't be welcome at my clinic any longer," she said.

"Sorry to hear that, Doc. You're the only vet for miles around and certainly the only one qualified to care for my four-legged soldiers," he said, knowing she spoke the truth.

A smirk of disbelief crossed her face as she gathered her clothing. "I appreciate the attempt to stroke my ego, Commander, but it's not going to get you what you want."

Not responding to that retort, he stood and led her to the door. Eros and a few others gathered beside him waiting for orders, waiting to see how the alpha would react when his potential mate drove off and left him in the dust.

Trista's taillights faded away into the night as he watched the heat signature in the vehicle, watched the last bit of her fade away from him.

"I'll follow her." Eros whipped off his shirt and handed it to Vic, then dropped his other clothing. It wasn't a question, and he wasn't asking for permission as he shifted into the giant, dark wolf who always had his back.

Eros loped forward a few yards on those long legs of his, then paused, looked back.

I'll see to her safety, sir.

Thank you. Be back by dawn.

Yes, sir.

Eros turned again and the dark night swallowed him whole.

CHAPTER
ELEVEN

Tears of pain and anger filled Trista's eyes and a deep ache tightened her chest. She'd only intimately been involved with Vic for less than thirty-six hours and her life had been turned upside down by him. Completely upside down.

"What the hell?" Slamming a fist against the steering wheel as she left the gravel and dirt lane, she turned the SUV onto the two-lane highway. Night deepened as she drove home. Her vision narrowed down to the bright halo of her headlights, but the flash of something, some glint of light, caught her eye on the left side of the road and she flung the tears of anger and hurt from her eyes.

A wolf. A huge wolf was following her. A black wolf raced along the edge of the road, parallel to the road. By now she was miles from the compound. Could one of them have followed her or was this a wild wolf? Slowing the SUV, she watched as the wolf slowed its pace to match hers.

"What the hell?" Again, she said the words out loud. "How is this even possible?" She'd been going forty miles per hour. How had a wolf kept up with her for so long? They could certainly haul ass for short bursts of speed while hunting prey, she knew that much. But this was miles at that speed.

With a glance in the rear-view mirror, the road was clear behind her, and she pulled over. She left the lights on and the motor running in case this went bad, and she got out. She could dive in through the open door and get away if she had to. Some unknown force compelled her. She had to find out if this individual was one of Vic's wolves or a lone wolf.

It stood in the middle of the road facing her. It dipped its head once, and panted, catching its breath, watching as she moved closer.

The glow in its eyes didn't match any of the wolves she'd met at the compound, didn't give her that same sense of ease she'd experienced with them. Maybe this was truly a wild wolf, and she'd just committed an act of utter stupidity. The thing could have rabies, for all she knew. It was behaving very strangely for a wild wolf, though, and didn't appear afraid of her. Not like a normal wild wolf. Not under the control of a master, the way Vic's wolves were. This one seemed to have a superior intellect. The fine hairs on her arms and the back of her neck stood upright, raising the tension in her to high alert.

The flash of a dark shadow sailed past her, the brush of wind and fur touched her skin. Trista screamed at the unexpected presence of another wolf launching itself past her to attack the wolf in front of her.

The sounds of a dog-fight always frightened her, no matter how many times she heard it. The squeal and high-pitched yowling. The flash and snap of teeth and jaws designed to kill, cut the silence of the night.

The skirmish lasted only a few seconds, ending with the larger, dark wolf skittering across the road and into the night, tail between its legs.

Now, she was faced with another animal she didn't know. Backing away from the wolf, she crossed the road toward her SUV and slammed the door once she was safely inside.

The big black wolf with yellow eyes followed her and stood in the light from her headlights right in front of the SUV. He wasn't afraid. He hardly looked like he'd even been in a skirmish just now. The head dipped once in acknowledgment and as it did so, the flash of silver caught her eye. It wore a pendant or *dog tags*. Like Vic's pack did, but she didn't recognize this wolf. Not that she'd memorized every wolf she'd seen there, but this one stood out. She'd have remembered it. It's sense of dignity. Of honor. If that wasn't assigning too many human qualities to an animal.

As it stood in the headlights, staring at her, she realized it knew her. It waited for her. Its presence was there to protect her. To keep her safe. Somehow, the massive animal was one of Vic's, and it knew to follow her.

The panic, the utter fear that had flooded her veins subsided in an instant, and she got out of the vehicle again.

"I know you, don't I?" The wolf bobbed its head again, allowed its jaw to go slack and its tongue loll out as it panted. "I'm insane to approach you, but I can't help it."

Having learned a few things from Vic, she stood tall, not giving it any sign of fear or submission, and it approached her, stuck its muzzle in her hand and licked it once.

"Let me see your tags. What's your name?" As Trista reached for the tag around its neck, the wolf turned away from her, its ear perked forward, its body alert and it stood in front of her in a posture of strength and protection.

Trista swallowed, having only caught part of a name that started with E, she felt the heart inside her chest flutter madly as an even bigger wolf approached, stopped in the middle of the road, its golden eyes glowing liquid fire. "Geez, you're big. I know I've never seen *you* before." She swallowed again. "God, I hope you're one of Vic's wolves." The bitter taste of fear filled her mouth and churned her stomach, the biggest timber wolf she'd ever seen walked slowly toward her, its long, lanky legs and giant paws bringing it closer.

A flash of herself and Vic making love filled her mind, her mouth, and her nipples tightened. The sensation of pure lust filled her, shoving aside any thoughts of fear. For a second, she felt as if she were back at the compound with Vic's hands, his mouth, his essence surrounding her and her lips parted as if his kiss touched her lips.

How odd that should fill her mind right now.

The wolf closed the distance between them as the blast of emotions washed over her. Without hesitation, the great multicolored wolf stuck his nose right in her crotch for a big sniff.

"Hey, now." That got her attention, and she took a step back from it as the memory faded from her. "You know you're not supposed to do that." With a gentle hand, she pushed its face away from her groin.

The other wolf, in submission posture raised one paw and placed it on second wolf's back and gave a small shove, pushing him away from Trista.

Suspicion rose strong in her. If the dark wolf sitting here was Vic's, then the other one certainly had to be. "Do you have your tags on, too, or is your commander a big, fat liar? He said you always wear them."

The lighter-colored wolf cocked its head at her, then took a step backward before she could reach for its tags. The shiny metal slipped from her fingers before she could read them. With her focus on the lighter wolf, she hadn't seen where the other one went. It disappeared before she realized it had slipped off into the night.

"Okay, dude. Time to head back to the compound before the commander realizes you're missing." She backed away from the wolf and slid into the driver's side from the open door, then startled and nearly screamed as she felt a presence beside her. "Geez! You can't be in here." She placed a hand over her racing heart. "You scared the hell out of me, dude."

While she was focused on the other wolf, the dark wolf had jumped into the SUV and now sat in the passenger seat, big as you please. He looked like he was just waiting to be buckled in, and they'd be on their way. Panting, he turned his head toward her, then looked ahead at the road, as if telling her it was time to get going.

Trista spent several fruitless minutes trying to shoo it out of the vehicle, but it wasn't budging. "Fine. I'll drive you as far as my place, then you have to go. You're on your own to get back to the compound, but I'm certain you know the way." She shook her head at the tenacity of the beast. With one finger on the control, she put down the window half way, and he leaned closer to the open window, sniffing and tasting the air.

The fear had left her as she was trying to extricate him, and she'd realized it was a him, when she'd inadvertently grabbed him between his legs and discovered his male parts fully intact. "One of these days, I'm going to get the commander to neuter the lot of you," she'd ground out between clenched teeth. "If I ever speak to him again, that is." The only answer was a quick chest growl from the beast, who faced forward again. "This is the most ridiculous thing I've ever done. Drove home with a wolf in my car." She shook her head as she looked in her rear-view mirror and pulled onto the road. "I must be out of my mind."

Twenty minutes later Trista pulled into the gravel driveway of the little adobe and stucco house she called home. The office sign had been turned off and in less than twelve hours she'd be turning it back on again, no matter how tired she was. Business went on whether you'd had the best sex of your life, had gotten into a fight with a man who turned you on like no other, and ultimately rejected you for reasons unknown. The world, and the animals within it, kept spinning, kept moving, kept needing her care.

"Okay, wolfie. End of the road. Now you have to get out." With an exhausted sigh, she turned off the engine and opened the passenger door. The black wolf jumped right out as if that had been his intention all along.

"Go home, dude. I'd call your commander, but I'm too tired, and I'm not speaking to him at the moment. He'll have to figure out where you are all by himself," she said. A heavy sigh rolled out of her. The wolf approached her, head down and tilted to the side, as if he were approaching his alpha, and sat at her feet. Then it licked her hand several times as if offering her comfort in its own way. Wolves were very intelligent, sentient beings, that much she knew, but Vic's wolves continued to amaze her.

Reaching toward him, she tried to grab his tag again, to see who this wolf was, but he resisted and pulled away from her. Slinking away, he moved into the shadows at the side of the house. He sat there, waiting, watching, the reflection of his eyes let her know he was still there.

Even though she'd just left the compound, she derived a bit of comfort from having the large wolf present outside her home. "Just leave my cat alone, okay? Anything happens to him, I'll have your hide on my wall," she said.

Exhausted at a cellular level, she entered the house. Seconds later, the black and white cat she'd raised from kitten-hood, raced past her legs and cowered under the table.

"It's okay, Pete. That big boy out there isn't going to hurt you," she said, trying to reassure him.

Pete stayed where he was, and she was too tired to care. Dropping the clothing Vic had given her on the floor beside the bed, she crawled between the cool sheets wishing that someone strong and comforting was lying beside her.

As her mind relaxed, her muscles loosened and she drifted off to sleep with only the heat of a memory holding her tight.

Morning came too early with Pete pawing at her, ready to be fed.

After the early morning tasks, she showered and readied for her usual office hours. Her bedroom was on the second floor and provided an amazing view of the mountains and valley that were once the bottom of a very ancient ocean. Now, it was filled with pines, cedar and juniper trees and a scattering of aspens that gave the forest a flaming yellow and orange brilliance in the fall.

With the weather turning slightly, cooler than the heat of the summer, the leaves would be changing soon, the forest hastening to ready itself for the sleep of winter.

Gazing outside, she searched for a wolf at the edge of

the forest, but saw nothing. "Maybe he's gone home, Pete." A heavy sigh rolled out of her. "Just as well. I shouldn't have any ties to Vic, the commander, anymore." She wasn't going to think of him by his given name any longer either. It was too personal. He was right. And it kept him too close to her heart. "It'll just make things more complicated than they already are."

Pete, not caring about the commander, yowled his displeasure at the slow manner in which she filled his bowl. He twined his way in and out of her legs as she poured the food for him, then ignored her as he settled down to eat.

The day wore on, interminably long, until she finally wrapped things up and closed the office after five PM. As she strolled outside into the early-evening sun, the sensation of being watched filled her. The hair on the back of her neck stood up in alarm as did the ones on her arms. Someone was definitely out there, staring at her.

Pete came screeching around the corner, scrambling to the door as a silver-colored wolf emerged from the shadows at the edge of her property. She froze. She knew that wolf.

Anger flared hot and burned bright within her. She pulled out her phone and called the commander. Irritated to the Nth degree, she wasn't going to put up with his manipulations any longer.

"Hello?" Vic answered the phone pleasantly.

"Commander, this is-" she started.

"I know who you are. What can I do for you, Doc?" he asked, like he hadn't just screwed her royally two nights ago.

"One of your wolves is staring at me, and I don't like it," she said as she continued to stare at Silver.

"Really?" he asked, fake disbelief in his voice. "How do

162

you know it's one of mine and not just a wild wolf staring at you?"

"It's Silver. I recognize him," she said, her voice flat.

"So, that's where he's gotten to. We were wondering. He disappeared, and we thought he'd caught the scent of a female or something," he said, amusement in his voice.

"Nothing here except my cat. If Pete disappears down the gullet of one of your wolves, Commander, I'm holding you responsible," she warned him.

"Nothing will happen to your cat. Our boys are well fed here. They don't need to scavenge," he reassured her.

"Come and get Silver. I don't want him here," she said, the irritation dissolving, leaving only sadness behind.

"We'll be there to collect him shortly. I'm sorry he bothered you," Vic said, sincerity in his voice, and she shivered once.

The line went dead, and she shoved the phone into her pocket.

Well? Wasn't that what she wanted? To end her association with a man who was dedicated to his work, his mission, and the animals he cared for? There wasn't room in all of that for a woman, a relationship, in the way she'd dreamed of having one.

He was good for one thing only.

Amazing. Hot. Sex.

A flush of heat, simmering desire washed over her at the thought. She took in a deep, steadying breath and blew it out. Silver took another step toward her, leaving the protection of the shadows.

"Just stay there, dude. Your commander is coming for you," she said and pointed a finger at him, as if that would stop him.

The great beast sat, then placed one front paw in front

of the other and lowered his weight to the ground, looking as if he were lying at attention. He remained there, even while Trista went inside to get a bowl of water for him. He rose, sniffed the bowl and drank his fill, then returned to his former position. He resembled a sentinel, on duty, watching for any sign of danger. Damn, these wolves were awesome and her grudging respect for Vic rose, despite her desire that his male parts shrivel into uselessness.

In twenty minutes, the wolf turned an ear toward the road. Trista heard the whine of the Hummer engine and her heart raced, knowing she'd see the commander again in seconds.

Silver looked at her, as if trying to tell her something and his ears lowered in submission.

"I know, boy. Hormones are a bitch, aren't they?" Hardening herself against any influence those steely eyes of the commander's might have on her. Disappointment rose harshly as she realized he wasn't in the vehicle when it came up the driveway.

Eros and Luke got out and approached her, their expressions giving away their personality. Eros severe and stern. Luke smiling and wide open, despite his loyalty to the commander.

"Ma'am," Eros said and gave a crisp nod.

"Where's that runaway of ours?" Luke asked, his eyes hidden behind dark shades, but the friendly smile of his immediately put her at ease. He was the easiest one she'd met.

"He's there, by the edge of the--he's gone," Trista said and dropped her hand to her leg. "He was just there a minute ago, just hanging out, until I looked for the Hummer. Now he's gone. Dammit. How are you going to find him now?"

"Don't worry, ma'am. We'll find him," Eros said.

"Where's your commander? He seemed to have a way of talking to the wolves, and they always listened to them," she said.

"Except for Dane." Luke shook his head with a grin. "That one doesn't listen to anyone."

"How is he? Is he up yet?" She'd almost forgotten about Dane in her concern for her own emotions and hurt.

"Yes, finally got his ass off the bed, but he's not himself yet." At those words, the lightness left Luke and his shoulders drooped a bit.

"Don't worry. Now that he's up, I'm sure he'll recover in no time." She offered the words of comfort to Luke who only nodded. "In the meantime, you've got another wolf to find," she said.

They searched and called for Silver, but to no avail.

"He's probably out there hiding from us, having a good laugh," Luke said. "That's what I'd be doing."

"I'm not amused," Eros said, his expression and energy clearly indicated that.

"Come on, guys. Come inside, and I'll get you a bottle of water. Then you can call the commander and figure out what to do." She led the way to the back of the building and entered, then stopped short at the sight of Pete perched on top of the refrigerator. He never got up there.

A second later, she realized why he was up there.

Silver lay on her couch. Asleep.

"Oh, for God's sake. Guys! He's in here," she said, calling out the door to them.

Silver roused at the sound of her voice and sat, but didn't get off the couch.

"You lazy-assed bitch!" Luke took in the scene, then

gave a short laugh. "You were in here all the time." He moved to Silver and rubbed his head.

"He's going to get some extra guard duty for this, I think." Eros snapped his fingers and pointed to the floor. The beast hopped down from the couch and moved to sit at Eros's feet, waiting a command.

"I guess you don't need the commander after all," Trista said, her brows rising in surprise. "You're as skilled as he is."

"No one is, ma'am," Eros said, slid her a sideways glance, then focused on Silver and seemed to be having a conversation with him. Silver demonstrated submissive behavior to Eros, curling his tail between his legs and turning his belly upward. After a second of hesitation, Eros placed his hands on his hips. "You're lucky I'm in a good mood today. Go get in the Hummer." He spoke the words to Silver who scrambled across the living room and out the front door.

"Thank you for collecting him, I hope he doesn't run off again," Trista said and pulled three cold bottles of water from the fridge and handed each of them one. "One's for Silver if you have a bowl or something."

"If he does return, let us know," Eros said and headed out the front door.

"Thanks for letting us know where he was," Luke said. He gave her a jaunty salute, tossed his water bottle into the air and caught it with one hand behind his back. The man was a character. How he'd gotten attached to this group of men and wolves, she didn't know, but he was obviously the comic relief in the group of severity. As the sound of the Hummer disappearing down the road faded, she realized it didn't matter. She wasn't going to be seeing the commander again.

As she turned, Pete jumped down from his perch, onto the counter and then onto the floor. He looked behind her and scrambled back up onto the counter and resumed his previous position, this time his fur spiked out.

"Now what's the matter with you?" she asked, but turned in the direction of where Pete stared.

The biggest black wolf she'd ever seen stood in her door.

CHAPTER
TWELVE

"**D**id you get him?" Vic asked once everyone was back home and to safety.

"Yes," Eros answered.

"Did she suspect anything?" Vic asked, despite not wanting to be, he hung on every word about Trista, his mind filling in the details of how she looked, how she smelled.

"No. Just thought Silver got out of the compound," Eros said.

"Good. We have to be more careful not let her see anyone, or she'll get more suspicious than she already is," Vic said. The woman was smart enough and tenacious enough to pursue anything that didn't make sense to her. The mind of a scientist. The body of a stripper. What a combination.

His phone rang. It was Trista again. Now what?

"Yes?" he asked, trying not to be pleased she'd called again.

The second she drew in her breath, he knew something was wrong. Seriously wrong. Senses on high alert, he snapped his fingers as Eros, who immediately responded at attention, awaiting orders. Vic put the call on speaker.

"There's another wolf here. Blocking my door. It's trying to get into my house." Her breath huffed in and out, distorting in the phone. "I don't like it. I don't know this one. It looks wild. Dangerous. Maybe has rabies." Another gasping breath, and her voice dropped to a hushed whisper. "I think it's the same one that followed me from the compound yesterday," she said.

"Don't move, Trista. Don't look it in the eye. Don't move too fast. We'll be there." He raced toward the Hummer with Eros and Luke fast on his heels. "Can you get into a bath-room or a locked room?"

"I think it could break down any door I have here," she said and the fear in her voice was killing him. "Hurry, Vic. Please hurry," she whispered.

"Hold on, Trista. I'll be there. I'll be right there," he cried.

The line went dead.

"There's a big-assed rogue wolf at Trista's place trying to get in. May be one of the Ridge Runners. She said it was the same one that followed her last night." Vic slowed long enough to get through the gates, scraping the side of the vehicle on the last one in his fever to get to Trista. The highway was just yards away down the rutted dirt lane, and he floored it.

"Apparently, the ass-whooping last night didn't faze him. It was Buster," Eros said and removed his shades to polish them on his shirt.

"Buster is pretty dense," Luke chimed in from the back seat as he took off his clothes. He'd fight in wolf form. Vic and Eros would protect Trista on two legs.

As Luke shifted in the back seat, his energy swirled in

the vehicle and tugged at the beasts hidden within Vic and Eros. In seconds Luke stood on the back seat.

"Watch the claws. I'm tired of having to fix the back seat 'cause you guys can't keep your feet trimmed," Vic said.

Yes, boss.

Luke jumped down from the back seat onto the floor and stuck his nose between Eros and the commander, his tongue hanging out, panting in eagerness as they sped along.

When's the last time you brushed your teeth, man? Eros asked.

Bite me, Eros. Been a little busy today, right? Luke said.

Settle down, you two. Something is changing with the Ridge Runners. I can feel it. They're ramping things up with this stunt. I'm not going to fuck with them any longer and risk Trista's life. It ends today, Vic said.

The boys remained silent for the rest of the short drive. Anger churned inside Vic. The oath he'd taken as a soldier to protect the homeland from enemies foreign and domestic merged with his oath to protect those in and around his pack. Though Trista wasn't a member of his pack and could never be one, she was under his protection. Having the Ridge Runners blatantly ignoring his warning of just a few days ago irritated the fuck out of him.

They were going to pay for it. If it was an all-out war Zane wanted, then he was gonna get it shoved up his ass.

By the time they arrived at Trista's place, the atmosphere was eerily silent. Vic turned off the Hummer, and they listened intently for any sign or sound out of place. Normally there would be sounds of birds or small flitting around the thicket of trees surrounding her house, but they were all quiet. Not even a cicada chirped.

I don't hear anything. Do you think she's...hurt? Luke asked.

No, Vic said.

Vic closed his eyes and pushed out his senses as far as he could in all directions, looking for something. Anything. Feeling for some sense of her, of what had happened. There were no sirens filling the air, so she hadn't called 911. She'd either handled the situation, or she was dead.

Fortunately, there was no coppery scent of fresh blood in the air. On stealthy feet they left the Hummer and searched in three different directions.

Luke, take the woods around the house. Eros, the front. I'm going in.

Vic moved toward the back entrance, the most likely place they'd be. He took a quick look around the corner. No movement. No wolf. No Trista.

He sniffed the air. That bastard. Buster had been there! Vic could still smell the stench the wolf exuded. A mix of bad cologne, body odor and stale beer.

He smelled like the fucking state fair.

Vic sidled alongside the house, and he drew his sidearm. He'd added a little something extra to the ammo in case the wolf wouldn't go down easily. If the bullet didn't get his attention, the poison in it would. Desert Nightshade, the toxic plant that converted werewolf poison in the right hands was very hard to come by. It was pricey, and he had a limited supply, but with Trista's life on the line, he wasn't taking any risks.

Heart racing, anger boiling, he could see the ass end of a wolf hanging out the door and down the outside steps. It wasn't moving, but it was breathing. Feet spread out at odd angles, it looked like he'd gone down like a ton of bricks.

Vic raced the last few steps, jumped behind the wolf, and shoved his weapon into its side. "Buster!"

He didn't twitch. Vic looked inside to find Trista splayed out on the floor, arms and legs going in all directions. Her breathing came fast in her throat, and her chest pumped with the effort.

Vic knelt beside her and holstered his weapon.

They're inside. Secure the perimeter, then come get this fucking wolf out of here.

On the way, boss.

On it!

"Doc?" Subduing the tremor rolling through him, Vic placed his hand on her neck to check her pulse. Though he knew she was alive he needed to feel it thrumming beneath his fingers. A large syringe lay a few feet from her outstretched hand. Large scratches covered her hands and arms, but they were minor and he relaxed a little. "Trista? Sweetheart? Can you wake up?" he said, his mouth speaking the words before his mind knew what to do. Tentatively, he tried to reach her on the psychic wavelength he'd already established with her. Not like it was a private line. The others would hear and know what he said to her. Right now, it didn't matter.

Trista, wake up now. It's okay. You're safe. I'm here.

Trista's hand twitched, then her arm, as the lifeblood, the energy she'd expended, returned to her body. "Vic? What happened?" She fluttered those green eyes at him as she roused to consciousness. For a few seconds, vulnerability shone through, the want, the pleasure at seeing him, then she remembered what had happened between them, remembered what had happened here, and she slammed the door shut to her soul.

"Help me up," she said. He slid an arm under her shoulder and eased her upright.

"Take it easy. You might be dizzy," he said, knowing it was true, he used it as an excuse to keep her close a few minutes longer.

"Whoa." She placed on hand on her forehead and took in a breath, then clutched his arm. "No kidding." Another breath, and her heartbeat settled down. Almost normal again.

"There's an unconscious wolf in your doorway. Wanna tell me what happened?" he asked? Now he could have a laugh at Buster's predicament, knowing she was safe. This was gonna be a good story.

"Oh. Oh, my God, Vic," she said. "Commander." Her eyes widened as she searched his face, his eyes. "After I called you, I got out my emergency pack. I always have a syringe of sedative in it in case I run across an animal on the road or something. After distracting him with cat food, I sedated him. He almost bit me. He knocked me on my back, and I hit my head on the floor." She raised one hand to the back of her head and felt around just as Luke and Eros came trotting through the front door. "Not sure if I was out or what."

"You were when I came in," Vic said.

"Lard ass," Eros said in disgust, his upper lip curling into a sneer as he stood in the doorway over the unconscious animal.

Luke sniffed the wolf's back and recoiled. *Ew. I'm gonna hurl.*

"So what's happening? Do you know this wolf, too? Is he one of yours? I didn't see any dog tags, so I'm not sure," she said and stood, but wobbled and clung to Vic.

"Yeah, we know him. Troublemaker. Been relocated

several times, but always manages to get back here and get into more trouble," Vic said. It wasn't quite a lie but wasn't quite the truth either. The less Trista knew about the world of shifters living around her, the safer she'd stay.

"Well, he's a sedated troublemaker, now. Maybe you guys can contact the Park Service and have him taken farther away than they have been doing. Obviously, it's not far enough," she said, her brows twitching upward.

"Eros, tie our friend up and get him to the Hummer. I want to see to the doc's injuries, then I know exactly where to take him," Vic said, anger simmering deep in his gut as a plan came together in his mind.

"You got it, boss," Eros replied. "I'll get some rope and the tarp out of the Hummer. That ought to hold him." Eros left with Luke trotting out the door behind him.

"What injuries are you talking about? I'm fine," Trista said.

"You've been knocked unconscious twice in as many days. You're not fine. You need an ice pack and some Tylenol for your head," Vic said, trying to doctor the doctor.

With her head cocked to the side and blazing green eyes giving him *the look*, she placed her hands on her hips. She'd be so ineffective as a drill sergeant. No one would do anything except look at her breasts sticking out the way they were. At least that's what he'd be looking at. *Bodacious*. "Don't even think you're going to tell me what to do in my own home," she said with a tone he didn't want to touch.

"Wouldn't dare," he said, and one side of his mouth lifted. "Just making a suggestion based on experience. If you don't like it, I'll stuff you in the Hummer and take you back to the compound. Then I'll tell what to do in *my* place," he said, offering her an alternative to choose from.

For a few seconds, she contemplated him, stared into

his face with her jaw set and cocked to the side. "Fine. What injuries are you talking about? Other than the lump on my head, I don't feel anything," she snapped.

Without a word, he took her hands in his and raised them to eye level. "These ones," he said gently.

Surprise flared in her eyes as she took in the bloody scratches that criss-crossed her hands and forearms. "Oh. I see," she said and raised her gaze to his, looked at him, confusion in her eyes. "I didn't even notice."

"That's what adrenaline does for you. If you'll lead the way to your medicine cabinet, I'll help you clean up," he said. "Then we'll get lard-ass off your property."

That made her smile. "You must know him well if you have that kind of pet name for him," she said and led the way to the bathroom down the short hall.

"Yeah, we do. He's gotten into fights with my wolves. Territory disputes and all that stuff. Thinks any tree he pisses on is his," Vic said and followed her, trying not to stare at her ass, but he couldn't help himself. He was a male. An alpha. And he wanted her.

Alpha males loved their females. He breathed in her scent as he followed her. That was a fragrance he'd never get out of his memory. No matter where she was, he'd find her by the unique scent burned into his memory.

"Here. The bathroom is kinda small." She washed at the sink while he stood by. After she dried her hands, he inspected the depth of the gashes.

"Doesn't look all that bad," he said. "That's good." That was a relief. If Buster had bitten her and gotten his blood into her, who knew what would happen. She could have turned into a werewolf, or she could simply have died from blood loss. Anger filled Vic's senses, and he pushed it back. If anyone was going to bite Trista, it was going to be *him*,

176

not some fucking rogue wolf only out for the pleasure of a kill.

"A little antibiotic ointment ought to do the trick," he said. "Keep an eye on them. If they start to get infected see your doctor right away. There's no telling where his paws have been," Vic said.

A slight uplifting of one side of her mouth drew his attention to its fullness. He stared at her lips, feeling the urge to bring them against his own, to stroke his tongue over them, to renew the memory of their sweetness, their softness, their passion.

"Sounds like what I said to you a few days ago, doesn't it?" she asked, her voice a husky whisper as she brought her gaze up to meet his. The fear was gone, replaced by attraction and heat. Vulnerability.

"Yes. Well. Those were wise words, and you should listen to them," he said. Unable to stop himself, he leaned toward her, placed one hand beneath her chin and lifted her face until her gaze met his. "I want to kiss you. Right now." He took a breath, filling his mind with her. "Tell me not to, and I won't. Tell me to walk away, and I will," he whispered.

A deep breath filled his chest as he struggled with the wanting of her, with the need to push her away, but the fierce urgency to take her against him overrode his good senses. In this moment, he couldn't be trusted to do the right thing.

"I see." That pink tongue came out to lick her lips, drawing his attention there, keeping his focus exactly where he didn't want it to be. The shiny moisture beckoned him. The wiles of a female in human or animal form were never to be underestimated. "I... have no objections to that."

Groaning out loud, he slid his hand to the left side of her face and brought her closer until she was millimeters from him. Then she closed the distance and pressed her lips to his. It was her tongue that sought his, her lips parting wide as he accepted her invitation to deepen the kiss, to take her as far as he wanted. Oh, by the gods, he wanted. Hearts racing, desire overwhelming, he brought her hips against his, let her feel the heat of desire in his cock.

We're ready to go out here. Buster is starting to come out of it, and he's not happy, Luke's voice interrupted.

Roger that. Gimme a minute.

Vic pulled back from her, straining against the fierce want and need to mate that his beast had unwittingly released. He wanted her. He was the alpha. He shouldn't have to stop. He shouldn't have to restrain himself. He could just take her here. Now. But the memory of her warm and willing coming into his arms overrode the baser senses of his beast.

"Vic?" The questions in her eyes couldn't be answered right now. He had to go. He had a job to do. He had a need to make his mark on her, to make her his own. But the job always came first. Would always come first. It had to be that way, or he'd be ineffective as the leader of his pack that was gaining ground as a group and in their community.

This human female could end it all.

"Look, Doc," he said and eased away, reluctance in every movement as he strained to let go of her. "I have to go deal with that idiot in the Hummer."

She raised a brow in amusement. "Which one?" she asked.

He barked out a laugh at her question. "The trouble-maker. Anesthesia's wearing off, now," he said.

A frown crossed her face. "How do you know that? You

haven't been out there to check on him." Now, she retreated from him, putting a little space between their bodies, her sharp mind spinning rapidly. "You have some sort of mental connection to your men, don't you?" Green eyes held his gaze. "They hear your thoughts, the way I did."

"Yes." It was the least he could give her.

"Since I was a little girl, I've heard about the military making breakthroughs in psychic connections, remote viewing, and that sort of thing, but I never knew they were successful." She curved her hand behind her ear, pushing her hair back to expose more of her face, more of her soft cheek to his view.

Grinding his teeth together, he had to move, had to get out of there before the lure of her threatened everything he'd worked for. Warring with that was his overwhelming need to protect her. He had to make sure she was safe, or he'd never forgive himself. Even now, the short, intimate association she'd had with him had jeopardized her safety. There was no telling what the Ridge Runners would have in store if she were left alone all the time.

He'd done exactly what he hadn't wanted to do.

He'd made her a target.

Gimme a minute. I have to convince the doc she's coming with us again, Vic said.

What do you mean she's coming with us? We just got rid of her, Eros said.

She's got a target on her back now. We're responsible for putting it there, Vic said.

Eros sighed, his displeasure obvious. *Roger that. Don't like it. But roger that.*

Vic took another step back from her, considering how he was going to broach this subject.

"What?" Those green eyes narrowed in suspicion. Rightfully so. "What's going on?"

"I think you need to come with us. You're not safe out here by yourself," he said. He wasn't sure how safe she was with him, but she was extremely vulnerable without him.

"What? No way. I'm not going with you again. I have a life and a business to run. I can't hide on your compound for no good reason," she said. "Forget it." Pushing away from him, she stalked down the hall to the open door and strode right out to the Hummer and spoke through the open window. "You guys need to go and take your commander and his crazy ideas with you," she said.

"I appreciate your input, but we only take orders from him," Eros said, but acknowledged her statement. Luke sat in the back seat, his tongue hanging out, watching the interaction, golden eyes taking in everything as if he understood and was eager for more.

"Commander, I'm giving you an order to get off my property. Take that wolf somewhere so he can't come back here, and leave me alone," she said. The piss and vinegar seemed to drain out of her in the next instant. "Don't come back. I won't have you trying to take over my life the way you've taken over theirs."

For the moment, she was right. "I'll keep in touch. This guy has friends that might show up looking for him, so be on watch and let me know if you--"

"I'll be fine. I was fine before I met you, and I'll be fine now," she said. Crossing her arms over her chest, she stood there strong and utterly looking like a female warrior with the breeze teasing her hair around her head, swirling, as if she'd created the breeze through the force of her will.

She would make someone a fine mate. Fierce. Protective. Sexual. All the qualities that went into a good partner.

Unfortunately, not for him. And having her only as a sexual partner would be unfair and disrespectful to her. So, this ended here and now. She was right.

Searching her eyes one last time, steeling himself against the pull of her, memorizing her features and the lines of her face, he committed the picture of her to memory. "Goodbye, Doc." Vic got into the vehicle and turned on the engine. There was nothing else to say as he backed out and headed down the road.

Aren't you going to say something to her? Anything? She's an amazing female and would make you a great mate, boss.

There's nothing to say, Luke. She doesn't belong with us. Me.

But--

Except that when I slow down, you jump out, go back and watch the house 'til I call you off.

Oh, I see. Stealth mode! Awesome.

Don't get caught like Silver did.

Got it.

Half a mile away from the doc's property, he slowed the vehicle to a crawl, and Luke jumped out the open window to land lightly on the highway. As Vic looked in the rear view mirror, Luke watched him for a few seconds before melding into the bushes and shadows at the edge of the forest.

Luke could do this. Vic had every confidence in him. Stealth was his middle name.

Silence, however, was not.

Don't worry, boss. I'm gonna keep her safe for you. No worries. You can count on me. I'll be at the perimeter in a few yards. I made good time...wasn't even distracted by that jackrabbit--

Christ, Luke. Shut it. Report when necessary, not a running commentary.

Oh. I thought you, like, wanted to know what she was doing. I think she's getting in the shower now. Let me get closer. I smell body wash.

Dane isn't the only pervert in the crowd, Eros said.

Shut up, Eros. I'm not a pervert. Only observing and reporting what I see, and may I say, I see a whole lotta skin--

Luke, so help me. If you don't cut it out, I'm going to give you extra guard duty, Vic growled.

That's okay, as long as I'm guarding this sweet naked goddess from heaven. I'm gonna howl!

That's it. Get back here. We're trading places. You and Eros can dispose of Buster. I'll keep watch over Trista. The doc.

Vic whipped the Hummer around, squealing tires and leaving black skid marks in the middle of the highway.

Are you sure, sir? I'm happy to stay here. Happy to.

Get back to where we dropped you off. Now. And that's an order.

Yes, sir.

In minutes, Vic had returned to the spot to wait for Luke. The seconds seemed like hours as he stripped and let the rage of his animal, let the power of his beast come through. The pain and flash of the change was always agonizing, but if he relaxed into it, the torturous sensations didn't last very long.

As Luke trotted up the road toward him, Vic raced to meet him. Dammit. The beast had gotten his eyes filled with images of Trista that should have been his alone.

Growling his displeasure, he nipped Luke on the ear and received a protesting squeal in return. Luke postured in submission, his tail between his legs, turning his belly up. The way he should be.

Get in the Hummer and do whatever Eros tells you. For now, he's in charge until I figure this thing out.

Got it, boss. Sorry.

Luke skittered away, flinging rocks and dirt from his back feet as he hurried to the Hummer.

Try to keep him outa trouble until I get back. If you don't hear from me by moonrise, check in with the doc and see what's going on.

Not waiting for any reply, he shook himself, arranging the fur on his back into place and settled into a slow trot toward Trista's house, determined to keep her safe and not get caught.

⁓

LUKE RETURNED to his human form with a laugh and reached for his clothing on the back seat with a laugh.

Eros watched as Vic trotted away. "Well, that worked," Eros said.

"Just a little too easy, don't you think?" Luke shoved his arms into his shirt and slung it over his head, then reached for his fatigues and yanked them on. "He's got it bad for her and doesn't even know it."

"Yes, you're right. I think he's got it worse than we imagined, but for whatever reason can't take that last step to make her his mate. Maybe because she's human. It's done, just not tradition." Eros adjusted the beret on his head to a better angle. "He needs to take a mate. It's well past time. I'm just not sure she's the one," Eros said.

"What are you talking about? She's *perfect* for him. Gives him shit when he needs it, and they're great in the sack," Luke said.

"Yes, but overhearing them couldn't be helped. It's none of our business." Eros twitched his brows at Luke.

"After he mated her at the compound, I was ready to

take her as *my* mate. Don't you remember how he felt, how crazy he was? I've never felt him like that with another female." Luke whistled and shoved his feet into his boots.

"Yes. I was trying not to," Eros said.

"You don't like her, do you?" Luke cocked his head at Eros, trying to see his reasoning.

"I don't like the changes I see coming if he takes her as mate. He should find another were to take as mate. Not a human woman who can't defend herself should the need arise. Like now," he said, offering the situation as evidence.

"What are you talking about? She defended herself pretty fucking well against Buster just now, didn't she? You're his second. You'll *always* be his second. No worries about that," Luke said and slapped Eros on the shoulder. "Not even a mate will replace you in the order of things. You worry too much, bro'. Just give her a chance. She could be good for him. For all of us." Luke shrugged. "You never know, do you?"

Eros took another glance down the road, then shoved away from the Hummer, moved around to the driver's side and slide behind the wheel. "I hope you're right, dude. I hope you're right."

Luke slammed the door after getting into the passenger seat. "It's all good, bro'. All good." He glanced over his shoulder to see a pair of very angry wolf eyes in the trussed-up animal taking up temporary residence on the back seat. "Let's get rid of Buster so we can go home. I'm starving," he said.

"You sound like Dane. Ruled by your stomach," Eros said and pulled the Hummer onto the road, heading for Tijeras and Maggie's Bar where they'd unceremoniously drop Buster in the parking lot with a note taped to him: *free to a good home.*

"My beast has no control," Luke said without any guilt whatsoever.

"I think Dane's going to turn around now. He's awake and hungry, too," Eros said. "Those are good signs. If his stomach is rumbling, we have to feed him."

"Let's stop at Costco and get a side of beef. We can celebrate. Dane is awake and the commander is after a bitch in heat. What more could we ask for?" Luke drummed his hands on the dashboard, his excitement palpable.

Eros grinned, the mood in the vehicle lightening. "Add a bottle of tequila, and I'm in." He raised his hand to Luke for a high five.

"Smokin'!" Luke said and howled. "*Ah-ooooh!*"

THIRTEEN

Vic waited in the shadows outside of Trista's house and clinic through the night and through the next three days. Humans came and went with their domestic pets and livestock of all sorts. Her business was thriving. Fortunately, there was no sign of the Ridge Runners.

Maybe they'd finally heeded his warning. Maybe they'd pulled back to lick their wounds and would come from another direction. Maybe he was overreacting.

The time had come for him to relinquish his post and get back to the compound and the pack. He had a business to run, too. Although a completely unorthodox one, it was still a business that needed managing on a daily basis, and he'd sat on his haunches for three days, letting Eros take on the burden when he didn't have to.

Several of the boys had come to visit him every night, to check in on him, bring him a few bunnies, but he was beginning to tire of the fare and of sleeping under the cedar and juniper trees.

He took one last look at the light in the window on the second floor and turned away, scented the air, and began the long trot back to the compound. Although he could send for the boys to bring the Hummer, he chose to romp through the trees and over downed logs one last time before heading to his own bed.

Then there was the matter of Dane. The report was that although he was awake now, he wasn't himself. He needed some intervention that couldn't be provided on the compound. Vic would have to meet with a psychiatrist sanctioned by the government and by the pack council, to see if she could help him.

He hated psychiatry, but this was the last thing he had to offer Dane. If he didn't respond to therapy, didn't recover and return to his position, he couldn't be a viable member of the pack and would be forced out by the others or killed. Though the others loved him like a brother, firm, long established rules and boundaries had been in place in the pack for centuries. They'd abide by what was best for the pack, no matter how unpopular it was. Issues like this, the old ways, needed to be upgraded, needed to be modified, needed to fit the current times. In that regard, Zane was right. Again.

The treaty was old, but it still needed to be followed until updates could be made. He knew things needed to change. As the Alpha, it was up to him to change them. No matter how painful. Changes were for the good of the pack. For the greater good, as the human in him would say.

After an hour of thinking and working his way back toward the compound, he came to a few conclusions and knew he had to act. Had to make some tough decisions regarding Dane and his place in the pack. There was no way around it. Something had to change.

Bunching up the muscles in his back legs, he leaped high, up and over the barbed wire fence, landing lightly on the other side. Within minutes, he was on approach to the house. He slowed his pace, caught his breath and eagerness filled his heart as this place, this scattering of odd buildings, they'd turned into a home, came into view. It was a place to be proud of. A place to call a real home. A place he loved, but was definitely missing something.

He needed a mate.

There were available females in nearby packs. Smaller packs that would be good to bring together with his for the stability of all. The last time he'd been to a gathering with the Canyon Creek pack, their female had snubbed him. Only later had he realized that she'd taken another *female* as her mate. Go figure. That situation wasn't going to work for him, but perhaps another female in the group would be receptive to him, and he could bring the two packs together, expanding their resources, expanding the protection of their females and pups.

The idea faded as he padded to the house and a memory from last night surfaced. His eyelids drooped as he allowed himself to sink into the memory of Trista standing just yards from him last night, her scent wafting toward him on the night air.

Trista had opened her door after midnight and stood in the entry, looking out at the stars, looking into the forest where he lay. Just yards from her.

Every night she called to her cat to come in. Every night it had responded. Except for last night. He felt the fear in her. The concern for her feline friend who'd never failed to show up when she called. Except for that night.

Despite sniffing around the area, he'd had no sense of the cat in the vicinity and had had no idea where Pete had gotten to. Maybe he'd scented Vic and headed for higher ground for a few days. Maybe he found himself a female, but Vic was pretty sure Trista'd neutered him. Possibly hiding on the top of the fridge again. It was her concern, her grief, that spoke to him, that pulled on his humanity, drew him closer to revealing himself to her.

"Are you out there, Vic? Somehow, I feel you. Sense you." She'd spoken aloud, the light mist of her breath in the cool night. "Have you sent your wolves to protect me, to look after me?" She'd pulled a shawl over her shoulders and walked toward the edge of the trees, only feet from him. The pull of her had been overwhelming. He'd stood, trembling with need, with want, with pure desire swirling in the heart of him, as a man and as a wolf.

He'd stood, prepared to go to her, but then something shifted, and she'd turned away, shut down the emotional channel she'd had open to him without even realizing it. She returned to the house and closed the door. If he'd wanted to, he could have shifted, gotten into the house, lay down beside her in that big bed of hers and mated with her as he'd wanted to. It was the duties of his position that held him back, that kept him from putting one paw in front of the other to seek her out. That's what he kept telling himself. He'd keep telling himself until he believed it.

He'd done the right thing. He'd had to. For his sake. For hers.

Now, after a deep breath, he focused on the human factor in himself, now in reverse to when his beast was dormant and allowed the muscles, tendons and everything to flash back to his human shape and form.

He dressed and returned to the infirmary.

"What's the status on Dane?" He approached and spoke to Blaze.

"He's awake, not eating enough. Still running IV fluids in him, but won't get down and turn back to his human form, sir," Blaze reported.

"Dane." Vic leaned over and growled into Dane's ear. Tired, hungry, irritated and sexually frustrated, Vic didn't hold back. He poked Dane in the ribs until he opened his eyes. "I know you can hear me. Get your ass up, soldier. You stink. You need a shower. You're reporting for duty in the morning, so get your ass moving," Vic ordered.

At the word *duty* Dane's eyes opened, and he looked at Vic, his breath coming in short, panicked gasps.

Duty? Really? I'm not ready.

Report to me at 0-600 hours and be ready to work.

Without answering, Dane jumped down from the stainless steel table, stretching the IV tubing to the breaking point. The energy in the air around him sizzled and snapped with electricity as Dane shifted into his human form. The pain of it reached Vic, and he pushed it back. The damned wolf had forgotten how to shift the right way. Dumb ass.

"Whoa." Dane wobbled a little bit and held onto the table. "I've been a wolf too long," he said.

"Yeah, your eyes are still wolf. See if you can get them back to human," Vic said. Even a pup knew how to do that.

Focusing internally, Dane worked on the transfer of energy to being completely in his human form. "How's that?"

"Better. Just a bit around the edges. It'll do for now," Vic said, the heat of his anger burned off as Dane followed orders.

"Can you take this thing out?" Dane lifted his arm toward Blaze who quickly removed the IV and placed a small bandage over the site.

"There you go," Blaze said.

"Thanks." Dane rubbed the spot. "Commander? What now, sir? I don't know if I'm fit for duty." They both knew what that meant. If he wasn't fit, there would be big changes coming for him. For all of them. There were no werewolves on desk duty.

"Get something to eat. Shower. Sleep. We'll deal with your assignment in the morning," Vic said. The delay would give Vic a chance to think about what he wanted to do and what he had to do. The two were not necessarily the same.

"Okay. Sorry I was out for so long, sir. Couldn't find the strength to come back," Dane said, and his brows twitched together once. He raised a hand to his chin and rubbed it, then gave a totally Dane grin and Vic sighed in relief. Maybe he was going to be all right after all. "Guess I need a shave in any case."

"Just glad to have you on your feet again," Vic said, squeezed his friend's shoulder once and left him there in the infirmary. He needed to clean up and eat as well. And brush his fucking teeth. After days in the forest eating only bunnies and drinking creek water, he stunk to high heaven, too. "I'll shower and join you in the kitchen for a meal," Vic said.

"Great. See you there, sir," Dane said.

Dane was definitely not himself if he were referring to Vic as *sir* so many times.

Half an hour later, Vic strode into the kitchen to find Dane sitting on one of the stools with half a rack of roast beef sitting in front of him. He chowed down on it, while Luke and Eros helped.

"Looks like I missed the party," Vic said, parked on a stool and pulled a plate of beef closer to him, grabbed a rib and took a bite, salivating at the rush of overwhelming flavors in his mouth. "This is so much better than rabbit." The beast in him howled in agreement, and he groaned out loud.

"Just getting started, boss." Luke tossed a rib into the trash bin beside him. "After we dropped lard-ass off, we stopped at Costco and got some meat. Since Dane was awake, we figured he'd need some extra protein." He shrugged and tossed another rib in the bin. "No reason we couldn't have some extra protein, too," Luke said, offering his pragmatic point.

"We put it on the Alpha Company tab," Eros added and grabbed another rib.

Silver joined the small group, needing some extra protein after his recent injury to his shoulder in the fight two days ago. He was obviously still sore, still favoring his right side. "I'm starved. Those jackrabbits don't last long enough. Pretty scrawny this year. Damned coyotes getting the best ones and leaving the little one for us." He reached for a rib with his good hand and took a bite, letting the juices run down his chin. "We oughta do something about them, too."

Vic nodded, acknowledging the coyote issue was a persistent and ongoing problem. "I'll add it to the list. We've got enough on our plates right now with the Ridge Runners being stupider than ever. The coyotes can have a few jackrabbits on our turf for a while. We'll survive," he said.

They'd eaten together this way too many times to count. Sharing food, trading outrageous stories, and more lies than any of them would admit to. For now it had all the appearances of being their norm, but for him, something was off. Something was missing. He'd always enjoyed the boys and their banter, even if he hadn't taken part. Just listening to them carry on relieved the stress of his duties, reminded him of times past, times they'd shared together, when all they'd had was each other.

"Boss, you okay?" Dane asked and cocked his head to the side, obviously, still deep in his wolf mind. "Energy seems flat."

"Yeah, spend too much time out in the woods by your-self staring at the doc's house?" Luke asked and snorted.

"What's going on? What did I miss?" Dane asked and the boys filled him in on the events while he'd been in the nether realm. "Are you kidding me?" His eyes popped wide. "She wanted to *neuter* me. And you're *sleeping* with her?" The shock in Dane's wide eyes made him laugh.

"I don't think you could technically call what they did sleeping," Eros added, with a sideways glance at Vic. "Whatever you call it, it was mighty fine." He blew out a slow breath and reached for a bottle of water. "Mighty fine."

"She's caught my attention, you might say, Dane," Vic said, admitting that much. "But everything is okay. I won't let her neuter you. Or anyone else."

"Uh, boss? I think that lady who's caught your attention is on her way in here." Eros nodded to the security monitors along the wall. "She's at the first gate honking the horn to beat hell."

"What?" He hadn't felt anything going on from her, but now, he tuned in and felt the panic, the fear and the rage bleeding out of her. "Open the gates."

Luke jumped over to the computer console and released both the first and second gates. "Guess dinner's over and the show has started," he aid.

"I'll figure out what's going on with her, then we need to get some sleep." Vic strode out of the kitchen, his hearing on high alert, and he caught what was going on behind him.

"Seriously? He thinks we're gonna go to bed when his female is racing in here with a head full of steam?" Eros said.

"I know, right?" Luke howled once.

Dane snorted, sounding much more like his old self. "Somebody make popcorn. This is a show I wanna see."

They scrambled to find a vantage point out of sight, but where they could see the action about to happen right in front of them. They raced up the stairs, their boots heavy on the flooring. Not that he could blame them. Anything that happened to the alpha affected them, so the sooner they knew what was going on, the better for them. Like a bunch of kids.

Or a pack of wolves.

He stood in front of the house as Trista brought her Jeep to a dusty halt.

"Whoa, lady. What's gotten into-" he started.

"Don't give me that shit, Commander." Ignoring his question, she stalked to the back of the vehicle and opened the hatch, pulled out a small cardboard box and shoved it in his face. "I told you this was going to happen." Tears of rage, of hurt and pain filled her eyes, turning them luminescent green. "I told you," she whispered, her voice cracking with emotion.

"What happened?" He accepted the box, but the flaps covered what was inside. His nose, however, detected the cause of Trista's distress.

"This. This is what happens when you let your wolves roam around loose. They kill things." The tears she'd been struggling to hold back overflowed.

"Pete?" He looked at the mangled wreckage of what had

been her beloved cat. "No. None of my boys did this, Doc. None of them," he said. At first he was seriously offended she'd even think it. That he or his boys would hurt anyone or anything around her. As the pure bitterness of her pain covered him, he tasted the acid in her mouth, felt the gnawing in her gut. The grief in her heart.

"I'm sorry, Trista." He set Pete's remains on top of the Jeep and stepped toward her, stepped into the circle of her pain, allowing it to wash over him, allowing her to shove it down his throat and choke him with it. It was hers. It was his. He'd share that pain with her. Take some of the burden from her. "Very sorry."

"Don't give me that." She lashed out at him with her words and with her fist. She socked him one in the gut that he wasn't prepared for, and his breath whooshed out before he braced himself.

This female who took on wolves, stood up to the commander of the Alpha Company special ops group and took no shit from any man, was losing it over her cat. She was a mix of tough and tender, sassy and sexy, hot and hotter. She was in his blood now and every cell in his body stood up to salute the beauty, the power, the strength and the vulnerability of her in front of him.

Oh, she's feisty this one, Silver said.

Shut up. He's gonna hear us, Luke said.

I hear you. Shut the fuck up before I neuter you myself, Eros said.

"Don't give you what? My sympathy? My compassion?" He was poking her. Deliberately. She was going to explode, and the sooner she did the better.

"You don't care about what happens outside this place, this compound, this utterly false reality of yours," she said. Tears streaked down her cheeks. The rattling pace of her heart transferred to his own. She was in so much pain. "Nothing can replace him to me. Nothing," she said struck out at him again.

Avoiding her right jab, he clasped her upper arms in his hands and brought her against him. He didn't know how to deal with tears, or grief, or the pain of her loss, other than to take the brunt of it himself. Those green eyes, filled with pain, with tears, opened up right into her soul and drew him in. His gut tightened, and his heart hammered away. "You're right. I can't replace Pete. But I am sorry, and I am going to find out what happened to him," Vic promised. He tucked her against his side and led her to the house. Some of the fire drained out of her and he held her closer, tighter to his body.

Overhead, he heard the boys scrambling to get back to the kitchen, to appear as if they hadn't been eavesdropping and hanging like a bunch of idiots out the upstairs window.

"I hate this. I hate you," she whispered. She sniffed in a ragged breath, but tears continued to pour out of her, but he didn't resist his touch, didn't resist being led to the house.

Put some tea on, Luke, Vic said.

Tea? What the fuck for? Luke asked.

For the doc, idiot, Vic said.

Oh, right. On it, boss," Luke said.

Don't think outside the box much, do you? Silver asked.

They got into it, arguing over who was more evolved in their thinking, more modern. Vic had to turn them off, tune them out. They were a bunch of cavemen where females were concerned. It was no small wonder none of them had found mates yet.

"Let's get you something to drink," Vic said. He led the way as she stretched one arm around his waist and held on.

"No. I don't want any alcohol. It won't help," she said. The pain in her voice dropped it an octave.

"I was thinking of something hot and soothing, like tea or cocoa," he said.

"Oh, sorry." She gave a quick glance at him. "I was thinking of the last time we had tequila..."

"Yes." He cleared his throat, the memory seared into his mind. Seared into the wall in his living room. "Well. Different circumstances now, I think." By the gods. How was he going to keep this female at arms' length if everything reminded him of how amazingly she fit his body, how sexy she was, and how much he wanted her?

"Thank you. I'd love something hot to drink." Then her eyes went wide, and she stopped short as they entered the kitchen. The four males were obviously pretending not to notice anything. "But it looks like you have a meeting or something going on."

"What? *This*?" Luke asked and waved away her words. "Pffft. Nah. Just a little snack since Dane's awake now." Luke slapped a hand over his mouth, as if that would take back the words he'd just uttered.

"Idiot," Silver said and slapped Luke one upside the head. "Now, look what you've done."

"Cut it out, Silver." Luke's long reach slapped him back.

The sharp silence that followed, paralyzed everyone in the room. Including Trista.

Her green eyes honed in on Dane who sat frozen, only his eyes darting to Vic, pleading for help. Then she looked at Silver, down at his bandaged arm, at his silver tinged hair.

What do I do? Dane asked.

Nothing. Just...fuck, Vic said.

The questions in her eyes focused on him. The shock.

The betrayal. The utter disbelief in her face all warred with one another. Steeling herself, she released him and backed away. She stopped when she hit the sink. Hyperventilating, her chest pulled in air at a rapid rate.

"What the hell is going on here?" she asked.

FOURTEEN

"Just hold on, now, Doc," Vic said and raised his hands toward her, palms out in a non-threatening manner. She wasn't buying it. They'd duped her. Thought she was stupid. They'd used her for her services, of several kinds, and then didn't let in on this? This *what*? This *insanity*.

"No. You hold on," she said. She pointed one finger at him, as if that would stop him from advancing on her, stop all of them advancing on her as they were doing now.

The four other men in the room spread out slowly, trying to surround her. Just like wild wolves would do with wounded prey. Encircle, then move in for the kill.

"We're not going to hurt you, but you've stumbled on something that's way over your head." That silky voice of Vic's tried to subdue her, tried to lull her, hypnotize her with its vibration, but it wasn't going to work again. She'd fallen for it once, but not again.

"Over my head? Seriously? You've threatened my life, put my business in jeopardy, killed my cat and only *now* you think to tell me I'm in over my head?" Yes, she had a temper. Yes, it had come out on occasion. Now? Now, she was pure fury.

"Maybe he said that badly," Eros said. He was the closest one to her and one of the most dangerous men she'd ever laid her eyes on. Those black eyes of his said it all. If he caught her, she was dead.

To her left the knife holder sat on the counter. She could grab one of the butcher knives and cut her way out of this situation, but she was pretty sure she'd only get one of them and then it would all be over. Not an option.

Don't do it, babe. I don't want to hurt you. Please relax. Look into my eyes. Just relax. Vic's voice was in her head.

"What are you trying to do?" She wasn't falling for that. Wasn't falling for some lame-assed attempt to hypnotize her. Unfortunately, the sound of his voice in her mind over-rode her desire to stick a fork in him. Those eyes that had been an icy blue were golden and glowing now. She couldn't look away. Couldn't tear her gaze from the man... the fucking man-wolf in front of her. Was that really the commander changing right in front of her? Was she dream-ing, having a hallucination brought on by the trauma of losing Pete.

Just listen to the sound of my voice, Trista. The knives won't help. You'll only hurt yourself. We don't want to hurt you. I won't let anything happen to you. I promise. His voice echoed again in her mind.

"Like the way you protected Pete?" Tears filled her eyes as the resistance in her body melted away. "I don't know what's going on here, Commander, but I don't like it," she said.

"I know. I'm sorry." He took a step closer to her then stopped. He held out his hand to her, but didn't try to touch her, didn't come any closer. Hesitation, caution and self-preservation in her mind, she looked at his hand and then back at his face. His eyes were blue again. His hand was just the hand of a man whom she had trusted with her body. Now she was going to have to trust him with her life.

Her breath came in short gasps as she made the most important decision of her life as she touched her fingertips to his. "Please don't hurt me," she whispered, her throat closing off with an unnamed emotion. "Don't hurt me."

"I won't. None of us will hurt you. You have our protection, and my word that you're safe here," Vic said. He clasped her hand in and reeled her in closer to him. He made a noise deep in his throat, a low growl, and the other men stood-down, as if that noise, that one sound commanded them to leave her alone.

"What's going on here?" She looked at all of them. These men, who somehow were more than men, who surrounded her, not just an illusion or delusion she'd come up with today. "I don't understand," she said. "It's making my brain hurt." Pain began to throb behind her eyes as her mind tried to make sense of what was going on.

"It's a hard thing to understand," he said, admitting part of the truth to her. He blew out a breath and his shoulders drooped. "Sometimes we don't even understand it."

"Start somewhere, please. I have to know, or I'm going to check myself into the mental hospital when I get out of here." She hesitated to say anything, hesitated to say what she knew or maybe they *would* take her to the nut house themselves. "I've seen things I shouldn't have, haven't I?" she asked the simple, but very serious question.

Vic didn't try to come any closer, draw her any nearer to him and for that she was grateful. He just kept her hand tucked into his. The pull of him was strong on any given day, but today, at this moment she didn't know if she could handle being any closer to him.

"Yes, you've seen some things. Been a little too close to the fire," Vic said.

"So, I was right about that black wolf at my house the other day. He wasn't yours, but you knew him... know him... somehow," she said.

"Yes. He belongs to a pack that doesn't get along with ours," Vic said.

Luke snorted, then straightened his face, but it was clear he was amused by the statement. Trista narrowed her eyes at him. Narrowed her eyes as she looked at Silver and his bandaged right arm. Then at the fourth man and stared the longest at him. The man looked like he'd just come out of a coma. His coloring was very pale. He was thin, and the clothing he wore hung loosely on him. The man looked as if he'd lost some weight in a short amount of time and his body wasn't happy about it. They hadn't told her his name, but she was pretty sure she could correctly guess.

Somehow, he was a wolf. *All of them were wolves.* She knew it.

"You don't just have the same names as the wolves, do you?" she asked, carefully. That would have been one way to clear things up, but she suspected it wasn't going to be that easy.

"That's true," Vic said and shook his head. She was so in denial. As a scientist she needed proof, not just some sort of evidence...

The *infirmary*. She had to get over there. The last time she'd seen him, Dane was laid out cold in the infirmary. Taking a deep breath, she released the commander's hand and sprinted for the door, racing through the kitchen,

knowing she wasn't going to get far, but fiercely determined to try.

In seconds a strong hand hooked around her waist and
dragged her to a halt against the front door, pressed his
body against hers, pressed his lips close to her ear. "Don't
do it, Doc. Don't run and make yourself a target like that. I
won't be responsible for what these beasts will do if you
tempt their baser instincts. They're barely on a leash as it
is," he said.

"I have to see with my own eyes," she said. The
commander held her back against him, eased his hips into
her ass and the heat of him, his chest, his fire. The rush of
his breath in her ear stirred her senses. Despite trying to
run for her life, she was held captive by her reaction. Sweat
poured out of her, off of him, the heat of the two of them
together scorched her skin and burned away her resistance.
Now wasn't the time to get cozy with him, but he overwhelmed her senses.

"Where do you think you're going to go?" His lips
pressed hot against her ear stirred the fine hairs along her
neck.

"Well," she licked her lips to moisten them, "I was
going to run to the infirmary and see Dane there." She swallowed as she watched his gaze drop to her mouth. "If Dane
is a wolf there on a table with an IV in his leg, then I'll know
I'm in a waking nightmare. I won't be thinking what I'm
thinking," she said. *That sounded rational, didn't it?*

"What are you thinking?" He leaned closer, the
fragrance of him washing over her. The clean soapy smell,
fresh from the shower, and she closed her eyes. Somehow,
some way, she felt him in her mind again, felt him push
aside her desire to bolt. She didn't want him in her mind,

but she didn't have the power, the skills, to resist his entry there.

"I...I don't know," she said and turned her face to his. She dropped her gaze from his eyes to his mouth."

"Relax," he whispered. "Let me in and I'll show you."

Fluttering her eyelids, she relaxed and opened her mind to Vic. What she felt, what she saw, stunned her. Images of the forest, the stand of trees surrounding her house. The fragrance of pine, juniper and cedar as sharp and clear as she'd ever sensed them. Enhanced, brilliant, more than ever before. Cocking one ear to the right, she heard the sounds of a mouse foraging beneath a pile of leaves behind her. Overhead, the laughing warble of a raven gained her attention. Then the door to her house opened and *she* stepped out, wrapped in a shawl as she called to Pete.

She gasped and opened her eyes, yanking herself out of whatever hypnotic-state she'd been in. "What was that?" she asked, studying him for deception.

"It's mine, Doc. My memory. I was watching you for days. Watching over you." The strong voice dropped to a whisper. "Protecting you," he said.

"How can you do that?" She searched his eyes for answers. "How can you be in my mind like that?"

"Practice," he said.

"I still don't understand," she said. "I know what words you're saying, but they don't make sense to me."

"How about I take you to the infirmary, and you can see Dane?" he asked. "Maybe the visual will help."

"Sure." Unable to shake the suspicion from her mind, she agreed to his suggestion. "You'll have to let me free, first."

Without speaking, Vic took a long look at her. From her mouth, down her neck over her breasts, and continued down her body. He cupped a breast, filled his hand with her curves and teased the nipple with his thumb. "You don't know what a temptation you are to me," he said.

Desire shot white-hot through her veins, and she swallowed it down. "Please?"

He took a breath and let it out slowly, then pushed away from her. Before he changed his mind, she opened the door and hurried toward the infirmary building with him right behind her. Trembling hands, moist with sweat, opened the door, and she burst through it to find three of the other four men standing around one of the tables and a wolf lay on it.

"I thought you said Dane was awake?" she asked Luke and gave him a hard stare.

"I was wrong. He *was* awake. For a while," Luke said, unable hold her gaze. Obvious sign of a liar.

"He had a relapse," Eros said, his expression rock solid and impassive.

"A relapse?" Trista asked, irritation shooting through her. There was nothing she hated more than liars, and she had the feeling they were all lying to her on a grand scale. She approached them before turning to Blaze who looked a bit pale and incredibly uncomfortable. "Soldier, is what he says true?" she asked and stared at him.

"Yes, ma'am." Blaze refused to look at her and maintained his rigid stance at attention, his eyes focused on a point over her shoulder.

"Look at me," she said. If anyone of the group could be duped, it would be him. "Soldier. What wolf is this?" she snapped. "He's not wearing his tags."

"Dane, ma'am," he said.

"I see," she said and paced in front of them, her mind spinning. "Is he unconscious?"

"Yes, ma'am," Blaze said and looked at Eros for confirmation. "He awakened for a while, but as Eros said, he had a relapse."

"How long ago was this relapse?" she asked.

"Just...recently, ma'am," Blaze said.

"I see. Perhaps I need to operate on him again. He might have another bleeder in his abdomen that caused this relapse. How are his vital signs?" she asked and held her hand out for the tablet in his hands.

"Stable at the moment," Blaze said and read off the numbers to her, but didn't hand the tablet over.

"I don't like the way those numbers sound. I'm going to have to go in again. Get him prepped for surgery," she said.

Dane jumped up on all fours and lowered his head, growling at her, baring his teeth at her.

"No. Dane!" Vic cried. All the men surged forward, jumped in front of him and put themselves between her and the snarling, snapping wolf.

Calmer than she'd been in hours, she turned to Vic, to the commander of this group of men and wolves. "He understands English. How is that possible?" she asked.

"Wolves are supremely intelligent animals. You know that," Vic said.

"Oh, come on. You can do better than that. I know you're not what you say you are." She cast a glance around that included them all. "None of you are, are you?" she asked.

"Boss, what are we gonna do? She *knows*. If we kill her, humans will come looking for her," Luke asked, his distress almost palpable. "I don't want to kill her. I like her."

"No one's going to kill her," Vic said and snapped his fingers. "Dane, get down." Vic cursed and ran a hand over his head in frustration. He shook his head. "I can't believe

I'm going to do this. It goes against everything I've worked for, but Dane, you're gonna have to show her. Otherwise, she's not going to believe it," Vic said.

"Show me what?" she asked.

Dane jumped down from the table, moving lightly on his feet, as if he hadn't been in a coma for a week. She watched him. Watched the others. They no longer felt threatening to her, but she didn't know what was going to happen next.

"This isn't the way I wanted things to come out. Not the way I wanted things to end." Vic turned away from her, cursing like she'd never heard him do before. "Not at all."

The way her heart raced, the way her mouth went dry, the way her body tingled in anticipation, she didn't know what was going to happen. When the energy in the room changed, when the flash of light and thrill of a vibration hit her, her jaw dropped, her knees went weak. "O-oh. Uh, oh... Vic?" she asked and reached for him, but then drew her hand back and placed both hands on her face.

A naked man stood in front of her.

A naked man who just seconds ago, had been a wolf.

Stars appeared in her vision, and she swallowed hard. "Vic?"

"She's going down," Blaze said and reached for her.

"She's not going down. Just relax," Vic said, but stepped closer to her, offering his support should she need it.

"I knew it. I *knew* it!" She stared at Dane. Now naked. The Dane she'd seen in the kitchen only moments ago. While Vic slowed her down, he and the others had left the house and come to the infirmary, he'd changed into a wolf to keep the ruse going. It hadn't worked. Gone was her fear and replaced with sanctimonious indignation and righteous validation. She'd been right. Despite all the denial to herself, she'd been right.

"You're very smart," Vic said and pressed his lips together as he contemplated her. "I just wish you weren't. Now, I don't know what to do with you."

"Do with me? Like kill me and bury my body in the lava fields where no one will ever find it or let me into your situation so I can help you for Christ sake?" she asked in a rush. God, she shouldn't be giving them ideas.

"Help? How can you possibly help us?" Eros gave her a scathing look. "Human."

"If you tell me the whole story, I'll figure out how I can help you," she said and pointed a finger at Eros and narrowed her eyes. "And don't ever call me human like that again."

All the males broke out in riotous laughter, pointing at Eros, slapping the table in hilarity as the dressing down of the second-in-command by a human female.

Before any of them could collect themselves, Vic's cell phone rang. He pulled it from his pocket, looked at the number and a look so dark came over his face, she took a step back from him.

"I have to take this," he said and stormed from the infirmary leaving her with four men surrounding her and one of them naked.

"Watch her," Eros instructed and followed Vic out the door. He appeared to be listening to a conversation in his head already.

"Why don't you have a seat?" Luke asked and approached her, directed her toward a couch and sitting area that looked like it'd been taken from a fraternity house. Certain there were virile specimens growing in the fabric that she didn't want to touch, shook her head.

"I'm just going to put my clothes back on now," Dane said and reached for his fatigues on a nearby shelf.

"Are you guys gonna tell me what's going on?" she asked. After another look at the couch, she didn't have much choice unless she wanted to stand until Vic returned. Bracing herself, she sat in the couch and tried not to inhale.

"No, ma'am. We can't tell you anything else without the commander's approval," Dane said and dropped onto the couch beside her, his hands trembling from the effort of his recent shift.

Leaning forward, she braced her elbows on her knees and dropped her face into her hands, took a deep breath and sobbed. "I don't know what I'm going to do." Tremors shook her shoulders.

"Don't cry. Please don't cry," Luke said and fidgeted in front of her. "I hate when the females cry."

"It's so crazy. I-I-I don't know what I'm going to do." Sobs rolled out of her until Luke dropped to one knee in front of her.

"Please. Stop. I'll tell you anything you want to know, just stop crying, it hurts my ears," Luke said, distress pouring out of him.

"Okay." She raised her head, any trace of tears gone and fixed a hard stare at him. She glared at them, now that she had the upper hand, had their sympathies, and they were out of earshot of Eros and the commander, she was going to get some information out of these two. "How long have you been a...whatever-you-are?"

"Werewolves?" Luke asked, the expression on his face baffled as he looked at her.

"Are you asking me or telling me?" she asked him.

"Telling you?" Luke asked.

"I don't think you are. Tell me what you are and sound like you mean it, Luke," she said.

"Okay," he said and took a deep breath, bolstering his confidence. "We're werewolves. We're definitely werewolves. Part of the greater shifter community."

"Greater shifter community?" she gaped, her eyes wide. "There's more than you guys?" she asked Luke and looked to Dane for confirmation.

"Oh, loads more. Lots of shifter communities around that you're not aware of," Dane said.

"This is amazing!" she cried.

"You're not upset? You're not freaked out?" Luke asked.

"No, I'm not upset. I'll freak out later. Right now, I need more answers," she said and grabbed Luke's forearm. "Tell me how you got this way. All of you." She glanced over her shoulder toward the door. "Quick. Before the commander comes back," she said.

"Sorry, woman," Eros said, clasped her hand and removed it from Luke's arm. "Not gonna fall for that helpless female routine."

"I already did. Well almost," Luke admitted.

"Dammit. Let go of me." She twisted her hand and ripped it from the man's grasp. "I want answers, and I want them, now."

"You'll get answers," Vic said as he strode across the room toward her. "But not right now." His glance included the other three men. "We've got a critical assignment. Out of town. A rescue. We leave in an hour."

"What? You're *leaving*?" How could he leave her at a time like this?

"Only for a day, maybe less." That outrageous grin split his face, and his eyes held secrets only she knew he was capable of. "Blaze, you'll go in place of Dane."

"Yes, sir," he said and snapped to attention. "Honored, sir."

"Dane, you'll stay here and protect the doc with Rico's help. I'll leave you, Silver and Rico behind."

"What about the Ridge Runners?" Dane asked. "They'll be watching for an opportunity to strike. This would be the time they'd do it, too."

Vic ground his teeth together for a few seconds, and a deep growl rumbled in his chest. "I know. But we have no choice."

"What's the assignment?" Blaze asked. "What's going on?"

After a glance at Trista, where she knew he debated how much to say in front of her, then he sighed. "We're going to recover the soldier we left behind in the Middle East," Vic said.

Dane, Eros and Luke stared at him, wide-eyed. "You mean-" Luke's eyes filled with excitement.

"Yes. My brother, Bragg, is still alive," Vic said and the room erupted in cheers.

FIFTEEN

Over the next thirty minutes men came and went from all directions moving equipment, gear, ammunition and other life-sustaining supplies to the staging area in a garage that was as big as an airplane hangar. They'd load the chopper, rendezvous with the jet, a recommissioned jet at the military base in Albuquerque. With its speed of Mach 3.3, they'd be in the Middle East in four hours.

The Middle East was a place where no man should have been left behind. The pain of leaving Bragg behind had eaten away at him for five years. He'd allowed his own brother to be forgotten and presumed dead. The guilt, the inability to forgive himself, the mental beatings he'd given himself hadn't made up for leaving one of his own behind. A soldier. A wolf. A brother.

"What's the latest?" Eros asked as the jet raced along. Ten other men had asked the same question. They'd dedicated their lives to saving others. They just needed to know the score, what they were walking into.

"He's been released in a prisoner exchange. We're going to go get him. That's all I know," Vic said and leaned his head back against the seat. "That's all that matters now."

"Released?" Luke asked. "I didn't know he'd been captured." Luke shot a look at Eros. "Did you know?"

"We all thought he was gone," Eros said. "All of us."

"There was no choice at the time. We had to leave. It's no one's fault except mine," he said, keeping his eyes closed, reliving the nightmare of that long-ago night when he thought he'd lost his brother in a battle that could have taken them all.

Silence filled the jet. Except for the blazing fast engines, the whine of the motors, there was nothing to hear. Not even on their internal psychic frequency. Silence filled the gaps between them. Their sorrow hung heavy around them.

They landed, made the exchange and got out as fast as they could before the other side changed their minds about giving back the sick soldier who'd been on the verge of death for a year.

"Brother," Vic said and stood over the thin wolf on the stretcher, guarding his heart, his mind and pushing back the beast that wanted to howl in pain, in grief, in sorrow. "How are you?"

There was no answer from the beast. Vic tried communicating with him on their own internal link, their own private line they'd had since childhood. It was a vibration no one else could hear. Perhaps he could connect there.

What happened to you? Vic asked.

I am wolf.

Did they torture you? Vic asked.

I am wolf.

Brother. Answer me. What happened to you? Let me help you, Vic pleaded with him.

Then his eyes, only his eyes moved, looked at Vic.

I am wolf.

With a sigh, Vic gave up for the moment. Frustration, anger and guilt warred within him as the medics loaded Bragg onto secluded area where he could be strapped down on the stretcher for safety. If the jet took some rough air and tossed Bragg around, it could be the end of him. The jet sliced through the night sky, and soon they'd be home. Soon he'd have other things to keep him busy. Soon, he'd have to figure out what to do with Trista. She was safe on the compound, and he hoped she hadn't done anything stupid, like try to go back to work without Rico or Dane beside her for protection.

The woman was headstrong. Powerful in her own right.

Who is the female? Bragg asked.

Who is who? This was the first response from Bragg. Excitement shot through Vic as he realized his brother wasn't totally gone.

The human woman. Who is she? Bragg asked again.

Our veterinarian.

Luke, Eros, Silver and the others coughed, snorted and laughed out loud at that. Apparently, he wasn't on the private wavelength with Bragg any longer.

"It's true," he said out loud, if only to hear it himself. Yeah. Sounded lame, even to his own ears.

You left her alone? Bragg asked, reminding Vic that an alpha never left women or children unprotected.

Only to come for you. She's safe at the compound. We don't have time to waste, though. The Ridge Runners are gearing up for something big, so I don't want to leave her alone for too long, Vic said, uncertain if Bragg would understand.

Assholes. You'd better get your ass back and make sure she's safe if she's as important to you as it feels from here. Bragg sighed and closed his eyes, ending the short conversation that had exhausted him.

Vic opened his mouth to protest, but then closed it without comment. Bragg was right. He needed to get back and see to the structure of the pack. Once again it was changing. His brother returning home changed everything, the structure of the pack, the hierarchy, the world around them.

For now, Vic was content to close his eyes, rest his brain, and connect with Rico to get an idea of what was going on at home. Another reason he'd left Rico with Trista was that Vic had a powerful psychic connection with the dog. A regular dog, even one as fabulous as Rico, was less likely to attract the attention of curious onlookers should Trista venture off the compound.

Sighing, he settled down against the seat, took a few breaths and searched for the connection that only Rico could understand.

~

"DID you do what I told you to?" Zane demanded. He pulled one hand back to cuff Buster in the ear for taking so long on yet another simple task.

"Yes, boss. I got it. Her," Buster said, his eyes shifting left and right, looking anywhere but at his alpha.

The grin that split Zane's face was one of pure delight others might consider evil. Pure lust, pure vengeance filled him as he anticipated seeing just what Buster had brought him. "Show her to me."

Buster hesitated.

"What's the matter with you? Show me my prize!" Zane demanded.

"Boss, she's a little messed up," Buster said and took a step back, wariness in his eyes, fear in his sweat.

"What do you mean, *messed up?*" He surged toward Buster and grabbed him by the leather lapels. "*Exactly.* What do you mean? You better not have soiled her. She is mine, remember?" Zane would never tolerate taking a female *after* one of his underlings.

"I'm sorry, Boss. I'm sorry. She put up a bigger fight than I expected," Buster said, swallowed hard, sweat glistened on his fat face.

Zane sniffed at Buster's face, then shoved him away. "Is that why you smell like pepper spray and have a black eye?"

"Yeah." He dropped his gaze, trying to be submissive in his human form, but sorely lacking. The wolf needed a lesson. "I took it from her."

"Where is it?" Zane asked, wanting to see the evidence.

"I don't know," Buster grumbled.

"Where. Is. It?" Zane ground out through clenched teeth.

"Okay! Okay! Here it is," Buster said and pulled the small can of nearly empty spray from his pocket. "I was gonna toss it, but didn't have time."

Zane took it from him and shook it, keeping his gaze on Buster. "Hold still."

"No. Boss. Don't!" Buster held his hands up to protect his face. Zane grabbed the front of his jeans and unloaded the remaining pepper spray onto the Buster's sad little package.

Buster screamed in pain and dashed away, howling his way to the nearest sink. "Good luck with that," he called after the retreating male and laughed, then sobered as he came back to the situation at hand. Zane would have to re-think his second in command. Buster wasn't cutting it. Not in any way that mattered.

That fucker Stone was right. Did Zane want to leave the pack, his legacy, to the idiots he'd surrounded himself with? He snorted. Hardly. They were easy to control and manipulate, but not good for much.

Buster hadn't even had the sense to bring the little present into the main part of his lair. Hadn't even offered her some refreshment. Or any entertainment. Zane's groin pulsed as he thought of the types of *entertainment* he'd so enjoy offering Stone's female.

The images he brought forth in his mind only fueled his desire for revenge. Only stimulated his imagination more. "Maybe I could take her as my mate since Stone hadn't done it yet," he said aloud. Speaking to himself often was the only intelligent conversation he got around there. He rubbed his hands together in anticipation and laughed out loud. "Oh, wouldn't that be the ultimate revenge? While Stone sat on his ass, I took his female and made her my mate."

"Seriously, Boss?" Eric, the ginger-haired wolf, asked. He was second after Buster and slightly more intelligent, but no one matched Buster in brains, brawn, or balls. Pity. "That's not a good idea."

"What are you talking about? It's a great idea!" Zane hurried toward the SUV in the garage with Eric keeping pace with him.

"It'll bring down the wrath of Hell and those Alpha Company bastards down on all of us, not just you. If that's what you want, then go ahead, but count me out. If you want to live, want any of us to live, you'll reconsider that plan," Eric said. Though the words were wise, Zane dismissed them. He had his teeth set on that particular bone, and he wasn't letting go because his males were pathetic.

"Reconsider my ass. I'm just pissed I didn't think of it sooner!" He reached for the back double doors of the SUV and hesitated. "Did Buster kill that fucking dog of theirs or is it in here, too?"

"How the hell should I know? I didn't go with him. You never keep any of us informed about your plans. How the fuck are we supposed to know anything about anything?" Eric said and stepped closer, getting in Zane's face, and pushed Zane back.

"You forget your place. You're expendable and don't ever forget it," Zane said. He snarled, bared his teeth and studied the upstart in front of him. Insolence of any sort wasn't going to be tolerated, especially not from this one.

"My place? How am I supposed to know my place when all you do is dictate?" Eric took another step closer, challenging him. The human eyes disappeared as his golden wolf eyes shone, as his canines sharpened to razor points and his hands flexed into claws.

"Think you can take me on?" Zane asked and released the handle of the SUV, salivating at the chance to fight. It would only increase his desire to fuck something, or someone, up after the fight. It would be Eric, who was proving himself as expendable as Zane knew he was, or it would be the female. Either way he was going to tear something to pieces.

"I don't want to fight you, but what you've got in mind isn't for the good of the pack. You've got the business end going. Why fuck it up now?" Eric asked, trying to turn Zane away from his blood lust.

"You mean with this?" Zane pointed to the SUV as he

allowed some of his beast to show. The feeling of his canines descending, the feel of his beast jumping to its feet, ready to tear anything to shreds only fueled his desire, fed his need to uphold his status as alpha in the pack. "This is only a tiny snack, compared to the main course I'm gonna lay on Alpha Company," he said, his voice deep from his beast.

As their energy poured out of them others appeared, kept to the shadows, drawn by the threat of a fight, the potential for blood and the possibility of a new leader. No one respected Zane, but all of them feared him and the brutality of his treatment of them all. Every one of them would relish slitting his throat and watching him bleed while they tore his body to shreds.

"Back off, Zane." Eric ripped his shirt off and threw it to the floor, preparing to shift. "Leave the female alone. She hasn't done anything and if you kill her, you'll bring down the wrath of Alpha Company *and* the human police. We don't need either. Not now," Eric said, trying again.

"What's the matter with you? Did you lose your balls somewhere along the way?" Zane asked.

"No. I'm the only one here who has enough balls to stand up to you, to even try to make you think straight. All you can think of is revenge, of getting back at them and for what? A little bit of money? A little inconvenience?" Eric asked, trying to destroy Zane's vengeance with logic.

Zane was going to implode and tear Eric to pieces. "Stone has single-handedly fucked my empire!" Zane roared to the ceiling.

"No, he hasn't. You've done it yourself. If your ideas, your strategies have been found out by them so easily, then it was a bad idea in the first place," Eric said and showed his teeth to Zane without any hint of proper submission.

That. Was. It. "Get him out of my way." Zane backed up to give them some room. He wasn't going to break a claw over this one.

The others descended on Eric in a flash. Before he even had a chance to defend himself, they were on him, biting, clawing and dragging him out of the garage into the woods. All Zane heard was a mass of cries, howls, and then silence. The boys would be busy for a while devouring the rebel wolf who'd sought to destroy his organization from the inside out. It was a lesson to all of them. Mutiny or challenge of any sort wouldn't be tolerated. Ever.

He opened the back door of the SUV.

Teeth and claws were all he saw as that fucking dog of Stone's came at him. With one swipe of his claw, Zane dispatched the animal across the room. It hit the wall and lay still.

"Buster, get that damned dog out of here before it starts to stink." He wasn't going to have the putrid smell of Alpha Company's mutt stinking up his warehouse.

Buster arrived, wearing nothing except a pair of loose shorts and walking like he'd just gotten off a horse. "On it, Boss," he said through a fake smile.

No sympathy arose in Zane at Buster's condition. The moron had brought it on himself by not following Zane's orders. None of them did what he said without threats. He might have to invest in a case of pepper spray to keep them all in line.

"See that I'm not disturbed until I call you. Give it to the others to deal with," Zane said, expecting his directive would be taken care of immediately, and he turned away from Buster.

"Got it." Buster clasped the unconscious dog by the collar and dragged its limp body toward the door.

"Hello, kitten." Zane grinned, letting his wolf teeth show, letting his wolf eyes rake over her body. He could more easily see the heat of her, see the racing heart in her chest, the breath coming fast in her throat. Breathing deeply, he took in her enticing female fragrance. "No wonder Stone has it bad for you."

"What did you do to Rico?" she demanded. Hostile green eyes peered at him. Intelligence shone bright in them. Yes, she would make a fine mate once he beat the defiance out of her and filled her with fear. Then he could control her. Then he would dominate her.

"That stupid dog?" Frowning, he tapped one finger on his cheek, as if he were thinking. "Oh, yes. He's being eaten right now. Devoured by my hungry wolves. They're always hungry, you know?" Zane laughed and watched for her reaction.

"What?" she asked, her eyes suddenly filled with fear. There was a pause in her confidence. A lapse in her certainty. Fear made her heart quiver in her chest.

Panic. Tears. Fear. All the things he loved in females Just before he fucked them. Or killed them. Whatever. They knew exactly what was going to happen.

"Yes, my lovely human. He's being gutted and the hide ripped off of him right now. Just the way I'm going to do to you," he said with a twitch of his brows.

Raising her chin, she glared at him, the defiance returning to those emerald eyes of hers. "The commander will come for me," she said and nodded. "Vic will come," she whispered. Somehow, her words gained strength in the face of her mortal enemy. Her fear subsided. Her tears dried up. Panic evaporated. She calmed.

"He won't come in time. He's out of the country and out of my sight. My boys will ensure that he never finds you,"

Zane said, relishing the feel of the words. He had to make her fear him again. Had to strike panic in her heart again. How was she not cowering in a corner already? Dammit. This female presented more of a challenge than he'd anticipated.

"We have a connection. One you'll never understand. Aren't capable of understanding," she said. Her words were somewhat garbled, probably from the bruise in her jaw. Buster said he'd messed her up. One of her eyes was almost swollen shut. Oh, well. She was still a lovely thing and would be even prettier bent over his couch where he didn't have to look at her face or hear her stupid words.

"Your connection has just been canceled," Zane said. He grabbed one of her boots and yanked her out of the vehicle. She fell at his feet where she tried to scramble upright, but dropped to her knees where a proper submissive belonged.

"What are you going to do?" she asked, her tone demanding. Lashing out with her feet she missed his leg and scrambled backward to land against a stack of old tires.

"Oh, I've got a plan for the commander, but one enjoyable thing at a time," he said and stalked her. He strode one step at a time toward her. He yanked off his shirt and unbuckled his jeans. "This is going to be so much fun."

Unbelievable. The bitch got to her feet and stared at him, green eyes cold, unafraid. "You'll never break me. Idiot." She pulled herself upright. "You might kill me. You might destroy me and think you've ended what I have with Vic, but you will never, *ever*, break my spirit." She raised her face in defiance. She leaned closer and narrowed her eyes. "Never." The whisper of certainty in her voice nearly rattled him.

"That sounds like a challenge to me, kitten. I never walk away from a challenge," he said. "Especially not one that looks like you." That gave her pause, and her eyes turned away from him for just a second, then continued to glare at him. "Reconsidering your options, are you? You know I'll win. You know what I am. What we all are, don't you?" he asked, but already knew the answer, otherwise she'd be in the corner cowering.

She nodded, and kept her gaze on him. "The option I hadn't considered is, you're an asshole. A small, dick-less little boy who thinks he can get what he wants by bullying others," she said, taunting him.

"Dick-less?" He grabbed the zipper of his jeans. "Just wait till you see what I got waiting for you in here, baby. You'll be crying out for more. Stone's got nothing compared to me," he said with assurance.

"Really? How do you know that?" A sly smile came over her face and those emerald eyes of hers glittered with amusement. "Been peeping in his window when he wasn't looking?" she asked.

"No, I--"

"Then you have no clue how your shriveled little prick compares to his," she said. Her gaze darted to the side, and he looked away from her to see Buster rushing in through the door. Still in his boxers. Still interrupting Zane's private time with his captive.

"Boss--" Buster started.

The female dashed past Buster, through the open doorway into the night.

"You idiot. She's getting away." Zane rushed toward him. "Go get her!"

"Sorry. No can do. I can't even walk yet," Buster said, put his hands on his hips and blew out a breath.

"Why not?" Zane asked. "What's wrong with you?"

"You pepper-sprayed my nuts!" Buster cried.

"Oh, right. Keep the others away. She's mine." Zane stripped the rest of his clothing off and shifted into his beast. He lifted his head into the air and sniffed, searching for her. With one last look at his disappointing second-in-command, he loped out the door after his prey.

CHAPTER
SIXTEEN

Vic, Eros, Luke and several others had set up a base camp at Trista's home. His essential soldiers were with him and the rest headed to the compromised compound. Bragg had to be taken to safety and the situation at the compound had to be assessed. Were there casualties? Injuries? What were the injuries and what was the state of the compound? Vic sent Bragg with the others to the compound for safety. The Ridge Runners were unlikely to return just yet and the compound was the safest place for Bragg.

For the time being, Trista's house was closer to the major roadways than the compromised compound. "Everyone and everything is blocked," Vic said and ground his teeth in frustration. He had psychic connections to Trista and to Rico. If those avenues failed, he'd call Trista on her phone. No signals, psychic or cell, were going through now and it could only be for one reason.

The Ridge Runners had struck while Alpha Company was gone. Dammit. The one vulnerable time where the compound was at its fewest number of soldiers and wolves, when Trista had become more and more important to him than he ever could have imagined, and the Ridge Runners knew it. When Alpha Company was occupied elsewhere, the Ridge Runners had known. Somehow, they knew it.

Could there be a spy in Alpha Company? Could one of the wolves have inadvertently let it slip they were going to be out of the country and it had gotten back to the Ridge Runners? How? How could his enemies have known exactly when to strike? Had one of Alpha Company been followed and not even known it?

He closed his eyes and groaned, then yelled out his frustration. *Pete.* It was those jackals who killed Trista's cat knowing she'd run right to Vic. In her distress, she'd inadvertently led their enemies straight to Alpha Company's gates.

"What?" Eros asked, his intensity vibrating the air.

"It was the cat," Vic said and narrowed his eyes.

"The cat?" Luke asked. "Doc's cat?" Luke frowned, then his expression turned to one of dismay and then anger. Luke ground his teeth together and clenched his fists. "Oh, man. They fucking killed her cat to get her to run to you, didn't they?"

Vic growled out his answer. "They did."

"And they followed her right to our doorstep," Eros said and stood. "See? I told you having an outsider around was going to cause nothing but trouble, and I was right."

"Eros, shut up," Luke said. "I like Trista. And I liked her cat. He didn't deserve to get torn apart by those assholes." Luke, always the most tender-hearted, but also the one who exacted the most revenge.

"Yeah, you were right," Vic said as his beast strained to

be released. "It doesn't matter who was right. Only who's gonna be dead when I get through with them."

Vic paced the office at Trista's house as his closest soldiers awaited orders. "Who's on patrol at the compound now?"

"Dingo and Silver. Western perimeter, where the Ridge Runners struck before," Eros said. "No sign of them there."

"Good." Vic paced, unable to settle down. Unable to ease the feeling in his gut that something terrible had gone down while his back had been turned. It was his fault. His responsibility. He'd chosen his brother over protecting Trista.

"Echo and Günther are to the south with a couple of the new guys," Eros said, continuing with the briefing.

"What's the status in the infirmary?" Vic asked.

"Dane has a concussion. Still seeing stars," Luke said. He stood by the door with his arms crossed over his chest, his face impassive, eyes black and glittering with gold flecks as the beast in him rumbled at the surface, waiting to be released. Ready to defend the honor of his pack and his leader.

"No sign of Rico or the doc anywhere?" Vic asked. He should be able to connect with them, get something, unless they were unconscious or dead. He'd take any crumb of evidence to show where they were.

"No, sir. Scouts are back. Ridge Runner stench is all over the place," Luke said.

"Looks like they're gone," Eros said, his mouth turned down, his voice dark.

"You don't suppose they got out somewhere they just can't communicate from, do you?" Luke, ever the hopeful one, asked. "Maybe they're in a low spot or a cave with no cell service or something."

"No. I'd feel at least something if that were the case." Vic said as his cell phone rang. "Dane, you're on speaker."

"That fucking pack of jackals was here, sir. Came through the neutral territory, distracted us while more came through the front gates." Dane took a few breaths. "They took your female and Rico. I'm sorry, sir. We couldn't stop them." He growled low in his throat and expressed his sorrow.

"At ease, Dane." Vic's hand clenched the phone in his hand as Dane confirmed his worst fears, that the Ridge Runners had violated everything Vic stood for and had taken those under his protection. There would be no quarter for them now. Treaty or no treaty, he was going to get Trista and Rico back or die trying. Then, he'd unleash his wrath on the Ridge Runners. His jaw tightened as he listened to his soldier report the incidents.

"Hold on," Dane said. Muffled voices on the other end, distorted so much that he couldn't hear. "Silver just made it back. I'm sorry to report sir, Rico and a wolf from the Ridge Runners have been found together. Dumped at the southern edge of the compound, but no sign of the doc," Dane said, his voice harsh with anger.

Although they were all psychic and could read each other, the atmosphere in the small office was tense with anticipation, filled with males needing action. Books on the shelves rattled from the intense energy swirling around. Something had to give.

"How bad?" The tension in Vic was about to explode as his beast chomped and clawed to get free, ached to sink its teeth into something and tear the flesh from their enemies' bones.

"They're beat up pretty bad," Dane said. "Blaze is working on Rico now."

"Who's the wolf?" Vic asked. Identifying the male could provide them essential information.

"No one I know," Dane said.

"Lock him up." If Dane didn't know the wolf, he was unlikely to be high in Zane's pack structure. He might have some intel. Vic wouldn't put it past Zane to come up with a ruse like this. Putting a mole, albeit a beat-up mole, on Alpha Company borders, hoping Vic would take the injured wolf in was a totally Zane move. He wouldn't hesitate to sacrifice one of his own to get to Vic.

"He's seriously hurt, too. Looks like Zane's boys chewed him up and spat him out," Dane said, and Vic paused.

Now *that* was interesting information. This might give Vic the opportunity he needed to find Trista and get her back while gutting their enemy and leaving the entrails for the scavengers.

"We'll be there directly." Vic shoved the phone into his pocket and hurried toward the first of two black SUVs waiting out front. Shadow government traveled in style, but they weren't exactly inconspicuous driving through the little mountain town of Tijeras, past Maggie's Bar and racing toward Alpha Company headquarters.

In silence, the entourage made it to the compound entrance in good time, determined to protect their home-lands and bring the doctor back. As they sped up the rutted lane, they didn't have to stop to get through the protective gates. They were blown to hell. Vic maneuvered around the mangled steel gates that should have protected them.

"Looks like they came in with a fucking bulldozer," Eros said and adjusted his beret low over his brow. "We're gonna roast them over the fire, boss. I want to feel their bones cracking in my teeth," he said.

"Me, too, Eros. Me, too." The pulse of Vic's wolf rose in anticipation of chewing up the bones of their enemies.

The group stormed into the infirmary. Blaze stood beside the first patient bay. Rico lay on his side, silent, but breathing, with an oxygen mask strapped to his face. Dane hovered nearby, a bandage wound around his head, claw marks and scratches covered his face, neck and arms. He might not be back to his full status yet, but he'd fought to protect Trista and Rico. The wolf was deserving of his position in the pack.

Wolves from other shifter groups gathered in the courtyard, in the infirmary and in the forest nearby. They'd heard the distress call for assistance sent out over the psychic airwaves. The alpha female of the Canyon Creek pack had sent members of her group to lend help in whatever way they could. As guards, as soldiers to run with the pack, or scouts. These females could do it all.

A foreign timber wolf lay on the floor, his paws chained to the wall. One eye was open, the other swollen shut. He struggled to his feet as Vic approached. The wolf hung his head and turned it to the side, pulled his tail in between his legs. The posturing didn't mean anything to Vic. It could be another trick to fool them. Anger, rage and a white hot heat filled him. He reached toward the wolf, ready to pull him up by the scruff when the sharp tang of blood hit him. Breathing deeply, he scented the gooey substance covering him.

Blood covered the wolf. His muzzle bore fresh bite marks and scratches. One of his eyes was closed from an injury and there was a piece missing from the tip of one ear. Both front legs bore severe bite marks, and he held one paw up, as if it were very painful.

Vic stood in front of the wolf trying to keep calm for a little bit longer. "Who is your alpha?" Vic demanded.

The wolf ground his words out, speaking human words through the structure of a wolf's throat. "I have none."

"As commander of this pack, *I* am your alpha while you are here. I command you to shift into your human form. Now," Vic said, exercising his authority.

The wolf lowered his head in acknowledgment. He'd taken a beating tonight. Long minutes passed before he could muster the energy to shift to his human form.

"Get on with it, will you?" Eros stood close by, arms crossed over his chest, any patience he might have had had been left behind hours ago.

Others gathered closer, drew nearer to Vic in case the prisoner tried to attack. The enemy shifter in human form sat on the floor, legs splayed out in front of him.

"What are you called?" Eros asked.

"I am...called Eric." He panted from the effort to speak and what the transformation had cost him in energy.

"Blaze, get an IV in him. Get him some pain medicine and evaluate his arm," Vic ordered.

"Yes, sir," Blaze said.

Vic wasn't without compassion, but Eric's condition was far down the chain of what he was concerned about now.

"Where is the female taken from here?" Eros asked. This was the most important question of the day. Where was she? Where was Trista? Where was his female? A tremor pulsed through Vic. "Where is she?"

"Zane has her." The man covered in blood, scratches and bites shook his head, trying to clear it. "Zane has your female."

"Where?" Vic asked. "Where is she?"

"Safe house." Eric closed his eyes as Blaze knelt beside him, inserted the IV and hooked him up with an electrolyte mix. Vic needed him to stabilize, needed information out of him to find Trista. After that, the bastard could die for all he cared. Eric was tough and hearty, so on the other hand, he could be of use to Alpha Company. If he didn't die or no one killed him first.

"Safe house? Where is it?" Eros asked and looked at Vic. "We don't have any intel on a safe house."

Eric looked up with his one good eye at Vic and the others surrounding him. "I hesitate to say, my alpha, as I'm uncertain of my safety here. I could give you the information, but what would stop you from killing me, after that?" he asked, right to be concerned for his safety.

"Where is she, jackal?" Eros demanded and struck the male in the chest, knocking him over onto the floor. "Do not defy your alpha's command."

"Your safety will be maintained," Vic said and paused for breath. He tried to infiltrate the male on a psychic level but couldn't. He either blocked Vic, which as a beta he shouldn't be able to do or was so shut down that his psychic channel had closed completely. "Don't give me cause to change my mind."

"Yes, alpha," Eric said and closed his eye.

"I'll release your shackles as a gesture of good faith. If you defy me, I will end you," Vic said making certain Eric knew the price of any defiance.

Eros removed the weighty restraints, and they clattered to the floor. Eric stood with great effort and accepted the blanket Blaze offered, then fell into the chair pushed to him. He cleared his throat, then swallowed several times. "The safe house is in the wilderness area near Mountainair. It's remote. It's wild," he said, his voice rough. He looked at

Vic with his good eye. "Your pack must be careful if you go there. You don't know how insane Zane is."

"We don't care. We must find his female," Eros said and growled deep in his chest.

"She won't be his female for long," Eric said and accepted a glass of water from Blaze, but it fell to the floor as Eros hauled him to his feet by his throat.

"What do you mean? Are you trying to trick us into leaving the compound again? Into going there when we'll be ambushed on the way? What's your game, jackal?" Eros demanded.

"No game." Eric struggled, his face turning red, his breath coming in short gasps as Eros strangled the life out of him.

"Release him," Vic said. "Let him talk freely. We can always kill him later."

Eros released Eric, and he collapsed back into the chair, gasping for breath. "Zane's going to take his ultimate revenge on you, alpha." Eric looked at him, only truth and fear showing in his eyes. "He's going to make her his mate since you haven't done it."

Red, black and gray filled Vic's vision, pushed everything else away. The air in his lungs burned as he fought for control of his beast who struggled for freedom, to tear the place apart.

"Commander." Eros called to him from a long way off. Pain sliced through his mind, and poked daggers of rage into his brain. "Vic!" Eros shook him once, but he ignored the male. "Control yourself. You can't let your beast control you now." Another shake and Vic took a breath, fought for control.

Luke grabbed Vic's arms, and Eros slapped him once across the face. The pain in his head, the jarring of his body jerked him from the haze of churning fury building inside him.

Vic shook his head, took in a deep breath and arched his back. Baring his teeth, he roared, trying to resist the pain of his transformation, struggling to control his feral beast. Sweat poured out of him, burned in his eyes. Thunder echoed in his ears as he shoved down his rage.

Eros was right. He had to maintain control. Had to keep his human brain intact if he had any chance of finding Trista. She was *his* female. She was *his* responsibility. He had to find her. Panting from his efforts, he struggled in Luke's arms as the red haze faded from his vision.

"Let me go," Vic said and shrugged away from Luke. He walked a few steps away, gathering his energy. Gathering the power he needed for the fight about to go down.

"We need a plan. We can't just roll in there and take her back," Eros said.

"We're going now. Plan on the way," Vic said. The storm of madness roiled within him, building power, and driving his fury to the highest level. He turned to Eros, allowing the male to feel the turmoil inside of him. Eros would take over, could be trusted to lead the pack should Vic die tonight. He wouldn't return without Trista. "I'll die before I let him take her as his mate."

"Dane, you're in charge while we're gone. Protect Rico. Kill the infiltrator if necessary." Maintaining eye contact with Vic, Eros started issuing orders. The human in Vic faded away as Eros gave commands to Luke and Silver, the others, to shift, follow behind in a second wave of teeth and claws. "It's gonna be ugly, Blaze. We're on foot. Pick a team. Bring the Hummer, the transport truck, and all the medical supplies you've got. We're gonna need all of it." The room filled with crackling electricity as the others shifted to their beasts.

Turning his focus inside, the rest of the men, the room, everything faded away and his vision narrowed to a small spot.

Vic unchained his raging beast.

The pain that emerged with the ferocity of his wolf made him roar, made him cry out. Muscles straining to their max, tendons contorted to their breaking point as energy fired to its maximum potential. His guts, his insides, his heart and brain shifted, morphed to his animal. To his wolf. To his savage beast. To the untamed one within.

Searing blue electricity shot across his nerves. His back arched from the savagery of it. He cried out again as fur and teeth, sinew and bone shifted into that of his most vicious, most primal, most dire wolf.

Dropping to all fours, the final shocks of electricity hit him, and he allowed his entire beast to take over.

Panting, he took a few breaths, feeding oxygen to the cells in his body, but there was no time to wait. His female was threatened. Nothing else mattered. Nothing, except death, would stop him from finding Trista.

Rushing into the evening air, he faced the sun as it clung to the horizon. Raising his head, lifting his nose, Vic scented the air, filtered it for any remote trace of her. Connecting to her remembered fragrance, he allowed his blood to boil, released any control he had over his beast.

Tonight there was nothing left of the human commander.

Tonight, there was nothing but the beast. Rearing back on his haunches, he lifted his head and howled into the night. The wolves around him raised their heads and howled out their solidarity, their unity to his mission.

He stepped forward in silence, focusing on his connection with Trista to lead him to her. Let his passion for her fill his mind. Let the power of his love for her guide him through the night.

~

TRISTA'S SHOULDERS burned like hot coals. Like nothing she'd ever experienced before. There was no position she could take to ease the force of her body weight on her shoulders.

Standing on the tips of her toes eased the pain for a few seconds. She couldn't hold it for long. She had to lower herself and let her bound arms take her weight again. The thick rope slung over a high tree branch ended at her bound arms. There was no way she could get out of this by herself.

No way Vic would ever find her.

She was in the middle of nowhere. With some ass-hat toying with her, torturing her, wanting her dead.

"How are you, kitten? Having a little trouble scratching your nose are you?" Zane asked her, as if she needed more sugar in her tea or something.

Zane had built a huge bonfire and poked the ends of several long sticks in it, looking too much like a cowboy readying his branding irons than someone enjoying the heat. He'd gathered willow branches and bundled them together into long, sharp whips that he'd beaten her with. The ends burned like electric shocks along her nerves, down her back, across her bare buttocks and legs. He'd even used the switch across her breasts and tender nipples, stirring red welts across the once-pristine flesh she'd been so proud of. Flogging her with her clothing on hadn't satisfied him. The beast had stripped her naked. He'd said the blood would make *the show* more interesting, draw Stone more easily to her, if he smelled her blood on the night air.

"Vic will come for me. You know that, right?" The only thing keeping her awake, keeping her alive, was her ability to verbally torment Zane. Though it was a small thing, it was the only thing to focus on. If she focused on the pain, she'd give in to it and die.

"Just keep telling yourself that," Zane said and snapped the switches in his hands. He didn't need to hit her with them. Just the sound of them cracking brought fear to her. "The only thing keeping you alive is my anticipation of torturing you in front of him while he's forced to watch. Watch the ultimate humiliation of his mate. Then I'll kill you both," he said.

"I'm not his mate, or whatever you call it. I don't know why you keep saying that," she said. Trying to stay focused on the words in her brain. Maybe she could convince him that they weren't a couple. Hell, she didn't even know what they were. She knew she'd fallen hard for Vic. Had fallen the first time they'd kissed.

"Really. That's why you stink like he's marked you?" Zane scoffed. "The alpha only marks a female with his scent when he plans to make her his mate." He moved closer, tracing one finger across her painful breast, around her tender nipple. "But he didn't move fast enough now, did he?" Zane asked, his tone quiet and wondering. His gaze settled on her breasts. He held her still with a vicious grip on her neck. He bent and settled his disgusting mouth over her nipple. A piercing pain shot through her when he bit her.

"No!" Trista screamed into the night, disturbing a flock of birds that had roosted nearby.

"That's it, kitten. Scream. *Scream some more*. Bring the

entire company down here. We're ready for them," Zane said. He shoved his dirty fingers into the center of her, where only Vic had the right to touch, had marked her, had pleased her. The pain of Zane's teeth on her tender flesh filled her body, filled her mind with anger. Her breast throbbed. Her core burned from the Zane's vulgar touch. She struggled against him, tried to find the ground with her toes, but she couldn't. On a sharply in-drawn breath, she braced herself for the pain her actions would bring and hoisted herself up to knee him in the gut.

He released her with a grunt. The hit she gave him wasn't hard. Hadn't hurt him. Only surprised him with her tenacity, and her ability to take the pain he inflicted. Somehow, the fire light revealed a measure of respect in his eyes as he placed a hand on his abdomen. "I see why the commander wants you as his mate. You're a strong female. Very pleasing to look at. I could change my mind and make you my own instead of killing you," he said as he contemplated his plan.

"I'd never be yours. *Never*," she said and spat at him. If she could wrap her legs around his neck and strangle him, she would, but she wasn't powerful enough to do that. "I'll always belong to Vic, and you won't want to claim what he claimed first, will you?" she asked.

Zane tilted his head to the side and listened intently for a few seconds before a delighted grin covered his face. "We'll see about that. When I've got your lover staked out and ready for slaughter, we'll see what you'll do to save his life." Zane slid into the bushes, hidden easily by dark shadows. "They're on the way. Everyone be ready for them, or I'll string you all up with her and let Alpha Company eat you for dinner," Zane said, and a long growl filled the air.

Tears filled her eyes and overflowed as she steeled

herself against the pain and suffering, that Vic and the others would see her this way, witnessing her humiliation. Listening as hard as she could for signs of help, for signs of Vic coming, she couldn't hear anything with her ears. Couldn't tell whether Alpha Company was coming for her, or if Vic was even out there. What if they'd been delayed on their recovery mission? What if they weren't even coming for her? What if they didn't even know she was missing? *What-ifs* raced through her mind, played on her fears, her determination, her energy and spirit. If Vic didn't come, tonight she would die. Of that she was certain.

Closing her eyes, she took a few rapid breaths, trying to find that place in her mind where she'd connected with Vic. Where he'd shown her his memory. Where he'd spoken gentle words to her. Loving words. *Passionate* words. Maybe that was the place she could find him, could get a message to him, could tell him she loved him before Zane took her life. If she could only tell Vic once, it would be worth the effort to try.

Warmth infused her despite the chill of the night. Another breath and another, she focused deep, ignored the pain in her body, pushed it back as long as she could. All of it faded as she recalled the desire, the full out lust, that had filled Vic's eyes when he'd looked at her. Breathing in, she could almost catch his fragrance, the memory of his cologne that lingered in her mind.

From that place, she knew she could survive a little longer. From that place, where she knew he cared about her, she could find him.

Commander? Vic? Are you out there? Only the silence of the night replied as it seemed to anticipate what was yet to come. *Vic? Are you out there? Can you hear me? I need you. Please. I need you now.*

Pain bubbled up from her darkest place, from where her deepest secrets lay, from the place no one knew about. Where she'd hidden her feelings for Vic from the first time he'd touched her. Was it just days ago? *I need you. God, Vic, I need you now. Please. Help me.*

The sob broke from her throat. He wasn't there. She leaned her head back and screamed out her frustration into the night.

I. Am. Here.

CHAPTER
SEVENTEEN

"He's here," she sobbed. "I knew he would come." Knowing Vic would end this night one way or another, Trista let her head fall back. No longer alone, she clung to the message she'd received in her mind. Vic had come for her. Dehydrated, shivering, beaten and bloody, she could let go now, could let Vic take over from here. She trusted him as no other.

From where Zane had disappeared, a black wolf burst from the shadows. Its jaws snapping, its feet pawing at the dirt, its great breath coming in a fetid stench even she could smell. The ominous wolf yipped three times, then gave a long howl, announcing his presence, calling to Vic.

"No!" Her scream echoed into the night. "Vic. It's a trap!" Struggling against the restraints was no use. The only thing she could use was her voice and her mind.

"He knows," Zane growled from his wolf throat. The beast approached her, stood on his hind legs and used his sharp claws to slice through the rope. She dropped to the ground like a sack of potatoes, her muscles strained and weakened, unable to hold her weight. Arms still tied together, she tried to push up with them, tried to sit, but was forced face down into the dirt as Zane shoved one paw on her back.

Zane rose over her as she lay gasping for breath. Using his weight, he forced the air from her lungs. Slowly, painfully, he suffocated her. Using the last of her strength, she sent her last message to Vic.

Vic, I'm dying. I love you.

"Where is he?" Zane scraped his claws into her back, demanding an answer.

"I told him...not to...come," she whispered.

Zane reared back. He picked her up in his giant claws and threw her toward a tree.

Helpless, Trista knew this would end her life. Another wolf, a huge timber wolf threw its body between hers and the tree. *Vic.* He took the brunt of the force and eased her to the ground. *It's me, my love.* Rising to his feet, he launched himself at the black wolf.

In pain, Trista could only watch as Vic attacked Zane. Her breath came in painful gasps as other wolves formed a circle around the two and protected her. Jaws snapped and cracked as they sized each other up. Tears filled her eyes as she watched the man, the wolf, that she loved, fight for her. She knew he'd never stop until one of them was dead.

I love you, Vic. Never forget. I love you.

Points of light filled her vision and expanded, blocking out all else. Closing her eyes, she knew no more.

~

Give it to him, Boss. He's a pussy. You can take him, Luke screamed in his mind.

See to Trista. When she's safe I'll take him down, Vic said.

246

Blaze is on the way, Eros said.

Don't wait. Get her out of here, Vic said.

On it, Boss, Luke said.

She's not breathing, Eros said.

Go!

Vic sized up Zane and kept him distracted while the others took Trista to safety. What Zane lacked in brains he made up for with raw power. They'd never fought each other despite their pack skirmishes over the years. Zane would fight dirty. Zane didn't know that Vic would, too. There were no rules, no treaties in this meeting of alphas. One of them would die tonight.

Circling each other, Vic felt the power of Zane's beast wash over him, the depravity oozing from him. Vic scented Trista's blood on his enemy. An insane shot of white light blazed through him, stirring the human and the beast together to avenge his beloved. She was dying. He knew it. Her life force was fading. Soon, there would be no more of her except for his memories. Vic would die to avenge her. Tonight Zane would die a traitor and a coward.

Nothing was more important to Vic than Trista. Nothing. Even though he hadn't officially made her his mate, she was in all other ways mate to him. From the time they'd met, had touched, she'd been his. He'd been hers.

Anger at his lack of action drove him on, drove him to take risks.

I got you this time. Took your mate from under your nose, and you didn't do a thing about it. Did you? Some alpha you are, Zane said in Vic's head.

Vic launched himself at Zane's throat. The fucking wolf was padded with muscle, fat and fur, protecting the vital and arteries in his neck. Shaking his head violently back and forth, Vic tried to break Zane's neck. Tried to end it quickly.

Zane broke free, circled around once and charged at Vic. Thunder filled Vic's ears at the intensity of the fight, the roar of the wolves around them, the blood in his eyes, the fever in his heart. The urge to kill. The need to destroy. It all fused together as his beast struck out with his paws, with his teeth, biting and clawing his enemy.

Zane went down, unable to keep his balance and his legs gave out from under him. The others of his pack circled around him, protecting the wolf they feared more than Vic.

Ready to meet death at the hands of his enemies, Vic rose on his hind legs. He raised his voice to the sky in his death howl. Crying out his pain, howling out his intent, he put everything into his voice. There was no reason for him to live. Not without Trista.

Zane slowly got to his feet. He was hurt. They both were. This would be Vic's last stand, his last chance to eliminate Zane. Tonight, he had to kill his enemy or die trying. The pack would go on without him. Eros would take over until Bragg could recover. Alpha Company would continue.

Tonight, he could be proud and die fighting as a warrior.

As wolf.

As--

Vic?

The voice in his head was a memory of her, and he shook it off. Focus. He had to focus, not go to Trista on the other side yet. Though she called to him, he had to finish this. After it was done then he'd release his spirit and journey to the other side with Trista.

Pulling his remaining power into his muscles, he prepared for one last strike at Zane.

Vic, I need you.

She's awake, boss. You'd better come now. Luke's voice was somber and serious. *She needs you.*

Vic hesitated. If there was ever a chance to kill Zane, it was now. The council would understand. There would be no repercussions to the pack due to his actions.

But his mate lived.

The draw of his mate's call was stronger than his need for vengeance. She needed him. He had to go to her. No matter how much time they had together it would never be enough. If there were only minutes, he'd honor them. Would treasure them, and then return to his mission. If she died in his arms, he had to savor those last precious moments with her.

Controlling his emotions, his elation, switching from murder to rescue, took a few seconds as he heaved in great breaths of air to bring his human mind to the surface.

Finish it! Zane said. *One of us is not walking away.*

Zane broke from the protection of his pack.

Peace. Calm. The clear understanding of Vic's place in his pack and the greater world of shifters stopped him. He'd never been more certain of anything. There'd be another time, another place for Zane's comeuppance. Now his mate needed him.

My mate is more important than you. We'll finish this another time. And you will die, Vic said. He raced away from the stunned group, his tail held high, without submission. He didn't run *away.* He sprinted *to* his beloved.

I'm here, Trista. I'm coming, Vic said, calling to her.

He arrived at the bivouac site Blaze had. The Ridge Runners wouldn't approach with so many Alpha Company wolves on guard.

Status, Blaze? Vic asked.

Internal injuries. She needs blood. Now, Blaze said.

Then let's go! Get a chopper her now!

She won't make it to a human hospital. I'm sorry, sir, Blaze said.

She can't die, Vic said as his breath panted in and out of him.

Panic filled him. Not *now.* She was safe now. She couldn't die. Placing his front paws up on the make-shift ambulance, he found Trista on her back, an IV in her arm, oxygen covering her face, her skin a ghastly gray color.

Jumping all the way into the small confines of the transport van, he approached her, sniffed her ear and licked her face, then lay his head on her chest and howled softly.

Her breathing quickened at his presence. She placed her hand on his head, stroked her fingers through his fur. In that position, he shifted.

Never more exposed. Never more vulnerable. On his knees, beside this woman whom he desperately wanted to save, desperately loved, desperately wanted to be his life-mate, he changed into the man he was.

Her hand paused during the shift, as his energy changed. Then her hand moved to his face and turned it toward her.

Those pain-filled green eyes of hers locked onto his and in them, he felt the wonder and the love she truly felt for him. "I knew you were different. I knew it was you outside my door. For days." Tears flowed down her face. Her chin trembled, and her breathing labored as she tried to talk. "Thank you," she whispered. "Thank you."

Save your energy. Don't talk now, Vic spoke in her mind.

I know I'm dying. I can feel it. I love you, Vic Stone. I just wanted to tell you again.

You can't die. Not now, Vic said.

Dread churned in his soul. This couldn't happen. Not after all they'd been through in such a short time.

You have to save me. Or let me die. I won't be a vegetable kept alive on a machine, she said.

Tell me what to do. I don't know what to do, Vic said.

I need blood. Give me yours, Trista said.

It could kill you.

It could save me.

She squeezed his hand. *Please. I love you, but if you don't love me, let me die now. Find another woman, another mate and go on,* she said.

You're so fragile.

I'll never be stronger. There isn't much time. I can feel it. I'm fading.

Vic stood and faced the males surrounding him, awaiting word, awaiting orders. Some in wolf form. Some in human form. All awaited their leader's guidance. The forest was alive with electricity.

"Flash, send for the chopper. Luke and Silver, get a fire going. We don't have time to get to the compound." The two hurried off. "Blaze, we need blood. Do you have any?"

"Yes, sir, but..." Blaze hesitated.

"What?" Vic asked.

"She needs *your* blood, sir. I can't guarantee what I have is yours," Blaze said.

"Get it ready. We'll use it if we have to," Vic said. He looked at the rest of the wolves. Some he recognized. Some he didn't. All were eager to help. Everyone knew this was a momentous occasion in the shifter community and the outcome would affect them all.

"The rest of you, set up a protective perimeter. Eros, you're in charge. Everyone reports to him," Vic said and kept his focus on Eros.

Eros, if this goes badly, I'm giving you orders to kill me. Take over the pack, Make it your own. Take care of Bragg, Vic said.

His second pivoted back to him, his eyes wide, mouth open in shock.

What? No!

Brother. Promise me, Vic said, begging for what only Eros could do.

Eros stilled as he stared into Vic's eyes. He nodded and held out his arm. They clasped arms as warriors.

I promise. My alpha. My brother, Eros swore the oath to Vic.

The energy and emotion pulsing from Eros was almost tangible. Right now, Vic could only focus on Trista. He removed the oxygen from her face. He kissed her bruised and battered lips. Kissed her black and swollen eye. He pulled his energy to a higher state, allowing it to flow out of him and into her through his hands on her face. He could heal some of the damage, to ease some of her pain, and take it on himself. He could take her pain better than he could watch her endure it.

"That's a little better," she said, her voice raw. "Thank you." He eased one arm behind her shoulders, one arm beneath her legs and picked her up. She curled her left arm into his chest, clung to him. Her head drooped onto his shoulder, and her hair hung in tangled waves, caked with blood, dirt and debris from her fight to survive.

Fury boiled like a raging storm inside him. He struggled to control it, to channel his rage into healing. "On my honor. With the souls of my ancestors to bear witness, I swear to you now. I will end him for you." Vic stepped from the van and his bare feet hit the dirt. He curled his toes into Mother Earth. Closing his eyes, he called to the power of earth energy, of healing, to pull inside him to heal Trista.

With his body as the conduit, he pushed away attempts the energy made to heal him. Everything was for her. First.

If she survived, then he would allow the energy to heal him.

He carried her to the fire that Luke and Silver had started. The heat of it blazed high and offered some comfort as the smoke wafted around their bodies. She'd begun to grow cold, and needed the warmth for her survival, more than he could give her from his body. One of the boys had placed a blanket close to the heat. Vic placed her carefully upon it, then lay down with her. He cradled her head on his shoulder, drawing her chest against his, and giving her as much of his body heat as possible. Another blanket was placed on top of them, sealing in the warmth.

Trista shivered as her body instinctively tried to generate heat and she opened her eyes.

"What's going to happen?" Her voice was so soft, so faint he strained to hear it, used his wolf hearing to understand it.

"I don't know, sweetheart. I've never done this before, only heard stories of it. From elders who are no longer with us," he said, shivers starting to overcome his body as well. By the gods, he hoped he'd remember all of it. He called to the spirits of the ancients to come to him now, fill him with their wisdom, carry him through.

Turning her face toward him, she licked her dry lips and reached for him. Tears again filled her eyes. *Kiss me again. Kiss me like you're never going to let me go,* she said.

I never will. He lowered his head and covered her mouth with his lips.

Filled with grief, knowing what he had to do to make this ceremony work, he focused on his love for her, not the sexual act required to fulfill the ritual. Right now, this union wasn't about sex, it was about survival and saving her life. Of keeping her on this plane as long as he could. He'd do what he had to do, though it wasn't the way he wanted to make love to her. He pulled her beneath him, breathed in her scent, connected with her mind, joined with her in the most psychic manner possible for a wolf and a human.

She accepted the deeper psychic connection that readied her body, and soul for him. Tears continued to fall from her eyes as she kept her gaze on his face. *I love you, Vic.*

Positioned between her thighs, he rose to his knees. With one hand, he lifted her hips upward and joined his body with her. She cried out as her body accepted him. He knew it wasn't pleasure in the way they had come together before. The perfection of their union had made him tremble, as man and as beast.

Pulling her upright onto his lap, he held her tight against his chest and her head dropped onto his shoulder.

The beast within him seemed to understand the need for care, the need for restraint and bowed to the human side of him. As needed, his teeth came in, but he forced back the rest of his animal. No harm would come to Trista. Not even from him.

He swept away her hair from her neck, exposing the vein pulsing frantically there, stirring his beast to rise again. A long, mournful howl rose within him.

By the gods, you are mine. I take you as my mate. For as long as we live, we are bonded. It is so. With the blessings of the ancients, it is so, Vic said. Fastening his mouth on her neck, he bit into her tender flesh. She cried out. His body reacted, pulsing, throbbing, shooting fire and electricity through him, centered in the juncture where they joined.

Her blood tasted so sweet on his tongue. So pure. So human. So *perfect*. He took only a mouthful and swallowed.

The sexual pressure in his body surged to a sharp peak. Gasping, he released her neck.

While his body throbbed in heightened desire, he used a claw to open a vessel at the base of his neck and guided her mouth to it.

Drink, my love. This bonds us forever. This will save you.

This was the moment that would save her life.

Or end it.

She turned her face to his neck. Slowly, her lips locked onto his wound, and she took in the healing essence contained in his blood. Clinging to him, she took in more. And more. In a powerful surge of transcendence, Vic released inside of her and cried out with the primal pleasure of it as he clutched her tightly against him.

The blood of his human *and* his beast flowed into her in pleasure and fulfillment, making Trista part of his body and his soul. Throwing her head back, she called out her sexual release and her nails dug into the flesh of his arms as she trembled. She held on, crying out with the power of the climax that consumed her.

Moving her gently to her knees, he rose behind her and entered her again as he would have done with a female wolf.

She lowered her shoulders, taking him in fully and the psychic bond between them fused when another climax overwhelmed her. It filled her mind, her heart and her soul. Her body clenched around him. Consumed with the pleasure their union gave her, and she cried out again and again, so her mate knew the satisfaction he gave her.

She cried out as the waves overpowered her. She cried out as the blood in her boiled. She cried out as she became his mate.

The gods and Vic's ancestors had blessed the union

between them, gifting them with a transformative experience that would bond them forever. No other could compare. No other would matter. Only each other.

Every muscle straining, the overwhelming orgasm that took over Vic's body pulsed inside Trista. Uncontrolled, his body pumped, and he clutched Trista's hips in his fingers, bringing her against him, drawing out the pleasure for both of them. He raised his face to the sky and howled his pleasure into the night. Nothing was as supreme as this moment when he'd joined with this female in the ceremony that tied them together forever.

Seconds later, howls of his pack and the Canyon Creek pack filled the air around him. The howling continued down through the canyons and up over the ridges, down arroyos and across the tops of the mountains, a chain of communication announced that the leader of the Alpha Company pack had taken his mate.

EIGHTEEN

The blades of the arriving chopper cut through the night air.

Vic collapsed beside Trista and cradled her against him, trying to muster the energy to hold her, to heal her, but the battle was rapidly being lost as stunning fatigue overcame his ability to create enough energy. He'd been through an endurance test of his own in the last few days, and his body gave up the fight.

"Sir, we need to get her on a stretcher," Blaze said and knelt beside them, but his words seemed so far away.

"Take her," Vic said, seeing his mate safety away before allowing anyone to help him. Muffled words surrounded him, and he felt Trista being eased away from him.

In what felt like seconds, Eros, Luke, Silver and Blaze placed him in the chopper beside Trista. He tried to connect with her. She was unconscious, her body trying to reject his blood. Her body raising its temperature to fend off what it perceived as a foreign invader.

Snatches of voices jarred him. Shards of light startled

257

him. Weightlessness as the chopper lifted off triggered him. He knew no more until hands roused him.

"Here. Drink this." Eros shoved a bottle of something under his nose Luke sat him up and held onto him.

"What is it?" he asked, he voice croaking.

"I don't know. Red Bulldozer or something. Blaze said you needed some fluids. This ought to jack you up in a hurry," Eros said.

Vic looked at the IV in his arm, becoming more conscious, more aware of his surroundings and realized he was home, in the infirmary. "That isn't enough?"

"No. Shut up and drink it." Eros put one finger on the bottom of the can and lifted it toward Vic's mouth.

Vic downed the noxious tasting drink as his mind awakened, and the full impact of the previous night hit him. His mind suddenly filled with flashing images. Fighting. Trista. Blood. Mating. Sweat.

His *mate*. He'd taken her as his mate. Had she survived the ordeal or had it been too much for her? Had she been in such a weakened condition that she'd succumbed to the ceremony? Searching quickly in his mind, he felt her nearby, but not in the infirmary.

"Where is she?" His breath huffed in an out, burning through his system as the oxygen lit him up, seared his body with healing energy.

"She's *your* fucking mate, dude. Shouldn't you know where she is?" Luke asked, simmering amusement on his face as his lips twitched upward.

"Eros. Kill him," Vic said and growled deep in his chest and his beast flashed in his eyes. "Now."

"Stand down!" Luke said, his eyes wide in panic. "Sir." Luke said and took the can of Bulldozer from Vic and drained the remainder.

"Put your fur down," Eros said. "She's fine. The females are with her and giving her some privacy from all the males who want to pay homage to their new alpha female."

"Okay. That's good," Vic said, then raised his brows and looked between Eros and Luke. "What females?"

"Canyon Creek," Eros said.

"You should see some of those females," Luke exclaimed. "They're very impressive, but I wouldn't want to take one on in a fight." Luke gave a whistle of admiration. "I'm just glad they're on our side."

Urgency overwhelmed him as he took in his next breath. He had to get to her. To see for himself. He threw his legs over the side of the metal table and struggled against the stars that obscured his vision. There was not time to be weak. No time to lay there like a weak pup. "I've got to see her." He stood and was yanked back by the IV still in his arm. "Get this out of me."

"Sir, you need the hydration," Blaze said and rushed forward, trying to stop Vic from bailing off the gurney.

"Yeah, you lost a lot of *fluids* last night," Dane said from the chair beside them. Their laughter surrounded him, teasing him, reminding him that he'd taken his mate last night.

"Oh. Shut. *Up!*" Luke howled at that, slapping a hand on his thigh. "Good one, bro'." He high-fived Dane.

"Fuck you. Every one of you." Vic reached for the IV. He was in no mood. If Blaze wouldn't do it, he'd rip the damned thing out himself.

"No, sir. Wait," Blaze said and grabbed his hands.

"Excuse me?" He narrowed his eyes at Blaze and growled low in his throat. "You forget yourself."

"No, sir. I mean...I'll take it out rather than you tear it

out." He dropped his gaze and cleared his throat. "You could damage the vessel. Sir."

"Do it. Fast. I need to see my mate," Vic growled through clenched teeth. Need filled him.

"Not like that you don't," Luke said, and Dane nodded, eyes wide in horror at Vic's statement.

"Like what?" Vic looked down at his body, then back at the males. Every body part necessary was intact. Just some bruises and scratches that would heal. "What's wrong?"

"You can't go see your mate for the first time stinking to high heaven." Dane stood. "You're going to shower, shave, and put some damned clothes on." Dane said that like he actually thought Vic was going to do it.

"Seriously? That's what you're worried about? Since when do you care how I smell?" Vic took the next Red Bull-dozer Eros handed him. With the heart of a wolf, he could handle it.

"We don't give a fuck how you smell, but the females do." Dane made a face and curled his upper lip. "They have standards, but I just don't get it."

"Your appearance and how you're received by your potential mate is important," Eros said. He crossed his arms over his chest and took a wide-legged stance in front of Vic, blocking him from going anywhere.

"What do you mean, my *potential* mate? We performed the ceremony last night. We're mated in front of the gods." Vic might not remember everything, but of that he was certain.

"Uh, not really," Luke said with a grimace. Something had happened.

"What does that mean?" Vic asked. Were they all out of their minds? "Didn't you all witness the ceremony?"

"Oh, yes, it was witnessed," Eros said. "And we all

witnessed that she was *under great duress* at the time you took her as your mate. The legality won't hold up to the council if she objects in the light of day. You know that. She could reject you now, and you'll be out on your ass. You'd better be on your best behavior when you see her for the first time, is what he means," Eros said, providing the synopsis of the situation.

"Oh. I see." He sipped from the can of go-juice, contemplating his next move. "I see what you mean. I kinda forgot about that clause. Busy saving her life." There was specific language written by the council to prevent alpha males from taking mates by force, threats, or *under great duress*. Never thought he'd fall into that category of restriction.

If Trista wanted to argue the legitimacy of the mating ceremony, there were ample witness to prove she'd had little choice when she'd agree to become his mate, and accept his blood. His own pack could provide proof against him if they chose to. Hell, Zane could even protest to the council, though he'd caused the *duress* situation in the first place. Vic would find a way to stick a knife between his ribs one day. The council would only censure Zane if there was ample evidence he'd deliberately caused trouble for other packs risking exposure to the humans.

Though his pack wouldn't want to, they could witness against him.

"Any sign of Zane?" Vic asked and swallowed more of the energy drink. He shivered, but whatever it was doing was waking him up.

"No. We sent scouts back to the area, and they're gone. Just smells like piss and blood," Eros said.

Vic relaxed a little at that report. At least that was one thing off his plate right now, but the situation with Trista was more precarious than it had ever been.

Fuck. This could destroy everything he'd worked for years for, building the pack. Bragg had just been returned to the pack, and this situation could ruin the homecoming Vic had hoped he'd have and deserved. This could end his relationship with Trista, and the love that stirred for her. Could ruin the hierarchy of the pack and the relationships he'd cultivated with other alphas in the area. Everything rested on one human female and her decision to accept him as her mate. Or *not*.

Eros wasn't fond of Trista. He'd made that abundantly clear from the beginning. Even he could contest the ceremony and take over the entire pack if he wanted to, though it had been offered to him last night.

"Everything's in your room. Then we'll take you to her," Dane said. He stood, then swayed a little, and sat down again. "Whoa. Guess I'll stay here for a bit longer." He waved a hand for them to go. "I'll catch up."

Blaze put a can of energy drink into Dane's hand. "Drink this."

"Awesome." Dane cracked the can open and slammed it down.

Before leaving the infirmary, Vic impatiently allowed Blaze to stitch up a few of the deeper gashes on his back, legs, and the self-inflicted one on his neck. Wouldn't do any good to take a shower and then bleed all over his clean clothes. The boys would make him start all over again. Though he could heal it in a few hours, the stitches would speed up the process. After shaving, showering alone with entirely too much time to think, he was desperately eager to see Trista. More than ready to see where his fate and their futures lay.

Nerves shot through his system, and he felt like a pup about to go on his first date with the prom queen. By the gods, he was shaking. How in the hell could he be an alpha, a leader, a commander of the greatest pack in the south-west, when he felt this out of control? The nerves of steel he'd been known for suddenly vacated. His hands were moist. His throat was dry. Even his beast hid in a deep, dark place. *Coward.*

Raising his hand to knock on her door, he paused, trying to get a sense of what was going on behind this door. Before he could figure that out, the door was yanked open by a very tall woman with angry, black eyes, a generous mouth and black hair that fell in wild waves over her shoulders.

"What?" She looked him up and down, didn't give him any quarter, no break because he was the alpha male of the pack. She held her position which barred him from entering the room. She had her duty, and she would see to it. Luke was right. Canyon Creek pack was fierce.

"I'm the alpha here, and I've come to see my mate," he said. By the gods, he was going to see Trista or this female's fur was going to be yanked out by the roots in a few seconds.

"Really?" The tall female with dark eyes and heavy eye makeup, placed one strong hand on a hip, and took a stance, looking at him in disbelief, raking her cool gaze over him and raised one high-arched brow. "What makes you think she's in here?"

"It's okay, Bobbie. You can let him in." Trista's tired voice came from within. The strength of her scent came to him. It was different than it had been yesterday. Had she been changed that much?

"Are you sure? He looks pretty mangy," Bobbie said and chewed her gum, blowing a bubble and popping it as she looked him over again.

"What do you mean, *mangy*? I'm at my best right now," Vic said, trying not to sound like Luke who obsessed over his appearance more than any of them. Though he wore his typical black shirt and camo pants, he was as proper as he could be. Dating rituals were pretty basic among wolves. If you liked each other, that was all you needed.

A small smile lifted one corner of her ruby lips. "Indeed."

Bobbie backed up a few steps and pulled the door wide, granting him entrance with a flourish of her hand.

He took one stepe, then stopped. The entire room was filled with females. All of them watched him, their golden glowing eyes following him, checking him out, assessing and wondering if he could satisfy his mate in the way she needed. Sexually and in all other ways. He could hear their voices, their questions, their speculation.

Is he as good as he looks?

Can he really satisfy her?

How big do you think that cock of his is?

The real question is, does he know how to use it?

Does he know how to use his tongue? That's what I wanna know!

Wonder if he'd take on two mates? That's legal, right?

Ignoring them all, he pushed the chatter out of his mind. He focused on Trista. She leaned back against the headboard, her long legs stretched out in front of her. Rico lay on the bed beside her, guarding her, his eyes intent, his nose working to scent out any danger and wondering what was going on with so many others present. Trista was pal. Dark circles hung beneath her eyes, and she looked like she'd been beaten up. If she were pure werewolf, she'd have healed her injuries by now. He'd hoped his blood would heal her faster than it had. Maybe the blood exchange hadn't been successful, or hadn't been enough, and she was still mostly human.

Trying to find their special psychic link, he wanted to push all the females away and link up with Trista, but she pushed him back. Obviously, she wasn't fully human with that response. She was a worthy mate. If only she'd accept him. This female was strong and totally deserved to be the alpha female. If something happened to him, she could take over the pack and it would thrive. Of that he had no doubt. A pulse of pleasure surged through him.

"What have you done to me, Commander?" She crossed her arms over her chest and gave him a hard, green-eyed stare. The set of her fine jaw bespoke her stubborn nature and left him no easy out. He had to answer her to her satisfaction or it would all end right here. Everything they'd created together would be over.

"I saved your life," he said simply.

"Is that what you did?" The tilt of her head and the tone of her voice, more than her words, bespoke her doubt.

"Yes," he said.

"I wanted you to *save* me, not turn me into a wolf," she said, her eyes sparkling with anger.

"It was the only way. You would have died without my blood." He took another step forward. "Even with the chopper, we couldn't have gotten you to help I time."

"Then you should have let me die," she whispered, her voice cracking with emotion.

"I couldn't." He'd taken an oath to protect and by the gods, he'd protected her.

"Why not? I asked you to save me or let me die and you didn't." A curious light shone in her eyes as she stared at him. And waited.

He hesitated to speak with so many witnesses. So many

females. So much estrogen. "We need to speak privately," he said, his intention clear. He wanted them out of there.

"What you have to say can be said now. They stay," Trista said. She looked around the room at the female warriors who surrounding her. "You've brought me a clan of new sisters, and I thank you for that. But you've yet to win my approval." Tears glistened in her eyes. "Or my understanding," she said.

Irritation formed in his gut, and his beast gave a low growl of warning. Even it knew when to back off. "I couldn't let you die...because I love you. You were the one destined to be my mate. The gods tried to tell me, but I wouldn't listen, and it almost cost you your life. For that, I am sorry." Pain burned in his chest as he said the words. He'd never been more vulnerable with a woman, or anyone, than he was at this moment.

"Your mate? You're out of luck pal. I'm no one's *mate*. Not like this," she said and sat bolt upright. For a second, he thought her eyes changed to her beast, but after she blinked, they were green again. "I'm sprouting fur in places there shouldn't be fur, Vic." She huffed out a breath.

Bobbie cast a stony stare at Vic, then patted Trista's arm in a comforting gesture. "Don't worry, baby. We'll take care of you. One of my females does a fantastic wax job," Bobbie said with a nod and gentle eyes settled on Trista's face. "You won't even notice it."

"Thanks, honey. I appreciate it," Trista said, her voice gentle as she spoke to Bobbie. For a second, he wondered how in the world they had bonded so quickly, then then decided he didn't want to know.

Females.

"If you don't accept me as your mate, then I can't take another. You can take another mate, but I'll be banished and alone. You don't know what it will do to the structure of this pack, and the other packs in the area," he said with a sigh, laying it all on the line. Everything was in her hands. Everything came down to this moment. He had to trust her as he'd trusted no female ever before, not even his mother.

"He's bullshitting you, baby," Bobbie said and glared at Vic again. "He's not that important. We'd find someone who could lead better than he's done," she said and snapped her gum for emphasis.

Trista placed a hand on Bobbie's arm. "I'll listen to what he has to say," she said, then looked at Vic and held his gaze. The others in the room seemed to fade away. "Tell me more." She cleared her throat and seemed to gain control of her emotions. "As I'm new to this...world, please fill me in."

He became aware of the arrival of his males behind him. His brothers. At least there was some solidarity for him in the room.

Eros. Luke. Silver. Dane. All stood at his back. They always would, but these were highly unusual circumstances. His men, the wolves of Alpha Company, may be forced to do things they didn't want to do. For the good of the pack, they'd do it and howl out their misery as they tore him limb from limb, scattering his bones in the desert.

"Alpha Company will collapse. They'll be compelled by the laws of the treaty, the decision of the council, to force me out. Or kill me. You became my mate under great duress, and that can be contested if you choose. But you will not, cannot, return to being fully human again. That part cannot be undone," he said and waited.

"What? That's so not right." She crossed her arms over her chest now, and he could feel the prickly irritation on their psychic link as she released the stranglehold she had on it. It took her anger, her sense of injustice, to open it to him. At least it was something. "So, if I don't accept you as my mate...God, I can't believe I'm even saying that...then it's a death sentence for you?" Anger and exasperation flared in her eyes. "That's not much of a choice either, is it?"

The atmosphere in the room sharpened, tightened, as everyone waited for his answer. Even the beast in him quieted, subdued by her energy. His honor demanded he answer her with truth.

"Correct."

"Well, that's just stupid," she said. She planted her feet on the floor and stood, then reached out for Bobbie's hand to steady herself. "Whoa." She raised a hand to her forehead. The spinning dizziness in her mind flashed to him and for a few seconds, he saw stars.

"Tell that to the council," Vic said, admiring her sass, while he feared what her temper could do. His brows twitched in amusement. He'd love to see this female give those aged and narrow-minded council members a talking-to. So many things must change to keep up with current times and she could be the one to make it happen. With him. He'd be so proud to stand beside her.

"I'll be happy to. Where are they?" Taking a few deep breaths, she regained her balance and equilibrium.

"Uh, they're wolves, too. They're in their summer grounds in the mountains," Vic said.

She took in a startled gasp and stepped closer to him. "Just how many werewolves are there here?" Her heart raced with anxiety, and he could feel her opening up to him, to the others and releasing the choke hold she'd had on their psychic link.

He turned to Dane who leaned against the dresser,

looking pale, but strong enough to check out the generous chest of one of the curvy females nearby.

"Dane." Vic repeated to get Dane's attention.

"What?" He dragged his gaze back to the situation at hand and realized he'd been caught staring. He stood upright. "Sorry, sir." He cleared his throat. "Uh, what was the question again?"

"My mate wants to know how many shifters are in the area," Vic said and kept his gaze locked on Trista.

"At last count, twenty, sir." Dane's gaze shifted to Trista. "I mean, my alpha female."

"Well, that's not so bad, I guess." She sighed in relief and the tension in her eased.

"Uh...thousand, that is." Dane clarified with a weak smile.

"Twenty...thousand... *Seriously*?" A sudden sheen of sweat glazed Trista's face, neck and hands. Panic made her heart flutter, and he felt the echo of it in his own chest.

"Yes, ma'am." Dane nodded. "We take a loose census every few years or so, but with some packs being more mobile than other, it's hard to get an accurate count."

"Oh. My. God." She looked at Vic, her eyes fastened on him as this new information sank into her brain. "Where have I been living? Under a rock?" She jumped and clawed at her neck where a number of bristly hairs sprouted. "Dammit!"

"Maybe some depilatory cream would be useful, too," Bobbie whispered.

Vic had to keep the topic on hand, and he growled at Bobbie, who glared back at him, unaffected by his displeasure. "Humans simply see what they want to see. You just saw a group of military men working with wolves," Vic said.

A calmness, a deadly focus spread through her. Her heart rate slowed, her breathing evened out. Even the nervous impulses he sensed slowed as she focused intently on him. By the gods, the female was going to be a predator. Arousal shot through him as he focused on her intensity. She was an amazing female. How had he not known this before? Vic scoffed at himself. He'd been a fucking idiot, that's how. Even the males around him had known she was the one for him before he did. So much for being the leader of the greatest shifter pack in the southwest. He should just let them kill him now for being so stupid.

"I see. So, everything I know about you, or thought I knew about you has all been a lie?" That green-eyed stare shot right to the heart of him. It all came down to this moment. This decision. This beat of her heart.

Silence filled the room. Trista looked at Bobbie who nodded to the other females, and they retreated. His males did the same, easing from the room now to give them the privacy they needed.

Vic approached Trista. She fell into the overstuffed chair beside the bed, her energy now low. Without a word, he dropped to his knees in front of her, not touching her, not trying to reach out to their psychic link, not trying to influence her decision in any way.

Now, he was just a male. Wanting his female. Wanting her to accept him. To move forward with her by his side.

"No. Everything you know about me that's important is true," he said.

"Except that you're a werewolf," she said and raised a brow.

"Except that," he said, admitting biggest thing he hid from her.

270

"What do I know about you that's real?" she asked, tears filling her eyes.

"I've been crazy about you since we met. When we kissed the first time, I saw stars. I knew you were the one, but I resisted it. I had so many responsibilities that required my attention and there wasn't room for a female. Or that's what I thought." Vic swallowed, choked down the emotions that threatened to spill over. "When I looked into your eyes and saw the sass, the smarts, the female deep inside you. Everything you are stirs the male in me, and my beast." He shook his head, trying not to touch her, trying not to reach out to her. Trying to hide his fear. "When you were taken it was your scent, and our mental connection that enabled me to find you," he said. "I've never been more scared in all my life. Not in wars. Not in battles. Never."

Unable to resist the pull of her, resist the pain in her eyes, resist the temptation of her, he placed his hands on her warm thighs, needing that physical connection with her. If only one more time before she kicked him out on his ass.

"That's it? That's all you have to say?" Her expression on the outside was unreadable, but on their link, he felt the easing of her tension, the pleasure she derived from his words. The need for him to say more.

He placed his hands on the arms of the chair and leaned closer to him and she let him. "When I go to bed, I want you beside me. When I reach out in the night I want to find you soft and sweet beside me. When I reach for you, bring you closer, and you close the gap between us, it makes me want you all the more." He paused and awaited her reaction.

"Go on." She touched his leg with her bare foot and tapped him. "Don't stop now." Imperiously, she arched her brows.

A smile flashed across Vic's face as she raised her nose a prim notch in the air. Wooing an alpha female was risky, but he wanted her, needed her, and she needed him in the same way. Her resistance was fading. Parting her knees with his hands, he leaned closer, easing into her space, deliberately pushing her a little, stretching those boundaries she was slowing removing. The heat of her reached out to him, and on their link he accepted her touch and held on. "When we're connected, when I'm inside you, when you open yourself to me, there's nothing else that will bring me to my knees faster," he whispered.

Tears overflowed, and she leaned forward, placing her hands on either side of his face. "Victor Stone. Commander. *Wolf*? Love of my life. I accept you as my mate," she said, giving him her acceptance as mate.

Vic hugged her tight, then pulled back. He lifted his face up and yipped his excitement. The others knew what that meant. Trista had accepted him. From the hall and downstairs, cheers and howls erupted as the packs celebrated.

The bonding was complete and legal.

At least in the world of wolves.

NINETEEN

"We've got to get you ready. The ceremony is in less than an hour, and you're hardly ready," Bobby said. She clucked her tongue and fussed over Trista's appearance, touching up her makeup, while Kiki, Ginger and Lupé stressed over her hair, dress and patches of fur that continued to sprout in unusual places at the oddest of times.

"I'm ready on the inside, that's what matters most, right?" Trista asked. Inside, she was a frightened little girl, not knowing what was going to happen to her, feeling as if she were being handed off to some dreadful ogre in a fairy tale. But she knew better. As she thought of Vic, and how he'd humbled himself for her, her heart tumbled in her chest and her pheromones shot into overdrive.

Bobbie said and sniffed the air and waved a hand in front of her nose. She raised her heavy brows and gave Trista a warning. "You'd better reel that in, too, baby."

"Reel in what?" A nervous laugh bubbled out of her.

If I can smell your lust for your mate, so can everyone

else. You could turn this ceremony into a furry orgy if you're not careful," Bobby said, and the other females laughed.

"Seriously?" Trista asked, wide-eyed.

"Mm-hmm." Bobby pressed her lips together and continued to touch up the makeup on Trista's eyes. "Like you weren't just thinking of your mate and how hot you are for him?"

"How could you know that?" Trista whispered, fascinated at the powers these females had.

"We *all* know it, baby," Kiki said and blew out a breath, then fanned her face with her hand. "Hot stuff."

"The heat in you shot up about fifty degrees," Lupé said as she pushed a curl into place. "I could see it."

Ginger struck a hip out, put a hand on it. She was the epitome of a pin-up girl with flaming red hair and curves that didn't stop. "If we can smell it on you, honey, then everyone will. Just try not to think of that hunk of wolf you're marrying and concentrate on keeping your beast locked in a cage." She shrugged and checked out her fingernails. "At least for the time being." She belted out a bawdy laugh. "I'd love to be there when you let her out though. Whew. I'll bet there'll be some howling going on when you take him the first time as your mate."

The other females joined in the bawdy laughter, and Trista had to admit it was funny. The conversation distracted her from her thoughts and she relaxed.

"You most certainly are not going to be there when I do," Trista said. She looked at herself in the mirror and was startled to see her normal reflection staring back. On the inside, she'd changed so much, felt so different, she was certain it would show on the outside. "Who knows? I may sprout fur the first time I have an orgasm," she said.

The females laughed and joined her in the joke. She

loved that they were so easy to be around, so quick to accept her as one of their own and to fill her in on the trials and tribulations of being a female wolf in these modern times.

"Or your nose might shoot out." Lupé slapped a hand on her thigh and high-fived Kiki.

"Or your claws could come in," Ginger said and winced. "That could hurt."

"Okay, okay. Enough razzing. I don't want her to mess up my excellent paint job," Bobbie said, put down the makeup brushes. She inspected Trista's face, hair, down over the deep red dress she wore that accentuated her curves and hinted at feminine secrets behind the fabric. Bobbie nodded. "You'll do."

"Do? Are you kidding?" Ginger stood upright, her hackles raised. "She's gorgeous!"

"Every male in the grove is going to be standing at attention when they see her," Kiki gave Bobbie a glare. "Do. My. Ass."

"Okay. Okay. Ladies, enough," Trista said, wanting them calm for the ceremony.

Bobbie snorted and the others chuckled. "Ladies? How long have you known us?"

"Uh, three days now. Why?" Trista asked.

"In that time, have you seen any of us behave remotely *lady like*?" Ginger asked.

Trista thought a second, then grinned. "No. I have not."

"There you go. How about you just call us *females* or our names. *Ladies* gives me the willies," Ginger said and gave a delicate shiver.

"Okay, then. *Females*, let's get out of here. I'm ready to marry my mate," Trista said and took a breath, ready to leave the room and bond to her mate again, this time in a civil ceremony that satisfied her needs.

The female entourage left the security of the big house. The day was a little cool, a perfect New Mexico day with glorious blue skies overhead and a light breeze that lifted a strand of Trista's hair to tease her cheek.

A strong and silent male approached her. His face impassive, he looked her over from head to her bare feet that peeked out from beneath the hem of her dress. He took a deep breath and bowed in his formal military dress. The beret he always wore had been cleaned and starched and fit him to perfection.

The severity of this male would never change. The honor in him would never change. The pain in his heart would never die. Even without being fully in command of her powers, she knew that. Had known it since she'd first met him. The man wore his heart, his emotions, on his sleeve, and they bled with raw pain.

The clean-shaven cheeks accentuated the strength of his jaw, the firmness of his mouth revealed his dedication to his commander, and the formal posture showed his commitment to his task.

"Are you ready, my alpha female?" Eros asked, his voice strong and solid in her world that rapidly tilted on its axis.

"Yes." She cleared her throat. "Are you sure you're okay with walking me down the aisle?" she asked and looked into his dark, dark eyes. As Vic's second, he took on many responsibilities to help the commander of Alpha Company, but she didn't want to come between them. There would be times when she stepped fully into her role as the alpha female when they could clash. For now, she was content to lean on Eros a little, if he was willing to offer his strength to her.

"I'm honored to present the alpha female to the alpha male today," he said. In deference to her newly elevated status in the pack, he gave one slow nod and offered his left arm to her.

Taking a steadying breath, she tucked her hand beneath his arm. This man who had been standoffish, outright hostile to her at times, now stood solid beside her, offering her his support, his acceptance of her and her position. Emotions she couldn't name hummed through her heart. The day was overly full with them.

"Thank you, Eros. I know this hasn't been easy for you. I appreciate your support," she said.

For a moment, he said nothing, his face impassive as he looked down at her. Maybe it was the new senses she was learning about, developing, or just her own feminine intuition, but something in him eased, loosened a little at her words.

"There has been no alpha female as beautiful or as strong as you." Eros said the words to her as the sun shone down on them through the tops of the trees. "You bring honor to this pack. To Vic."

Tears pricked her eyes at the words that he didn't have to offer to her. "Thank you," she whispered.

"Dry your eyes, alpha female. Come and marry your mate. He's waiting for you with considerable impatience," Eros said, his humor dry, but correct.

A soft laugh rolled out of her at his words and the tension in her shoulders eased. "I'm certain he is." Squaring her shoulders and taking a deep breath, she gave an regal nod. "Let's go end his torture," she said.

The four-legged shadow, Rico, hurried toward her and sat at attention by her side, ever her protector. With a snap of her fingers, he was on his feet and ready to go. Though *canis lupus familiaris* and not *canis lupus*, his silent strength offered her comfort as well. This was a day she'd never forget, and her new friends, all of them, helped to guide her path forward.

Eros escorted her across the compound to a grove, a copse of trees where the men ate, entertained other packs, made bonfires and honored the pagan gods. The area had been cleaned up from their last event, party lights had been strung through the trees, and tables strained under the weight of food and drink. Even a keg sat in a tub of ice.

Dane and Luke stood guard beside the beer, looking serious and sharp in their dress blues. On the periphery of her vision, maybe it was the wolf eyes she'd heard about, she viewed shifters on patrol. They protected the sanctity of the ceremony from unwanted intruders or from the Ridge Runners who might stage a *coup* while everyone was occupied in celebration.

People, wolves, stood as she approached the circle. Everywhere she looked, there were people she was coming to know as shifters. Still coming to terms with the world that had changed madly around her, at least her perception of the world she knew had changed. She clung to Eros's arm and hoped she didn't fall on her face. In this moment she felt like a princess in a fairy tale, uncertain of her future beyond this day as she trembled on the verge of a new life.

She thought of her family who couldn't be present. Her brother was somewhere on a mission. There was no way for her to contact him. No way for him to be here, even if she wanted him to be. Her mother would have loved to have fussed over her the way the females had, but her mother couldn't be trusted to keep a secret, so there was no way she could come to the compound. *Ever.*

One day, Trista would explain something to them. One

day she hoped to see them again and reconnect with the family she'd left behind when she'd come to New Mexico. Seeing everyone around her, this new family of hers, made her want to reach out to her own. She would when the time was right. Now, she had a duty to learn and a new role to step into.

As she walked barefoot across the grove, sparks of electricity crackled as she reached out to the earth, drawing energy from it into her body, the way she remembered Vic doing on the night he'd saved her life. Was it just three days ago? It seemed like a lifetime yet only a moment ago. Now, there was a real physical connection to the earth, to nature, that she'd never known, and one she'd already begun to cherish. Tastes, sights, smells all sharpened to a new depth of sensation. She saw the world through new eyes in a way she never could have imagined.

When she looked forward, past the shifters to the center of the grove, her heart paused, then fluttered wildly in her chest. Unable to stop it, unable to control it, a swell of pheromones shot through her system at the site of her mate standing in the center of his pack, looking strong, handsome, powerful and outrageously sexy in his dress blues. Today, he also wore a beret befitting his position as commander of Alpha Company and alpha male of his pack. He could never be one without being the other.

Part of him would always be human. Part of him would always be wolf. The two parts of him blended perfectly together to challenge her beliefs, her heart and her love.

The fluttering in her chest wouldn't stop, and the beast within her that was emerging from the blood exchange with Vic, now roared to life. Howling inside, it cried out her emotions as Trista neared her mate, whom she would stand beside the remainder of this life.

The rest of the grove, the people and wolves around them disappeared from her vision as she looked at Vic. The world faded to just the two of them. The icy blue eyes remained unchanged, his face as strong and handsome as it had ever been, though a few more scratches and scars added to the beauty of him.

"Trista." Vic leaned over and pressed his cheek to hers, pressed a kiss to her lips, inhaled her fragrance. "You're beautiful. More beautiful than I could have imagined."

"It's the ladies, the *females*, who've made me beautiful," she said, correcting herself. The hot flush of desire and pleasure at his words surged through her. She relinquished Eros's arm and accepted Vic's. The warmth of Vic by her side ignited her sensuality, set fire to her core, and shot rockets of desire through her system.

"Hardly. You are worthy to be my mate. You match me in temperament, in passion and in your heart," he said.

"Vic, we haven't even exchanged our vows, and you're going to make me cry," she whispered. Since her change, emotions simmered at the surface.

"I'm sorry." He raised her hand from his arm and brought her hand to his lips, kissed the back of it gently, breathing in her scent. "My baser nature is on overdrive today," he said. He leaned closer and his lips against her ear raised goosebumps across her spine, her neck and her breasts. "I want to have you all to myself. *Very soon.*" The timbre of his voice sent chills of desire across her spine.

"Patience, my mate. We have guests," she said, deftly reminding him of their position. They weren't just a bride and groom exchanging vows in front of friends. Theirs was a union that had huge political implications to the entire southwest. "And a few council members to charm before you can unleash your beast on me," she said.

Turning to Eros, she pulled him closer and kissed his cheek. "Thank you." Nothing more had to be said.

Together she and Vic faced the clergyman who'd been *commandeered* from the military organization that the Alpha Company was associated with. His calendar hadn't included a werewolf wedding ceremony, but under the influence of a few of the Alpha Company members, he'd relented and agreed to officiate. The high ball glass in his hand trembled.

"Today, the hearts of these two, Trista and Victor, join together to create a new life," he started, calling everyone's attention to them.

The voice of the human man faded away as she looked into Vic's eyes. His wolf eyes flashed golden, and her vision changed briefly as her wolf acknowledged him.

After the words, the ceremony, smiling and being introduced to hundreds of people she knew she'd never remember the names of, they feasted on elk, deer, and other wild game. She ate enough to fill her belly and then some. As the sun leaned toward the horizon, she touched Vic on the arm as fatigue overwhelmed her. "I'm ready."

"You're exhausted," he said and placed his hand over hers. For a few seconds, she felt his energy seep into her as he shared his greater strength with her. "You should have said something sooner." He placed a hand around her waist and drew her against him, giving her his support and strength.

"I didn't want to offend anyone. I'm not sure the proper protocols yet," she whispered. Who knew what protocols she'd have to learn?

"You almost died a few days ago. They'll understand," he said. He made the wolf-equivalent sound of clucking his tongue at her. "You're the alpha female. You can do whatever you want to," he said.

"That's right. I am, aren't I?" she asked. The title was going to take some getting used to, but she'd do it. She'd do it all for Vic. For them.

"Come with me and let's go inside," Vic said. Without further preamble, Vic swept her up into his arms. With a squeal of surprise, she clasped onto his neck.

The sudden action got the attention of the surrounding guests who began to cheer, calling out ribald and unhelpful suggestions of what Vic should be doing to his bride in the next few minutes.

As Vic carried her into the house, a chorus of many howls and yips followed them.

"Seems everyone is pleased with our union," Vic said and carried her up the stairs to his bedroom and paused at the doorway.

"How can you tell?" She was going to have to get better at reading wolf behavior and fast.

"Hear those howls and vocalizations out there?" Vic asked.

"Yes. It's hard not to," she said.

"If they didn't approve, there would be silence," he said.

"I see," she said and dropped her gaze to his mouth. She brought his face closer to her, sniffing in his scent and for a second or two, she understood how powerful her abilities were going to be.

"You're looking at me like you're no longer exhausted," he said.

"I'm not."

Vic swallowed, looked into her eyes and pressed his lips to hers for a tender kiss that was all too short. "Shall I take you to bed, then, my alpha female?"

"Please."

She turned the doorknob before Vic kicked in the door. He strode straight from the doorway and fell backwards with her onto the massive four-poster bed, kissing and touching, pulling and tugging at her clothing.

A laugh bubbled out of her as she looked around the room in awe. "Look at this place. Oh my God. Just look at it," she said.

Vic eased the hem of her skirt upward, revealing her shapely legs to his gaze and hands. "I'd rather look at *this* place." His hand grazed between her legs, his fingers tugging at the fragile lace covering her body from his view.

"Vic." She grabbed him by the face and kissed him. "Someone went to a lot of trouble for us. The least we could do is see what they've done," she said.

Vic raised his gaze from his bride to look around the room at the candles, the flowers picked from the surrounding forest and desert, the mound of sweet-smelling hay on the floor.

"It's beautiful, but I'm more interested in you right now," he said.

"Let me just wash up a bit." Rising from the bed that had been turned down to reveal fantastically soft sheets, she kissed his forehead. "I'll be right back. I'm a little worse for wear."

Vic kissed her hand and escorted her to the bathroom where his large tub had been filled with fragrant steaming water. Candles flickered on every surface and cast a warm glow on everything.

"Oohh," Trista said in a hushed voice. "It's so beautiful."

"Don't take too long." He removed the beret and placed it on top of his dresser.

Trista looked through the doorway at the tub and chewed her lip in indecision. As the alpha female she could dictate anything she wanted to, right? She was about to give her first decree. "Join me. There's room for two."

Vic clasped her face in his hands and brought her mouth to his. With parted lips, he devoured her, the silky glide of his tongue across hers, the heat of his mouth threatened to set her on fire.

They stripped each other, their clothing landing in piles on the floor. Vic picked her up and set her feet first into the tub, then joined her, sloshing water over the sides of the claw-foot tub. He leaned back against the porcelain. Trista knelt between his legs, her bared body proud and unashamed at having her scars revealed to him. He knew they were present, so any attempt to hide them were futile.

This is who she was now, and she was proud of it.

His gaze roamed over her face, over her hair that still held its coiffure, across the scratches and healing wounds on her neck. Slashes crossed her breasts and stirred his ire. His gaze lingered on her breasts and her nipples tightened. His gaze continued downward over her abdomen and the claw marks there. His jaw tightened slightly at the blatant reminder of how she'd nearly died not long ago at the hands of his worst enemy. Staying in the moment, he focused on her hips and the juncture of her thighs.

"There are too many bubbles," he said and scooped them away. "I can't see all of you."

Her body was so ready for him, she now regretted the suggestion of the bath. The water stirred as he raised his hands to her breasts and teased her nipples with his thumbs. Closing her eyes, she reveled in the sensations he created in her, wanted more of them, wanted to join with him right now.

As her husband.

As her mate.

Easing forward, she reached for the rim of the tub and lowered her body until her breasts touched his chest. His erection pressed against her lower abdomen and a pulse of reaction shot through her core. She would never tire of her physical reaction to him.

"You please me, mate." Vic slid his hands down her back to cup her ass, bringing her fully against him, adjusted his legs between hers so that hers rested outside of his, giving her the greater control and power over him.

"You please me as well. Husband." Wrapping her arms around his neck, she kissed him deeply, tenderly, wanting to crawl inside of him, to revel in the sensations he teased to the surface in her as no other had.

The tender kiss evolved as mouths slanted across each other, hands reached for body parts beneath the water.

Vic pulled her hips up higher and eased her body down onto the tip of his cock, not taking it any farther. His ragged breathing matched hers. His erratic heart rate raced in time with hers. His psychic connection to her melded with hers and opened her mind, her soul, her body to him in a way they'd never connected before.

Are you ready?

Yes.

Vic eased her down. Trista gasped as the sensations of fullness, of completion, of perfection as her body accommodated him.

Together they moved. Vic pressed his fingers into her hips and led their dance. Trista sat upright and thrilled in the sensations he stirred in her. On fire, she felt the beast of Vic nudging to gain entrance to her inner sanctum, to where her beast now lived.

It's okay to let it in.

I'm afraid.

I'll keep you safe.

Loosening the control of their link, she allowed Vic's beast to enter her. She gasped as the size of him filled her mind, her body, her soul.

Are you okay?

Unable to speak, overwhelmed by the experience, she nodded. As she gained strength from him and rocked her hips in time with his, her beast, newly emerged, rose to its feet to greet Vic's.

Their inner beasts gained familiarity as Vic and Trista rocked against each other.

Vic brought his hands to her breasts and caressed her. A groan escaped her throat as sensations rose to the edge. Leaning back, she rode him harder, deeper.

Take me home, my mate.

You are my home.

On the edge of fulfillment, Vic took her into the abyss of pleasure. Her release peaked as their beasts came together.

Crying out her pleasure, she rocked against Vic, using his body, joining with his emotions and his love, he let her to take what she wanted, what she needed from him.

His body responded, and he arched his back as the strength of their pairing overwhelmed him, overpowered his control, and he exploded, spilling his power into her.

Trista fell forward, her energy spent and renewed at the same time as she collapsed onto Vic's chest. Her focus had narrowed to just the two of them. As she recovered, she rubbed her face against his like a female wolf would do with her mate.

Low howls began outside. A chorus rose in the night as wolf after wolf joined its voice to the others. Howls rose inside the house, outside their window, everywhere. Wolf voices rose together, carried on the wind to celebrate with Vic and Trista.

Alpha Company was complete.

*****

IF YOU ENJOYED THIS BOOK, please give a review wherever you purchased Alpha Wolf at. Authors are dependent on reader review to get the word out to other readers and your input is invaluable.

Thanks in advance for taking the time to leave a review. You're awesome!

Love,

Sierra

CHAPTER 20
OTHER BOOKS BY SIERRA WOODS

W olf Royale
Wolf Song

CHAPTER 21

FREE BOOK

Dear Readers,
Here's one more shameless plug to get your free book and sign up for my newsletter.

This is Gigi's story, *Always A Wolf*. She's a side character that occurs in book two. She's an older wolf, but she's not dead yet!

If you click the link here, you'll be taken to where you can download this book for free and to sign up for my newsletter.

I appreciate you all.

Love,

Sierra Woods

CHAPTER 22
SNEAK PEAK OF BOOK 2- WOLF ROYALE

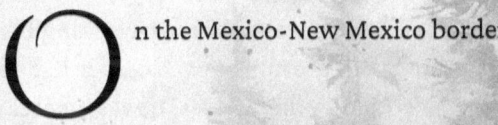

On the Mexico-New Mexico border

Chapter 1

Three members of Alpha Company hunkered down in a foxhole in the ground. Hot. Tired. Thirsty. Sweat burning his eyes, Eros was ready to beat something up. Or someone. Didn't know what. Didn't care what. Something had to go. Something had to give, or he would implode. The temper of a wolf was volatile at best. Put one in a hole with two idiots?

It was gonna get ugly.

Someone had to pay for keeping him away from home for three days straight in a dugout with Luke and Dane, smelling their sorry asses every second of the day. With no wind, not a hint of a breeze, it was like sitting in a cesspool of wolves, humans and dirt.

As a wolf, he wouldn't have minded so much. Wolves

loved the dirt, the coolness of it, the intricate smells. Unfortunately, in his human form, the whole thing sucked. His clothing stuck to him, his boots hurt his feet, and he was pretty sure he'd sat on a fucking ant hill last night.

The three of them were supposed to be on recon, supposed to be gathering intel on the Ridge Runner pack, the gang of rival shifters currently causing chaos and problems throughout New Mexico. The kind of chaos that could get them all killed by bringing too much attention to the secret groups and clans of shifters living in the area. All shifter groups maintained a strict code of ethics, maintained their secrecy above all things. Secrets, layers of them, ensured the safety of all. If they wanted to survive mingling alongside and entwined with the human world, they had to blend in, not draw attention to themselves. It was a necessity all shifter groups practiced in the modern age. Except for the Ridge Runners.

With their outrageous behavior, the Ridge Runners had blown secrecy all to hell. For everyone. Someone had to rein the delinquents in. Someone had to trip them up. Someone had to silence them before they silenced everyone else. And Alpha Company was going to do it.

That Eros' alpha had decreed they would end the Ridge Runners, was just one more reason to hate Zane Cavalier and his pack of furry idiots. They'd caused more chaos in the last year than all of the other shifter groups combined. Even the coyotes were more well-behaved than the Ridge Runners, and that was saying something about that lot of mischief-makers.

By the gods, Eros wanted to be done with this mission, pack all their gear, go home and curl up in front of the fire with a glass of brandy and a good cigar. Except he didn't smoke. And he didn't like brandy all that much either. But the sentiment felt good.

Plinking noises caught his attention as dribbles of moisture dropped onto his Gore-Tex jacket from the sky overhead. People thought it didn't rain in the desert. If that were the case, what the hell was falling out of the sky? It sure wasn't tequila.

Eros ground his teeth and closed his eyes, trying to push down the beast that wanted to break free and leap out of this hell hole.

They *had* to be doing this recon right in the middle of monsoon season. When it rained, it poured buckets onto unsuspecting citizens below. Then the skies cleared up and the sun beat down on a body to scorch and cook it. Desert temperatures dropped significantly after dark and cold, damp clothing turned to wet blankets.

Hell had frozen over and it was called the high desert.

After Dane's injury on the last assignment, Eros and the commander, Vic Stone, had decided to give him a try on this one. Dane had recovered and rested enough, so it was time to get his ass moving. When in wolf form, he'd been knifed in the gut, nearly eviscerated, underwent an operation and the vet had wanted to neuter him, too. Fortunately, Vic, had intervened on that point before she took the blade to him.

Dane, ever the crack up, always the first one to be ready for a mission, just wasn't himself, wasn't up to his usual self and that worried the commander. Worried Eros. Dane was their brother in arms, and teeth. Nothing was going to stop Alpha Company from giving him the best support to get back to his normal, weird self, both as soldier and as wolf.

Now, Eros was beginning to regret the decision to bring Dane along, to test him out on this assignment. Maybe he should have left Dane at home and brought Silver instead. Silver, at least, had all his marbles. Dane, however, had lost a few on that mission.

"Dammit, Dane," Eros growled. "When's the last time you got new boots?"

"Two years ago, why?" Dane asked and bit off a piece of their custom-made protein bars and chewed. Wolves and men needed lots of protein, especially on intense assignments like they were on now.

"You're eating? Now?" Luke asked and gave him a shove. Being the mature, adult male that he was, Dane shoved him back.

"Last time, you told me to eat *before* a mission, so I'm eating, fool." Dane gave a sound of exasperation, glared at Luke, and ripped off another bite, chewed it in Luke's face, like a two-year-old trying to make a point.

They both had issues. Serious, serious issues.

"You're an idiot. You're supposed to eat beforehand. Not thirty seconds before we go out," Luke said and growled deep in his throat and poked Dane in the shoulder. Not one to leave an insult unchallenged, Dane poked him back.

It was on.

The two of them started arguing, but Eros was going to end it. It stopped, or he was going to kill them. Or himself. Killing them would be so much more satisfying. Taking a deep breath, he considered his options, wondering how much ammo he had available. Oh, the temptation. He clenched his jaw and fondled his sidearm, trying to decide who to kill first.

"You know, you two should get mated to each other, 'cause the way you argue, no one else is going to want your sorry asses," Eros said.

Wide eyed, they looked at him. Blinked twice. Obviously dumbfounded, they looked at each other. Luke shrugged, dismissing Eros' words. "Fighting? We're not fighting," Luke said.

"It's a heated debate at best," Dane said, downplaying their argument. Seconds later, they returned to their squabbling as the blood in Eros' veins boiled past the point of no return. If he blew an aneurysm right now, it would be no surprise. At least it would end the misery of listening to his packmates disagree. Endlessly. Over nothing.

So much for silent-and-deadly. The only thing these two killed was his patience.

And his sense of smell. That might never be the same again.

"Shut it," Eros said and held up one hand to stop their commotion. "Commander's sending a message." Damn, how he wished he could cock his ears to the left and right like when in wolf form. Wolf ears picked up everything. He could hear a mouse crawling beneath a pile of leaves half a mile away. Down in this hole, at this angle, he couldn't hear shit. His human hearing seriously hampered him. Even cupping his hands around his ears to amplify the sound didn't help.

Their missions before Dane's injury hadn't been this miserable. Most of their secret missions were outside of their home turf, usually out of the state, sometimes out of the country. That's why they had protocols set up. Everyone knew the drill. They followed procedures that kept the team from getting hurt and returned home safe, happy and whole.

On the last mission they'd rescued a rich kid who'd been kidnapped in their own back yard, the assignment went pretty much as planned. Until Dane got hit with a knife. Then things went to hell, but normally, they went in, got the job done and went home. But this? This mission was trying his patience in all ways. The sooner this fact-finding mission was over, the better.

He loved his packmates, his brothers in arms, but he needed more personal space than this hole allowed for. The beast inside of him pawed, eager to be out and running through the desert, chasing bunnies. At least that would get his blood pumping.

"What's he say? When are we getting out of here? I got a hot date tomorrow I need to get ready for," Dane said and flipped out his pocket knife and began cleaning his fingernails.

"Yeah, it's gonna take that long to get the stench off," Luke said and slapped his thigh, cracking himself up.

"Garbled. Unclear," Eros said. Dammit. Rain interfered with the reception. The radio they had was useless with the weather bearing down on them. "Rain's screwing with my ears."

"Let me give it a try," Dane said. He crawled over to Eros and focused for a few seconds, trying to get the message just beyond their range. He closed his eyes and focused inward, the energy swirling around them, pulling at Eros' beast. What the hell was he doing?

Dane shifted *only his head* into his wolf. The rest of him remained in human form.

"Dude. That's truly disturbing," Eros said. He'd never been more grossed out in his life, and he'd seen some pretty nasty things.

"Oh, bro'. That is *soooo* wrong," Luke said as throat worked as he swallowed several times. "I may hurl." Luke made a face of clear disgust, his lip curling, his eyes glaring hard at Dane. Luke tried to put some distance between them, but it was kinda hard in a dirt bunker. "I'm never gonna look at you the same way again." Another gag tried to force its way up his throat, but he coughed it out. "I may never look at you again. Period," Luke said.

Ignoring them, shaking off the dregs of his own repugnance, Eros waited for Dane to listen with his sensitive hearing and figure out what the fuck was going on out there.

Report, Eros said.

Still out of range, sir, Dane said.

Try again. Get out of the bunker. See if you can get anything topside, Eros said.

Roger that.

Eros closed his eyes and tried not to hear or *think* about what they were doing. All the fumbling around overcame his desire to murder them both, and he opened his eyes. Dane was standing on Luke's shoulders. Or at least trying to. Luke braced himself against the wall of dirt, struggling to balance Dane's weight.

How much weight did you gain, dude? You weigh a fucking ton, Luke said.

I don't know. I lost like forty pounds when I was recovering from surgery, Dane said.

Dane swiveled his ears, trying to catch any audio the commander might be sending their way. They had to get the message, or they were going to lose track of the quarry they'd struggled to hunt down over the last three days.

I think you put that on and twenty more. Holy fuck! Luke grumbled. His face burned red. A vein bulging in his forehead revealed his effort. If he had a stroke right now, Eros wouldn't be surprised. It would at least save Eros the effort of killing him.

You haven't been in the gym in months, Luke said.

Cause I run, okay, Mr. Body Builder, Dane said.

Running doesn't help your upper body, Luke said.

Shut up and listen! Eros growled at them.

Got it. Sir, Luke said.

Not Vic. I hear a convoy coming, Dane said.

Is it the guns? Eros asked.

Dane sniffed the air, his sensitive nose twitching and wriggling with the efforts to draw in the scents around him.

All I get is diesel. Can't tell. Dane cocked his head to the side and took in another tasting whiff of the air. *And bad Mexican food. Tamales. Ew . . . menudo,* Dane said.

What is it with you? You're food obsessed. I'm gonna call that psychiatrist Vic keeps threatening you with if you don't cut it out, Eros said.

Obsessed is such a harsh word. I prefer intensely focused, Dane said.

Dane.

Eros.

Bullets whizzed by his head. Dane collapsed on top of Luke and Eros. Curses, punches, growls and snapping teeth cut the air as the three extricated themselves from each other.

"For fuck's sake, get off me," Eros said. He couldn't take it anymore. Just as he focused on his beast to shift and slaughter the both of them, something changed. A weight lifted from his chest. He could breathe again. His beast settled down.

Dane shook his head and shifted back to fully human again. "I think they spotted us," Dane said.

"No shit," Luke said and shoved Dane again, then dove on top of him as another cascade of deadly projectiles hit the dirt beside them.

"Down!" Did he really have to tell them to duck? Were they

that stupid today? Or had the last three days in such limited confinement robbed them of any remaining brain cells they had left. They hadn't been able to run in the wild, tap in to their beasts for days, and it was wearing on all of them. It was a basic survival requirement for them. If they didn't get what they needed, the pressure built up and pretty soon, the body found some kind of relief. That's when fights started.

The three of them stripped and shifted. What a relief. To stretch out his muscles. To feel the dirt beneath his feet and connect to the earth. To sniff the air and taste the variety of scents waiting for his brain to interpret. Nothing in life was as awesome as being a wolf. Nothing. Nothing could ever compete with that. Nothing. He would die before he'd stop being a wolf. It was who he was. A hunter. A predator. A protector.

Side by side, the three big males raced through the desert terrain, chasing the speeding truck. Past shrubs, over bushes, mesquite, cedar, pinõn. All the familiar scents of the desert sped past them as they tried to catch up with the vehicle whose red taillights disappeared as the truck outdistanced them. Luke was the leanest and fastest of them, had the most stamina, but even he couldn't keep up the pace for long. Wolves were good for short bursts at high speed, but they were designed for a longer, slower pace, taking down animal prey over natural terrain, not chasing vehicles on a man-made road that hurt the feet and injured joints.

Up ahead a flash of white caught Eros's eye.

Weaving in and out of the shadows. Through the sage and around the scrubby bushes. Something moved. Something chased. Something stalked.

Something didn't see them.

Surprised, Eros didn't know whether to fall back or give chase. Slowing his pace, he connected with the others.

What the hell is that? Eros asked.

Where? Luke asked.

Up ahead. Some white shadow, Eros said.

What the . . . Luke sniffed the air, his ears and tail shot up, then he kicked it into high gear. *I don't know what it is, but it ain't gonna get in our way. Ain't gonna stop us. Wahoo! I'm on it,* Luke said.

Luke took off with speed he'd never demonstrated before. He must have some kind of stamina to kick in that fast. Like he was in supersonic mode. Wiley Coyote on steroids.

I can't keep up. Dane fell behind, his breath wheezing in and out of his lungs. *I can't keep going.* The strain of his injury and his unfinished recovery were taxing his body systems. If he didn't stop now, he could give out, and they'd be dragging his carcass back to camp. *Go on. Leave me here. I'll stay here. Catch my breath, then I'll catch up,* Dane said.

No. We're not leaving you behind, Dane. Ever, Eros said.

Pulling up, Eros hesitated, thinking of a mission a few years ago where they'd had to leave Vic's brother behind in the Middle East and the far-reaching effects that had had on all of them. It wasn't going to happen again. Not now. Not if he could help it.

Luke, reel it in, Eros commanded.

What? No! I'm right behind it, Luke said.

That's an order. Get back here. Dane's gassed, Eros said.

At the mention of Luke's bro' falling behind, he gave up the chase and trotted back to them, tongue lolling out the side of his mouth, chest surging as he recovered his breath.

I told you, you should be in the gym, building stamina, Luke said.

Shut it. Dane gasped for breath. He stopped, his feet wide apart, head hanging down. Chest heaving with the effort, he struggled to breath. Wolves were athletes and this athlete had been at his prime two months ago. Today, he was struggling to keep up with the team. That decided it for Eros.

Dane was benched until he could prove himself physically, that he could pull his weight with the rest. If one team member failed, it put them all in jeopardy, and that was never acceptable. The safety of the team, of the pack, came first. Always.

Move it. I'm not carrying your sorry ass all the way back to the bunker, Luke said and nipped Dane on the ear, expressing his displeasure, which only resulted in retaliation as Dane slapped his paw down on Luke's head.

As Eros stood watch over the two of them, the snap of dry brush cracked through the air ending the play, putting them on high alert.

They froze.

No one moved except to find the source of the sound. Each of them sent out their signals, sent out their energy to discover whether the sound of a snapping branch belonged to a frightened little rabbit displaced by their chase or a vicious enemy come back to do them harm.

What the . . . Luke started to turn, then halted, his eyes going wonky in his head. Eros felt the rapid pulse of his heart, sensed his eagerness, the desire to chase, follow, capture. *Submit?* What the hell had Luke just seen?

Slowly, Eros turned his head and experienced the same sensations. The fur on his spine stood out as he took in the creature behind them.

Standing tall and strong in front of them was a pure white wolf.

A *female.*

Her golden eyes flashed to all of them. Staring them down, she exuded no fear, no concern. She was in charge and a powerful female.

Then he caught her eyes, made direct contact with her, and he felt like he'd been hypnotized. His heart raced, his desire to chase matched that of Luke and Dane. He'd heard about the legendary white wolf of lore, but had never seriously believed one existed. They were of pure, royal blood, but had been destroyed by rival packs long ago. Just like humans, what wolves feared they destroyed.

Standing in the rays of the waning sun, she was cast in a golden glow, as if she were a statue, not a living breathing creature.

Ears perked forward, every sense focused on her, Luke took a hesitant step forward. One paw lifted, then stepped onto the ground, pushed him forward. Tremors from Luke shot through Eros. He knew Luke wanted her. Wanted to get close to her.

They *all* did.

Something magical was happening. Something he'd never experienced. Something he didn't like. Electricity snapped in the air around them, as if they were in a vortex of energy. He shook his head, and looked away, breaking the spell she'd so easily cast on the three of them.

Maybe she was a spirit, a phantom of a long-ago legend. Maybe they'd just been out in the desert for too long. Stories of old had been handed down for centuries, but he'd never believed them. Never considered it. Until now. He still had a duty to protect the two under his charge, even if they couldn't help themselves and stood there with their tongues hanging out and their dicks dragging the ground.

Eros kept his gaze away from her glowing eyes. Away from the aura surrounding her. Challenge in his demeanor, he took a step forward, putting his body between her and his soldiers.

Who are you and what do you want here? Eros demanded.

Daring further, Eros took a step closer even as he fought to take that step. Something held him back. Pushed against him. He tried to move another paw forward, but again was repelled from doing so. Was it the force of this female standing in front of them? Could she truly be the magical wolf of legend? Seriously?

Luke growled at him, warning him off, but Eros ignored him. He was in charge, not Luke. A wolf in the throes of full-blown lust couldn't be trusted. With anything.

Don't interfere.

That was the only message she gave them. Paralyzed by the sound of her voice, by the buzz in his head, Eros remained still, not about to give chase when there were so many unknown factors. Before he knew it, she took off, skimming lightly over the surface of the ground, as if she were flying, her long legs stretching forward as her paws chewed up the ground beneath her. How had she gotten so far so quickly? Maybe they were just all dehydrated and having mass hysteria. Mass hallucination? Mass lust?

Wow! What the hell was that? Luke asked, jumped up and down, arching his back and kicking up little puffs of dust with his paws.

I don't know, Eros said and was forced to admit as he watched the white wolf race away after the truck they hadn't been able to catch. *I just don't know.*

I'm in love, Luke said.

You're always in love, hound dog, Eros said.

No, in lust, my furry friend. I'm always in lust, but that one? She's something else, Luke said.

What I want to know is why she's here, chasing down that truck, Eros said. He watched until she and the truck were out of sight.

The radio back in the foxhole crackled. Eros swiveled his left ear to better pick up the sound.

That's the commander. I'll handle it, Eros said. He glanced at Dane, assessing the wolf's condition, sending out his energy to connect with Dane's. *Are you rested enough to continue?*

Yes, sir. Maybe you should have brought Rico instead of me. He probably could have kept up, Dane said and tucked his head to his chest, and dropped his ears. Classic submissive behavior. Eros didn't want to see it. Didn't need it.

You idiot, we don't bring Rico on missions. Luke said and snapped at Dane's tail. *He's a German Shepherd and retired from military life. He's living in luxury at the compound, protecting the alpha female. That's his job now, not sitting in the dirt with us.*

Cool it, Dane. Keep your head up and your ears forward. You've only been out of rehab for a few weeks. It was probably too early to take you on a mission Eros said. He should have thought harder about the timing, but he wanted and needed Dane back in action, back in the field.

Sir. I'm sorry, sir. Dane said and sat quickly, his demeanor upright and rigid. Panting, he continued to gasp for air. Unlike him. Unfortunately unacceptable. They needed Dane back to his usual self, his usual protector mode at peak performance, his usual heart and soul. Now.

Eros narrowed his eyes, uncertain if the wolf was yanking his chain or was serious. With Dane it was hard to tell. In any case, nothing was going to change his mind.

Dane was going back to rehab at the compound until he could physically handle going on another mission. However long that took.

Let's go. I'll speak to the commander about how we lost the truck, Eros said.

And I'll tell him about the white wolf, Luke said, his tongue hanging out as he fell into line behind Dane. The weakest member of the pack was always protected on both ends by the stronger ones.

You will not, Eros snapped. *The commander is newly mated. He doesn't need to hear about how you're hot after some female you just met.*

But . . . but . . . he always wants to hear my stories, Luke whined and dropped his tail in disappointment.

Times are changing, Luke. Eros said and made his way around a fallen cedar tree in the path and returned to the trail a few feet later.

I know, sir. I just don't want them to.

Always A Wolf free novella-https://BookHip.com/CZZXTM